LIFE GOES ON

Emmy's Story, Part 19

by
Kenneth Lee McGee

For the family of
Adalynn Joy Sooter

I wish to thank Pastor Tyler Hubbell

for his excellent service to our church.

Nearly all of the words in the resignation letter belong to him.

I borrowed them for this book with his kind permission.

Thank you Liz for everything you do.

Thank you Teresa W. for your continued help

with the details about COVID-19.

A special thanks to Gina L. for her assistance

with the rules, regulations and other medical

advice so I could kinda keep things real.

May God keep all our healthcare workers safe.

Prologue

The helicopter pilot cleared the final peak of the Sawtooth Mountains and dropped in altitude.

Bill Robertson used his binoculars and then pointed. "There's the barn, and I can see the herd a few miles up the valley."

Tobias Tawney, the ranch foreman, also spotted the herd of close to two hundred animals. "They haven't moved far from their position last week."

The pilot, Lyle Claypool, slowed the helicopter to avoid exciting the animals. "Should I find a spot to set down?" he asked.

Mr. Robertson replied, "Yes, but keep it running. I want to head north and check the line cabin by the creek."

The pilot set the craft down in a clearing on the opposite side of the barn and outbuildings from the herd of Scottish Highland cattle and Mr. Robertson and Tobias jumped out.

"Keep your head low," Tobias shouted though he doubted he could be heard.

Mr. Robertson put a hand to his head to keep his baseball cap from blowing away. He ducked and stayed low until well past the rotor blades. He walked quickly around the buildings and used his binoculars to check his herd of prized animals.

Tobias joined his boss and pointed. "We can bale enough grass from this valley to support a herd of five hundred. Maybe more. In the summer it's green as far as the eye can see. There is enough grass in the barn to feed the herd for another month or more. "

"That's why I bought this valley ten years ago," Mr. Robertson said. "Let's check the line cabin now. I want to make sure it's well stocked."

They returned to the chopper and Claypool set down within a hundred yards of the rustic cabin.

"Should I shut down, Mr. Robertson?"

"Yes. I want to enjoy the fresh air."

"I'll keep it idling for now."

Mr. Robertson and Tobias checked the exterior before entering.

"Someone has been chopping wood," Mr. Robertson said.

"I kept the guys working," Tobias answered with a laugh. He removed his weathered cowboy hat, ran his hand over his close-cropped gray hair and rubbed his equally gray beard. "They earned their keep."

Mr. Robertson opened the door and they stepped inside. The light through the windows on either side of the one-room cabin created a haze of dust particles.

Mr. Robertson smiled as he noticed the shelves along the north wall were stocked with various types of pork and beans and large cans of Dinfield Miller beef stew.

"The winter crew knows how to eat well," Tobias said. "That's my favorite kind of stew. I been eatin' it since I was a kid."

"I am rather fond of it myself," Mr. Robertson said.

Suddenly, he hunched over and grabbed his arm.

"What is it, boss?"

"Chest pain," he muttered. "Hurts like a mother."

Tobias looked at his boss. "You don't look too good." He didn't waste any time. He hustled Mr. Robertson outside, caught Claypool's attention and made a whirling motion. He heard the pilot start powering up the idling turbine.

"We can make it to the hospital in Ketchum Fork in ten minutes. Hang on, boss. We'll get you some help."

Chapter One

"Anyone home?" Father James asked from the mudroom doorway.

"Come on in," Kenny Colwell said. "You just missed breakfast. Isabella made blueberry pancakes."

"Thanks, but I ate earlier." He glanced into the kitchen then the living room. "Where's the birthday girl?"

Kenny chuckled. "In bed. I told her she could sleep while we get the house ready for the party."

"I can't believe she's forty. She was only thirty when I met her." He sat on one of the island barstools. "I've aged twenty years since then, but she doesn't look any older."

"She was giggling last night like a little kid," Kevin said. He looked at his father and grinned.

Father James inspected the bananas in the wicker basket.

"You weren't supposed to hear anything," Kenny said.

Heather walked up and poked his side. "You shouldn't leave your door open. I had to close it for you."

"We were tickling each other."

"I would drop it before it's too late," Father James said.

"Is that what it's called now," Heather asked.

"We weren't..."

Father James tossed a banana at him. "That one's rotten. Do something with it."

Kenny checked it. "It's only starting to get ripe. Isa likes them this way."

"Are you doubting my word as a man of the cloth?" Father James stood up, winked at Heather and they both whispered, "He's a dork."

Emmy walked into the kitchen only minutes before ten. She rubbed her eyes and stretched her arms over her head.

"Happy birthday, Mommy," Isabella said. "I can make pancakes for you. Would you like some, too, Uncle James?"

"I'm good," he said while reading his newspaper in the breakfast nook.

Emmy lowered her arms to her sides. "I didn't know you were here."

"Obviously," he said without looking up again.

"I'm dressed," she said.

"You're still in your pajamas, Mom," Isabella replied.

She sat at the island. "Where is everyone? Have the caterers arrived?"

"Not yet. It's early. Daddy and Kevin ran to the store to pick up water, pop and beer."

Father James raised a hand. "The beer's for me in case you're wondering. Not Kevin."

"Where's Heather?"

Isabella answered, "She went to Aunt Diane's to help with something. Maybe she was going to make a cake."

"Heather can't bake a cake," Emmy said.

"She's not here. Maybe she went to Uncle Tony's house to see Peter."

"You don't have to cover for her, Isa."

"Peter is showing off his new car. It's not serious, Mom. She likes boys."

"She reminds me of myself too much," Emmy said.

Isabella made the pancakes, and Emmy ate at the island.

"Thank you, sweetie. They were delicious. I better take a shower and get dressed."

"Good idea," Father James said because Tony just got out of his truck."

Emmy ran upstairs before Tony walked into the kitchen.

"Morning, Isa. Mama sent me over with the potato salad. Where should I put it?"

"There's room in the garage fridge, or in the basement."

Tony looked around. "Where's your mother? Still in bed?"

"She's in the shower, I think," Isabella said. "Were you going to wish her a happy birthday?"

"I have three months to tease her before I turn forty. I'm going to take advantage of every minute. I'll put the potato salad in the fridge and come back later."

Emmy came downstairs ten minutes later. "Did Tony leave?"

"He will be back later to tease you." Father James closed the fridge and looked at her. "You still look like the girls..."

"Thank you."

"Only smaller," he finished. "Nice t-shirt and shorts. Did you borrow them from Isa or Heather?"

"Neither. They're mine."

Kenny and Kevin walked in carrying groceries.

"Your beer's in the fridge, Uncle James. I gotta shower, so me and the guys can go swimming then play army in the woods."

Emmy shook her head. "Why bother? He will need another shower before the party."

"He's twelve," Father James said. "He's supposed to smell."

"Who's supposed to smell?" Heather asked as she and Peter walked into the room.

"Your brother. Morning, Peter."

"Happy birthday, Aunt Emmy." He stared at her.

"What?" she asked. "I got dressed."

Father James rolled his eyes and shook his head. "This should be good," he whispered to Heather.

"Is that really you, Aunt Emmy? You sound like her, but you look different."

Emmy finally caught on. "You can tell your father I don't look or feel any different today, and his birthday is coming up."

"He made me promise to tease you. I don't think you look any different than when I was a kid."

"Thank you. Please thank Mama for the potato salad."

"I will."

"We're going downstairs to watch a movie. Call me if you need help," Heather said.

"Okay," Emmy answered without hearing as she sorted through the groceries.

Kenny watched Heather and Peter leave. "Don't you have something for her to do?"

"Who?" She held up a can of whole black olives. "We need sliced not whole."

5

He grabbed the can and looked. "Sorry, I grabbed the wrong one. I can slice them if you want."

"No, you'll cut off a finger. I'll do it."

The caterers arrived at noon followed by Kenny's parents and some of the Bristol Ridge neighbors and family.

"You're early," Emmy said. "And you can tease me later when everyone's here."

Mama hugged her and kissed the top of her head. "You don't look any older than yesterday, dear."

"Did Tony tell you to tease me?"

"He's telling everyone, but it's okay. You will have the last laugh in October."

Emmy walked outside and heard the kids playing in the pool. She walked through the gate and stood by the edge. "Make sure you look out for the little ones. Phoebe and David aren't used to this many kids in the pool," she said to the guys sitting at a table.

"We're watching them," Tyler said.

"Where's Liz? I haven't seen her yet." Emmy made a face at Tony and said, "You will get yours later, buddy boy."

"She saw Bobby and Shay with the baby. She's still talking to them." He pointed to the place where the driveway split off to go to the guesthouse. "Here they come."

"Does she plan on swimming?"

"Probably not," he answered. "Too many people."

"I understand, but I'm going in the pool later." She looked at Kenny and said, "Without my clothes on this time."

Kenny, Tyler and Father James stared at her.

It took a few seconds for her to realize what she said. "I didn't mean it like that. You are such a dork."

"What did she say?" Dad Colwell asked. "I was listening to the kids."

"She said she wasn't going to wear her clothes when she goes swimming," Kenny said.

Father James looked at Tyler and they chuckled.

"This should be good," Father James whispered.

6

"Kenneth Travis Robert Colwell, did you hear what you said?" she asked with her hands on her hips.

"Yes, I heard. What did I say?"

"You made it sound like she wasn't going to wear anything when she goes swimming," Tyler explained.

"Oh," he said. "That's not what I meant. Sorry, Em. You can wear your clothes this time."

Everyone laughed.

"What did I miss?" Bobby asked. "All I heard was something about Emmy wearing clothes."

Tony explained.

"Way to embarrass your wife, Kenny."

"I didn't mean to."

"You do it without thinking. Like last night when you... never mind. No one needs to know." She stuck out her tongue and headed inside.

Tony looked at Father James. "What happened?"

"You don't want to know."

"Are we going to sing after the prayer, or before we eat the cake?" Kenny asked shortly after one.

"After we eat," Kevin hollered. "We're starving."

"After we eat is okay with me." Emmy stood beside Kenny and looked around. "Where are Diane and Brady? They should have been here by now. Do you think they got lost, or forgot about it?"

"Carson, Caden and the little ones are here," Kenny said.

He pointed to Diane's four kids.

Emmy's cell phone chirped, and she pulled it out of her pocket.

"It's Diane," she said. "Hang on while I ream her a new one for being late."

"We can't wait too long, Em. Those boys look ready to attack," Kenny said with a laugh.

"Hey, Diane. What's up? Why aren't you here? We're ready to eat."

"Sorry, Emmy, but we aren't going to make it."

7

"Why not? Are you sick?"

"No, sweetie, but Mona called. Mr. Robertson had a heart attack..."

Emmy dropped her phone.

"Em, what is it?" Kenny picked up her phone. "What's going on?"

She held up her arms and whispered, "Hold me."

Kenny held her in his arms until her tears stopped. "Can you tell me what happened?"

"Mr. Robertson suffered a heart attack."

He waved at Tyler and Liz, and they hurried over.

"Is something wrong?" Liz asked.

"Mr. Robertson suffered a heart attack." Kenny looked at Emmy. "What did Diane say? How much does she know?"

Liz put her arm around Emmy as Emmy explained the call from Diane.

"Should we cancel the party?" Kenny asked.

"No, I don't want to ruin it for everyone, but I might need to go inside for a moment."

Kenny opened the door leading into the family room.

"Maybe you should tell Tony and Kristen," Emmy said. She held onto Liz's hand and they stepped inside.

Tony approached Kenny and Tyler. "What's going on? I saw Emmy drop her phone and start crying."

Kenny looked at Tony then Tyler.

Tyler whispered, "Mr. Robertson suffered a heart attack."

Tony's shoulders slumped. He took a deep breath and asked, "How much do we know?"

"Not a lot at this point," Tyler answered. "Emmy wants the party to continue, so maybe we shouldn't tell the kids."

Kenny spotted his parents talking to Mama Bertucci and headed in their direction.

"What is going on, son?" Mrs. Colwell asked.

Kenny started to explain before he was distracted by the sound of someone rushing onto the deck.

"Where is she?" Diane asked.

Kenny pointed. "In the family room with Liz."

Diane scurried past and entered through the French doors. "Emmy, the call got dropped or something."

"Sorry, I dropped my phone. How is he? How's Mona doing?"

"I didn't get a chance to explain everything."

Liz said, "Let's sit on the couch, and you can share what details you know."

"He's in the hospital and Mona said the attack was not as severe as the doctors first thought. He's..."

"He's still alive, right?" Emmy asked.

"Yes, sweetie."

"Thank God!"

"I didn't mean to spoil your birthday," Diane said as she hugged Emmy.

"It would have been worse if you didn't tell me, and I found out later."

Kenny, Tony and Tyler huddled together to discuss who to tell and how to keep the party going without alarming the kids.

"Let's go ahead and eat," Tony suggested. "The kids are starving, and it will be a way to keep it under wraps for now."

The ladies returned to the deck and slowly the news spread among the adults.

Emmy got everyone's attention, smiled and said, "I'm sorry for the interruption, but please, enjoy the food."

"Mom, is it true about Grandpa Robertson?" Isabella asked. "Did he really have a heart attack?"

"Yes, but he's going to be okay," Emmy answered hugging Isabella. "Diane hasn't told Lily or Conor yet, but as soon as she does, you can tell everyone. Just don't make it sound like he's going to die."

Although the news subdued the mood, the party continued. Emmy blew out the candles after everyone sang.

"Way to go, Mom," Kevin cheered. "You got all of them on the first try. You aren't as old as Uncle Tony said."

Chapter Two

"Kenny, Diane called. They're ready for you to take them to the airport," Emmy said Thursday morning.

He walked into the kitchen and grabbed the keys to the Odyssey. "I'll be back as soon as I can. Are you going to pick up Lily and Conor, or am I bringing them here?"

"I will get them. Carson is staying at the house, but I'm not sure about Caden. Diane said he has been pretty upset about this. More than the other kids."

"I understand why. He and Mr. Robertson are really close."

Kenny bumped fists with Brady and Bennett then the men loaded the luggage.

"Thanks for driving us to the airport," Brady said.

"You're welcome. We are praying for your father."

Marissa Robertson, Bennett's wife, waited for someone to open the sliding door.

"Marissa, just pull on the handle," Diane said rolling her eyes. "Kenny isn't your chauffeur."

Marissa huffed but she pulled the handle and got in.

Kenny parked close to the waiting Gulfstream III. He and Brady unloaded the luggage and the pilots helped load the plane.

"Sorry, but my sister-in-law in law doesn't understand the concept of traveling light," Brady said.

"It's okay. We have flown her to Atlanta numerous times," the pilot said. "I'm Devin Boone and that's my brother Noel. He's the co-pilot."

"I'm sure we've met before, but I'm not good with names," Brady said.

"I filed the flight plan, and we should be cleared to take off immediately. We will be cruising at 400 mph. We could push it, but that's a good speed for this craft. We should be in Boise in four hours. Give or take a few minutes."

"Thank you, Devin. We appreciate it."

"I hope he will be all right."

10

They landed in Boise, picked up a rental vehicle and drove to Ketchum Fork.

Brady called his stepmother's cell phone. "We are getting into town now, Mona. Where is the hospital?"

Diane pointed and said, "There's a sign. Go straight."

"You should see it almost immediately," Mona said. "It will be on the right. It's the only four-story building in town."

"There it is!" Diane yelled. "Turn in here."

Brady parked in the relatively small lot and everyone hustled inside.

"May I help you?" an elderly volunteer asked.

Diane explained who they wanted to see.

The volunteer smiled and used one finger to type the name into the computer.

Diane looked at Marissa, who appeared ready to blow a gasket, then turned away to stifle a laugh.

"Yes. He is here," the volunteer said. "William Robertson. That names sounds familiar." She put a finger to her chin and tilted her head. "Robertson."

"Could you tell us what room, please?" Diane asked.

"Oh, sorry, dearie. He's in the CICU. That's on the second floor." She pointed to her right. "The elevator is over there..."

Brady led the way to the lone elevator.

"... but you can't go up there," the volunteer said softly.

Mona was standing in the hallway when the elevator door opened. Diane rushed forward and hugged her stepmother-in-law.

"How's he doing, Mona?" Brady asked.

Diane released Mona and took a step back. "We got here as quick as we could."

Mona took a deep breath, smiled and said, "He is going to be all right." She explained where he had been when the attack occurred.

"He was fortunate the helicopter could land here," Marissa said disdainfully. "From what I have seen of this... medical facility... I would move him immediately."

"We might be able to move him soon," a man in a white coat said as he approached. "How did you get up here?"

11

Mona grinned and said, "This is Dr. Roland Brideweiser. He's in charge of this little facility and also teaches at the University of Washington's Coeling-Feist School of Medicine. You might have heard of it. They specialize in heart transplants and other minor medical issues."

Bennett frowned at Marissa, who suddenly developed an interest in a floral water color painting.

"Bill is doing okay for a man in his condition," Dr. Brideweiser said. "We're going to move him into the only empty room we have. Third floor. Room 301."

"Thank you, Roland," Mona said.

"No problem. I will see him again in the morning. I'll be around for a few days. I love to fish." He adjusted his Colorado Rockies baseball cap and said, "Mona has to stay until he is released because of our pandemic policies. I should have security escort you out of the building, but if you are still here in an hour, I will quarantine the lot of you. Understand?"

"Yes, doctor. We will leave immediately," Brady said.

Dr. Brideweiser headed down the hall.

"Bill was fortunate Roland was fly fishing and was able to get here shortly after the helicopter."

"Can we see him, Mona?" Brady asked. "For a minute."

"I don't think it's wise, but the regulations are... flexible here. Give them a few minutes to move him. They are making him use the gurney. He wanted to walk to his new room. You and Bennett can see him, but Diane and Marissa need to leave."

"I came all this way," Marissa said with indignation. "I should be allowed to visit."

"If you wish," Mona said. "The quarantine rooms are rather basic, but I'm sure you will find them... quaint."

Marissa did an about-face, harrumphed and waited in front of the elevator.

"You need to push the button, Marissa," Diane kissed Brady and said, "I'll take her to the hotel. Call me if you're going to end up staying here."

"Bennett and I will leave after we see Dad."

"Diane, are you at the hospital? How is he? What in the world happened? Have you seen him? Is he in pain? He is going to come home soon, right?" Emmy rattled off the questions.

"If you give me a chance, I will tell you," Diane replied.

"Tell me."

"We are leaving the hospital as we speak. I have Marissa with me. Brady, Bennett and Mona are still inside. We had to leave because of the COVID policies. If you want to know more, call Mona. She can explain."

"Thanks. I'll call her."

Mona answered with a smile.

"Is he okay? Can I talk to him? Are you okay, Mona?' Emmy asked.

"He is going to be all right, Emmy, and I am fine. He is waving at me as we speak..."

"Can I talk to him?" Emmy asked.

"Yes, but not for long. He did suffer a heart attack, so he needs rest." Mona walked across the room and handed her cell phone to her husband. "It's Emmy."

He took the phone, put his hand over it and asked, "How did they keep her from coming with Brady and Bennett?"

"They probably didn't give her an option. That's the only thing I can think of. Maybe they told her she needed to watch the kids," Mona answered.

He nodded and smiled. "Hello, Emmy..."

"Mr. Robertson! Are you okay? Are you going to be all right? Does it hurt? Should I fly to Idaho, so I can see you?"

"Slow down, Emmy. You don't need to fly out here. I'm doing much better, and my friend, Dr. Brideweiser, told me I will make a full recovery."

"I was so worried when Diane called me. I said a thousand prayers for you."

"I appreciate that, and I'm sure God heard every one."

Chapter Three

"Can we order pizzas for dinner?" Kevin Michael asked. "Caden is getting hungry, and Lily and Conor said they like pizza."

"What kind should we order?" Emmy smiled as she looked up at her twelve-year-old son and opened an app for Kerry Lynn's Pizza and Pasta on her phone.

They decided on the pizzas, and Kevin asked about the delivery time.

"They should be here within an hour," she answered.

Caden Garrett walked into the kitchen, put his arms around Emmy and rested his head on her shoulder.

She patted his back and whispered, "It's okay to cry. I know how much he means to you."

He sobbed quietly for a moment before straightening up. "I love him much more than my real grandfather. I haven't seen or heard from my other grandparents in ages. I haven't talked to my father in a long time either. He's a jerk."

Emmy reached up and put her hands on his shoulders. "I don't blame you for feeling like that, but he is still your father."

"Just because he and Mom... you know."

Emmy grinned and said, "He hasn't been much of a father, and Brady loves you and Carson as much as Conor and Lily."

"I know, Aunt Emmy. When Carson told me about the heart attack, I ran into the woods and sat by a tree and cried. I didn't want anyone to see me. After a while Kevin sat next to me and put his arm around me. We didn't really talk, but he was there in case I needed anything."

"He surprises me. Sometimes he can be an immature kid who drives me nuts. Then other times he does something to make me so proud."

That evening in the music suite of the Crest Ridge United Nazarene church, Emmy gathered the worship team together. "Please take a seat. Many of you know, or have heard about Mr. Robertson's heart attack."

"How's he doing?" Bobby asked.

"I talked to him this afternoon, and he is doing better." She bit her lip and and added, "For a man his age who just suffered a heart attack, I mean."

"We understand," Liz Hammond said with a smile.

"Would you mind if I took a few minutes to tell you about him?"

"Go ahead, Emmy," Pastor Rebecca said as she held her almost-three-month-old baby, Hannah Ruth, in her arms.

"Mr. Robertson worked for my grandfather Colasanti a long, long time ago..." Emmy explained how Mr. Robertson and his wife Lily would occasionally take care of her when she was a baby.

"After I graduated and worked for Coventry Shield Healthcare for a time, I got a job with Robertson Industries..." She continued the story about how she met him at a dance and his generosity toward her and Diane. "To make a long story a little shorter, he is like a father to me and a grandpa to my kids. We love him so much." She stopped because her tears were flowing faster than the Kinmundy River in the spring.

Liz and Rebecca put their arms around Emmy. Liz used a tissue to dry Emmy's eyes while Rebecca balanced Hannah in one arm.

"You are so good to me," Emmy said after clearing her throat. "I know God is in control, but it could have been Mr. Robertson's time, if you know what I mean."

"We will continue to pray for his physical and spiritual health," Liz said.

"Thank you, and now we really need to rehearse the songs for this week. I chose a new one, and we need to learn it."

"Hi, Dany, how was your doctor visit? Any news?" Liz asked her younger sister the next afternoon.

"He confirmed it. I am officially expecting again."

"Tell me everything you know," Liz ordered. "Phoebe, come here. Aunt Dany's on the phone."

Phoebe Grace Hammond hurried to her mother's side. "Is she going to have another baby?"

"Yes. Let's listen."

Dany Michaelis told them all the details she knew.

"I'm happy you're going to have another baby, Aunt Dany. I'm old enough now to help you take care of her. You better have a baby girl because you already have Patrick."

"I'll try," Dany said. "Let me talk to your mother."

Five minutes after Liz got off the phone with Dany, her cell phone buzzed again.

"Hi, Allie, how are you?"

"I'm expecting number three," Allie announced to her sister-in-law. "Larry is sure this one will be a boy."

"If it is, are you going to follow the family tradition?" Liz asked.

"I already promised your brother he will be named Lawrence Dustin Kimmerle the fifth."

"I hope it's a boy," Liz said. She hollered for the girls.

"What, Mommy?" Natalie asked. "Phoebe and I were talking about Aunt Dany's new baby. I'm old enough to babysit."

"And I can help," Phoebe added.

Liz smiled and said, "I have more good news. Aunt Allie is going to have a baby, too."

Phoebe's eyes sparkled. "I think every mommy should have another baby. You can have one. Aunt Emmy should have one, and Miss Kristen is going to have one." Phoebe held out both hands. "I love babies. When I get married, I want to have ten babies."

Liz texted her friends with the news.

Emmy opened the text and called to the girls, "Dany and Allie are expecting."

Heather and Isabella rushed into the kitchen.

"Did you hear me?"

"We did," Isabella said.

Emmy read the rest of the text, grinned and said, "Phoebe thinks everyone should have another baby, including me."

"Mom! You said you couldn't have another baby because of Kevin Michael."

Emmy grinned and answered, "No I can't, Heather, but it wasn't because of your brother." She sighed and took a deep breath. "I'd love to have another baby to hold."

"Hey! Don't look at us, Mom. We're just kids," Heather said as she and Isabella dashed back to the family room.

"Thanks for calling, Diane. I wanted to see your face, so I can tell how you are." Emmy she sat in her recliner in the den and watched Diane on her iPad. "I know we shouldn't worry because God is in control of everything, but I have been praying for him all day."

"We aren't sure when we will fly home, but when we do, Bill and Mona will be coming with us," Diane said but didn't get a response. "Em, are you there? Did you hear me?"

"Sorry, but I gotta go," Emmy replied.

"What's going on?"

"The weather siren is going off, and the National Weather Service issued a tornado warning for the area. It's getting real windy and starting to rain. I think I can hear hail. Talk to you later."

Emmy tapped the iPad and hollered for the kids.

"Mom, we just got texts about a storm. Should we go to the basement?" Isabella asked.

"Yes, where is your brother?"

Heather pointed outside. "He's on the deck."

"Go to the basement. Now! I will get your brother. Where's your father?"

"He isn't home yet. He went to see Uncle Andy about band business."

"He's supposed to be home before dinner. I hope they have enough sense to seek shelter." Emmy opened the French doors and hollered, "Kevin Michael, get your butt inside this instant!"

"Look, Mom! It's hailing." He held up a golf-ball sized hailstone. "Isn't it cool?"

"Very cool. Now throw them down and get inside, please." She checked the sky. "It's getting rather dark, and there is a tornado warning for SoHam. Can't you hear the siren?"

"What siren?" he asked with a shrug.

She stared at him.

"I'm kidding. I hear it. I remember when Uncle Andy moved here. He heard the siren going off and didn't know why. His neighbors had to tell him."

"They don't have tornadoes in Albuquerque or San Diego." Emmy glanced at the sky again and heard a tree crashing to the ground somewhere in the woods. "Please, Kevin. Come in now."

"I'm coming." He tossed the hailstones into the yard.

"Where have you been?" Emmy asked when Kenny walked into the kitchen. "Why didn't you come home sooner?"

He hugged her, kissed her cheek and replied, "I was with Andy. You knew that, right?"

"Yes, but didn't you hear the tornado siren?"

"I heard it, but I knew you and the kids would be safe in the basement. You did go to the basement, right?"

"Of course! We know better than to take a chance. Kevin checked out the woods after the storm passed. It knocked over a few trees. Bobby called and said that big one behind the house lost a large branch. He said it came within a couple feet of hitting the house. He also said the driveway is partially blocked."

"It was clear enough for me. A few small branches and leaves scattered about, but nothing big enough to block it."

She put her hands on her hips. "He meant the driveway to the guesthouse. He can't get past it."

"Oh. I didn't check there. If they need to get out, I can use the Jeep to go through the woods."

"I talked to Liz a few minutes ago. They have no power, and neither does the church. She said Crest Ridge suffered more damage than most sections of SoHam. Will we be able to have church if the power's still out Sunday?"

"Even if the power company doesn't restore it, the church has generators to provide power to most of the building. The essential areas at least."

"We should check Diane's house and Mr. Robertson's place. There could be damage."

18

"I'll call Tony. He can drive his truck. He claims it will go everywhere and through everything."

"Yeah, well he's a doofus. Be careful."

Kenny and Tony checked their Bristol Ridge neighbors and found everyone safe and secure.

"Did you check Kristen's house?" Emmy asked when Kenny and Tony returned. "Can they get to the hospital if she needs to go because of the baby?"

"Emmy, she's not due until the middle of September. She's not going to have the baby tonight," Tony said.

"If she does, it will be your responsibility to get her and Wyatt to St. Bart's."

Tony grinned and saluted. "Yes, ma'am."

She stuck out her tongue and whispered, "You are such a dork."

Chapter Four

"Are you ready to worship?" Pastor Tyler asked the crowd at the early service.

"Yes!" they responded loudly.

"Why do we worship?"

"Because Jesus is alive!" they answered with a shout.

"Wow! That was amazing for the early group."

"All righty then," Jim Rosek said drawing a laugh from those around him.

His wife, Sheila, rolled her eyes.

"Do we have any stories of how God has been working in your life this week?" Tyler asked.

Richard Cornejo stood up and adjusted his mask. "I have a story."

Tyler hurried with a wireless mic to where Richard was sitting. "Go ahead."

Richard held the microphone at stomach height and started to talk which resulted in a ringing noise in the sanctuary.

"You need to hold the mic higher," Tyler whispered. "Otherwise it sounds terrible."

Richard stared at the mic like it was going to bite him, but held it higher. "The part of SoHam where we live was hit pretty hard by the storms Friday night. Many homes in the area were damaged and the power is out and will be for some time." He paused to get his voice under control and looked at the people sitting nearby. "The large trees in our front yard were blown over and barely missed taking out the house. I feel God protected us from the worst of the storm." He opened his Bible and continued using scripture passages to illustrate his point. He closed the Bible and said, "It could have been worse, and if it had been, I would still be praising God."

Several other people commented on the storm which ended the lives of three people.

"If there are no more stories, I will pray while the worship team takes their place," Tyler said.

"Did anyone do a head count?" Tyler asked Wyatt after the second service.

"I asked the tech team to count. Josh told me there were over a thousand people all total."

"Does that include the people in the nursery and the ones who stayed in the foyer?"

Wyatt shrugged. "I couldn't tell you, but will it cause a problem if we have so many people in the building?"

Tyler chuckled. "It's a better problem than if we didn't have anyone in the building."

"They might have counted a few people twice."

Tyler furrowed his brow. "Why? Who would be here for both services?"

Wyatt laughed and answered, "The worship and tech team."

"Do we have enough fuel for the bonfire?" Daryl Wiley asked Tyler Wednesday afternoon.

Tyler chuckled and replied, "Wait till you see this go up in flames. It will surprise you."

"Do we need a permit to do this?"

Tyler shook his head. "We are technically in an unincorporated section of Crest Ridge, but I always call the station on Ellington and let them know about our plans. Sometimes they stop by to keep an eye on things, but they trust us."

"The teens are anxious for tonight," Daryl said. "They haven't met as a group since the government shut down churches. Was that in March or April? I can't remember."

"March 15th was the last Sunday before the shutdown," Tyler answered. "Is Brenda bringing the kids later? Liz is bringing ours. Phoebe and David want to see the fire, but they won't stay.

"Brendan and Carissa are old enough to enjoy the bonfire, and since we invited the junior high kids, they want to be part of everything. Ryan and Rebecca are going to help, and she lined up a sitter for the kids. They can use the nursery, right?"

Tyler nodded. "We have opened it for worship team practice."

"Kenny, are you taking the kids to church, or am I?" Emmy asked as she put the leftover lasagna in the fridge. "If you want me to take them, I need to shower."

He walked into the kitchen. "Haven't you showered today?"

"No, I was lazy this morning."

"You brushed your teeth though, right? I did kiss you earlier."

She rolled her eyes. "I wasn't a total slob."

"Would you mind taking them? I really don't want to hang around. Some of the newer teens ask me a ton of questions."

"Why?" she asked with a straight face. "You're just a dorky father."

"You know why."

She tilted her head, put a finger to her mouth and asked, "Are you that famous musician who plays guitar for Fridays At Five? You look rather familiar. Are you a for real rock star?"

"Very funny, Em."

She moved closer and whispered, "Can I be your groupie? I've always wanted to..."

"What are you guys doing?" Kevin asked as he tromped into the kitchen and opened the fridge. "Do we have anything to eat? I'm hungry again."

"We just ate twenty minutes ago," Emmy said.

"Who's taking us to church?"

Emmy looked at Kenny and sighed. "I will take you. Are your sisters ready? We should leave soon."

"They were putting on makeup. Heather chased me out of her room. They're dressed up like it's a party or a date."

"They are not going on dates," Kenny insisted. "They are twelve, and that's much too young."

Kevin looked at his mother. She made a circular motion around her ear and pointed at Kenny.

"Yeah, he can't count," Kevin said.

"You could roast a marshmallow on the fire from fifty feet away," Emmy said later at the church. "I think it might melt the siding of the storage shed.

Liz laughed and observed the teens conversing in small groups around the bonfire. "They are trying to maintain social distancing, but without much success."

"Emmy, are your girls wearing makeup tonight?" Rebecca asked.

"I told them they could." Emmy giggled and added, "Their father is doing everything in his power to prevent them from growing up. He can't remember how he felt about me at their age."

Liz and Rebecca stared at Emmy as the wind shifted and blew smoke on them.

"What?" Emmy asked as they moved away."

"You said 'how Kenny felt about you.' Did you mean the opposite?" Liz asked.

"Maybe."

"I've heard enough stories about your childhood to know you and Kenny were close friends at that age."

"We grew up together. Well, I was seven when we met."

"Rory Porter lived down the street," Liz said looking at Rebecca then Emmy. "Were you friends?"

"Yes, but he was... how should I put it? A little more adventuresome than Kenny."

"Is it true you would sneak out at night to hang with Kenny?" Rebecca asked.

"No," Emmy said putting her hands on her hips.

"Emmy, tell the whole truth," Liz said with a grin.

Rebecca looked at Liz then Emmy. "What is the whole truth?"

"I didn't sneak out to be with Kenny," Emmy said.

"Emmy," Liz said slowly then giggled.

"I would sneak out to hang with Rory, but he wasn't my boyfriend. I didn't have to sneak out to be with Kenny."

"Okay," Rebecca said. "I think I've met Rory, but I don't need to know the whole story between you guys."

Emmy watched Heather and Isabella talking to Peter Bertucci. "Kenny is a year older than Rory, and he was more interested in music than girls. My parents trusted him. Rory liked girls. He had a thing for my sister, but she liked older men."

"You've mentioned Rory had an older brother who died at an early age. Did you know him very well?" Liz asked.

"Not like Rory. He was twenty-five, I think," Emmy said. "Wow! It was twenty years ago."

"Why did you sneak out to be with Rory?" Rebecca asked.

"To have fun. Nothing more," Emmy answered.

"Let's gather together," Daryl said. "I want read a short devotional..."

"We need to help Daryl and Brenda," Liz said.

Rebecca giggled and whispered, "I want to hear more about you and Rory."

"There's not much to tell," Emmy replied.

Emmy waited until Tyler dismissed the group to approach Liz and Rebecca.

"Are you going to tell me more about Rory and Kenny?" Rebecca asked. "I should check on my babies."

Liz looked at Emmy and knew something was up. "Let's all check on the babies."

Emmy followed Liz and Rebecca into the building and down the hall to the daycare center.

"What is on your mind, Em?" Liz asked.

"I need to tell you something tonight, so you aren't blindsided tomorrow."

Rebecca held Hannah while Isaiah played with a toy drum. "I don't understand."

Emmy took a deep breath, looked at her friends and said, "I need to take time away from the worship team."

"What? Why?" Rebecca asked. "I don't understand."

"This isn't an easy choice, but it's something I need to do. I've been on the team close to twenty years, and right now I feel burned out. Part of it is because of the virus thing." She took another deep breath. "This has been the craziest year ever."

"For all of us," Liz said.

"I'm not saying I won't ever be a part of the team again. I'm not cut out to be in charge. I know that."

"You've done a great job leading the team through this situation," Liz said.

24

"Who will be in charge," Rebecca asked.

"Duh!" Emmy said. "You, of course. You have a college degree to lead the worship team. You're more organized than me. You know more music theory and everything."

"I have two babies."

"That made this more difficult, but the girls and I can help you. We can watch the kids while you work."

"Have you told anyone else?" Liz asked.

Emmy shook her head. "Kenny knows, but I haven't told anyone else."

"We won't say anything until you tell the team," Liz promised.

"Mom, what is so important that you have to tell us all together?" Kevin asked as the entire family sat at the breakfast nook table.

"You aren't pregnant, are you?" Heather grinned.

"Of course not." Emmy shook her head.

"Do you have the virus now," Isabella asked. "Did you catch it from Daddy, and it took this long to show up?"

"No, I am not sick. This concerns the worship team."

Kenny looked up from his phone.

"Did you get fired?" Kevin asked. "Did you mess up and Pastor Tyler had to fire you?"

"No, but tonight I'm telling the team I have to take time away. I'm burned out. I've been singing at church for eighteen years. I need a break."

"Oh, we thought it was something serious. Take a couple weeks off, Mom. It's no big deal," Isabella said.

"You didn't sing every week when the Schulenbergs were here," Heather said.

"I need more than a couple weeks off. More like six months before I consider singing again."

"Do you have a problem with your throat like Uncle Andy?" Isabella asked.

"No. This is not related to my physical health. It's more about my mental health," Emmy said.

Kevin laughed. "Did Uncle Tony say you were crazy again?"

"No, but I feel like it at times." She checked the clock. "I need to go. I might be home earlier than normal. After I tell them my news, they might decide they don't need me this week."

"If we could settle down, I'm going to pray and we can get started."

The worship team stopped socializing and took their seats in the music suite.

Rebecca prayed and held up squares of paper. "I would like to start something new. Please write your praises and prayer requests on the paper."

"What if we can't think of anything?" Ryan asked.

Rebecca put her hands on her hips and frowned at her husband. "You have plenty of things to be thankful for."

They filled out slips of paper as they talked about the latest news and political scandals.

"Do I have everyone's lists?" Rebecca asked.

Josh Belanger handed his to Rebecca. "Sorry. I'm always the last one."

Rebecca shuffled the slips and returned them to the team. "Please remember to pray for the requests this week. Before we move into the sanctuary to rehearse, Emmy would like to talk to you."

Emmy moved to the front of the room, took a deep breath, wiped away a tear and said, "I am taking time away from you starting next week."

"What?" Bobby O'Connor said.

Several people expressed disbelief.

Emmy closed her eyes for a moment then said, "I've been on the team since 2002, and I need a break."

Robby Collins looked at Bobby and asked, "What did you do now?"

Bobby shrugged.

Emmy shook her head. "This isn't because of something one of you did. Not even Bobby."

Bobby looked at Robby and nodded. "Not my fault this time."

"Bobby is the only one still on the team from when I started."

"Maybe we should make him take time off," Josh said. "We have younger drummers who need a chance to play."

Rebecca glared at him, and he shut up.

"This isn't something I'm doing without a lot of thought and prayer. I don't feel God has called me to be a worship pastor forever. Rebecca is back and more capable than me of leading you."

"Did the old people complain again?" Josh asked. "They always complain if we don't sing enough hymns or when we try something new with the lights."

"It wasn't anything like that," Emmy said. "Before this drags out any longer, I would appreciate your prayers, and hope you will understand my decision. Respect it, I mean. Whatever."

"If this is your last week with the team, should we sing your songs instead of the ones you picked out?" Regina Collins asked.

"No, let's sing what Rebecca chose, and I will not be announcing anything from the platform about this being my last week or anything."

"People will wonder why you aren't singing after a few weeks, Em," Bobby said. "What should we tell people?"

"Tell them God is moving me into a different phase of my spiritual journey."

"How about we tell them you have a sore throat instead?" Bobby said with a grin.

Chapter Five

"Who is picking everyone up at the airport?" Emmy asked Saturday afternoon. "Should I do it?"

Kenny grabbed his wallet and the keys to the Odyssey. "Brady asked me to drive them home. Mr. Robertson needs to rest. You can see him later "

"Okay, I won't bother him right away," she replied with her hands behind her back.

Kenny laughed and asked, "Aren't you a little old to cross your fingers and lie?"

"Hush. I'm not exactly lying. It will be later than it is now when I see him," she explained.

He put his hands on her shoulders and asked, "Are you going to stay here until I get back?"

Emmy sighed. "Fine. I will remain at home until you return. I can't promise anything more."

Kenny parked next to the hanger where Mr. Robertson's Gulfstream III was stored when not in use. After checking the time, he got out, walked around the building and stood where he could see the runway. The plane landed within a few minutes, taxied to the front of the hanger and shut down. Kenny walked toward the plane and watched as the door opened and the stairs were lowered.

"Hello, Brady," Kenny hollered as he waved.

"We made it back," Brady replied.

Kenny watched as Brady exited followed by Bennett and then Mr. Robertson with Mona at his side.

Mr. Robertson paused and looked at the blue clear sky. He spotted Kenny and whispered to Mona, "I wonder how he managed to keep Emmy from coming with."

"Maybe she's driving herself and hasn't arrived yet," Mona replied.

Eventually, the six passengers were on the tarmac. Kenny brought the Odyssey around and the men helped the pilots and the one flight attendant unload the plane and then load the luggage into the minivan.

"If it all doesn't fit, we can put it in the hanger and come back," Brady said while looking at Marissa's luggage.

"I called an Uber and it should arrive shortly," Bennett said. "I assumed we would need two vehicles."

Diane nudged Mona and whispered, "I'm surprised the plane could take off with everything Marissa brought. She would fill the luggage hold in a jumbo jet."

The Uber arrived and Marissa's and Bennett's luggage was loaded.

"I will call my parents and let them know we are back," Marissa said. "Mother has been worried sick. She will be pleased to know Bill is doing much better."

"We better not tell Emmy about the Uber. She will be upset knowing there would have been room for her," Kenny said.

Emmy waited at home until Kenny returned.

"I'm back," he said hanging up the keys. "Everyone is home now, and Mr. Robertson is tired from the flight."

Emmy brushed past him and hollered, "I'm outta here." She ran to the garage and jumped in her BMW.

"Emmy!" Kenny hollered to no avail.

"Hi, Dad. Where's Mom going?" Kevin asked. "She drove away in a big hurry."

"She's probably going to see Mr. Robertson."

"How is he?" Kevin searched the pantry for something to eat.

"Tired. He's been through quite an ordeal this year with the virus and now a heart attack."

"I guess he won't be doing any fishing soon." Kevin grabbed an apple from the island and headed outside.

"I'm sorry to bother you, Mona, but can I see him for just one second?" Emmy asked holding up a finger.

Mona hugged her and whispered, "He's in the front parlor, and you can talk to him for a whole minute."

"I won't stay too long. I promise," Emmy said holding up her hands for Mona to see.

29

"I need to unpack. I'll be upstairs if you need me," Mona said allowing Emmy to have time alone with Mr. Robertson.

Emmy entered the formal parlor, which would look perfect for a movie set of a Southern plantation though with modern amenities. Mr. Robertson waved from the couch and patted the spot next to him.

"I had to see you." She settled beside him and touched his arm.

"I feel so much better now that I can see you," he said with a smile. "I'm sorry about your phone. I'll buy you a new one."

"Only if you can find one with a purple case," she said softly. "You look tired."

"I'm regaining my strength and feeling better each day. The nurses and aides made me walk or sit up. They don't let you sleep very long."

"Kenny's father complained about the lack of sleep. He slept for twelve hours when he got home."

Emmy kept her promise and only stayed for ten minutes.

"I will come and see you every day." She leaned toward him and kissed his cheek.

"I will look forward to your visits."

Before the worship team left the music suite Sunday morning, Shaun Runyon stood up and announced, "Most of you know I asked Tinsley to be my wife a while back. We originally planned to get married this fall, but because of the virus and the lockdown, we can't have the wedding Tinsley envisioned, so our plans have changed. We have decided to get married right away. In two weeks, actually. I will be moving to South Dakota next week. I'm sorry for the short notice, but it's the way everything has worked out."

"We knew we would lose you the day you introduced us to Tinsley," Emmy said.

"Tinsley is a very blessed lady," Rebecca added.

The men shook Shaun's hand and offer congratulations.

"We are losing two members of the team today," Liz whispered to Rebecca.

30

"I know, and she made me promise not to mention anything to the congregation about this being her last Sunday."

"At least she's not moving. God may tell her to start singing again in a few months," Liz replied.

"I'm counting in it," Rebecca said.

As the worship team walked off the platform after the close of the second service, Liz put her arm around Emmy's shoulders. "You didn't cry. I was sure you would break down during your last song."

Emmy put an arm around Liz's waist. "A year ago I would have bawled like a baby, but I don't feel sad right now. Yeah, I will miss being on the team, but I am sure God wants me to do something else now."

"Maybe Jesus wants you to concentrate on your books for a while. I love reading them, and I'm sure so do thousands of other readers." Liz waited for a response but Emmy was quiet. Liz took Emmy in her arms and held her.

"Great! Now I'm going to lose it," Emmy said as the tears erupted.

Chapter Six

"The deal is done," Brady said walking onto the back deck Monday shortly before noon. "Bennett and I signed all the papers. Carson & Caden no longer exists as a company on its own. It has been absorbed into the PLMZ Technology Group. I am free to stay home."

"Until you get bored again." Diane shielded her eyes from the sun and looked at her husband.

Brady sat across the table from Diane. "I have thought of that." He etched a squiggle through the condensation on the pitcher of iced, sweet tea. "I have neglected my photography hobby for too long. When Emmy asked me to do the photography for the album cover, I realized how much I enjoyed it. It's relaxing yet challenging in a way, and I get to use the creative part of my brain."

Diane grinned and added, "Plus, you get to stay home with me and the kids." She stood and walked around the table.

"I promise not to start any more companies unless I can work from home."

Diane shook her head. "Brady, say these words 'no more companies.'"

He pulled her into his arms and whispered, "No more companies."

"Show me your hands."

"Why?"

"Making sure you haven't learned from Emmy."

"Though her face isn't new to us, we have a new member on the team," Tyler said Monday morning at the weekly staff meeting. "Now that Emmy has officially stepped down as co-leader of the worship team, Pastor Rebecca has agreed to take over full-time. She will need help with childcare, but we can handle it."

"My mother has agreed to watch the kids during the week," Rebecca replied.

"Have you decided which days you are taking off?" Tyler asked.

"Tuesday and Friday are the logical choices, but Saturday is an easy day, too, since by then everything is set for the services."

After discussing the technical needs of the worship team, Rebecca mentioned, "We used to have enough volunteers to maintain four separate teams but the pandemic changed that. We should ask for more volunteers."

"Do you feel people are less inclined to volunteer because of the time commitment?" Wyatt asked. "The team still rehearses Thursday evenings and early Sunday morning. That doesn't include the time people practice on their own."

"One needs to be intentional and have a willingness to sacrifice time for other personal endeavors, but our rehearsals are not as long as when I first joined the team," Rebecca said. She giggled and added, "I sounded rather formal, but you understand my meaning, right?"

"I'll look up the fancy words you used later," Jonah said with a smile.

"Concerning our Hispanic congregation, Dr. Schofield now considers them to be part of the Nazarene denomination. Donte Flores has been granted a district license, and he will continue to lead them in the old sanctuary Sunday mornings. I don't see an issue with traffic for the time being," Tyler said.

"Where is Pastor Flores?" Daryl asked. "I thought I saw him earlier."

"He is giving our new intern a thorough tour of the buildings and grounds. They should be back soon, and you can meet Quinn Moore. He comes highly recommended by Dr. Behren. The family is from Bellchester, Indiana, and Dr. Behren has known Quinn for years. He will graduate from Olivet after the fall semester."

"What is he going to do?" Wade Dickinson, the childrens' pastor, asked. "Will he be available to assist in all departments?"

Tyler chuckled and replied, "When Dr. Behren hired me as an intern, I helped with everything. I answered the phone, I helped the maintenance crew, sorted mail and even mowed the property."

"Wait! Don't you still do all that stuff?" Wyatt asked. "I saw you mowing last week."

Tyler chuckled. "I enjoy mowing, but I have learned to delegate a bit better through the years."

Dave Persching parked his black 2018 Porsche 911 on the edge of the asphalt across from the garage wing of the Colwell house. He jumped out, hurried to the passenger side and opened the door.

"This is it. Are you ready to meet everyone?" He watched as Claudia Hall's feet and long, slim legs emerged from the car. He thought about the first time he saw the twenty-three-year-old, blonde, Australian model in person after seeing her on the covers of numerous fashion magazines. "If Emmy or the twins are downstairs, they will ask you a thousand questions about makeup, fashions and everything else teens are interested in."

"Did you tell her I was coming today?" Claudia asked in her seductive, husky voice which had instantly captured Dave's heart.

"I had to tell her because Deborah told the twins about us," Dave replied closing the door and smiling up at Claudia. "Emmy's twins. Not mine."

"I want to meet the rest of your kids soon." Claudia gazed at the house. "It looks normal compared to the house where your ex lives."

Dave laughed and took her hand as they walked toward the service door. "Macy hates the house. She calls it a spaceship and wants to sell it, but the price is too high for the current market. I offered to buy it back at a reasonable price, but she refused."

They entered the garage, walked down the concrete steps and into the lounge outside the basement recording studio.

"This is Claudia Hall," Dave said to the members of Fridays At Five, who stared at her. He pointed to each man and introduced them.

"Are you guys going to say something, or are you going to stand there like idiots with your mouths open?" Emmy asked with a laugh.

Kenny closed his mouth.

"I'm going to be an idiot," Jeff said.

Emmy walked up to Claudia and smiled. "I'm Emmy. I promised the girls they could meet you before you leave. I hope you don't mind. The guys are not usually complete dorks, but they're acting like it now." She shook her head and poked Kenny's side. "Say something."

"Hello, Ms. Hall." Kenny cleared the cloud from his mind. "You're taller than I imagined."

Emmy rolled her eyes. *Such a dork.*

Claudia smiled and bumped his fist. "It's a requirement in my profession and please call me Claudia. We have to be tall and slender. I love Foster's beer, but have to limit my intake. I workout more than some pro athletes I know."

Eventually, the rest of the guys relaxed and talked to Claudia.

"If you don't mind, I'm going to take Claudia upstairs to meet the girls. You can have her back later, Dave," Emmy said with a grin.

Claudia kissed Dave then grinned at the guys and waved. She followed Emmy to the stairs.

"Wow! You said she was gorgeous, but she's like a fifteen on a scale of one-to-ten." Jeff high-fived Dave.

"I thought you were joking when you told me you met her," Jeremy said. "Are you guys dating or something?"

"You could say that," Dave answered with a grin.

"She's from Australia, right?" Adam asked.

"What gave it away?"

"I love her accent," P.J. said.

"She is a knockout," Dave said in his best Aussie accent.

After talking about Claudia for several minutes, Kenny asked, "Are we going to work on the demos or not?"

The band moved into the studio where Will Consoli and Stuart Lederer were busy setting up mics. Kenny played a new tune on his acoustic guitar.

"I like it, but will we date the record if we sing about the virus?" Jeff asked.

"That's kinda the point," Kenny answered.

He played snippets of other songs.

"Are they all about current events?" Jeremy asked. He shrugged and added, "It's okay, but we've never done a project about politics or been very open about our views."

"Maybe it's time we change," Dave said. "Let's face it. We're considered an old band by the kids now. We aren't going to sell anywhere close to as many CDs as in the past. We should make an album for the fans who still listen to us."

Heather and Isabella raced out of their bedrooms and down the stairs after Emmy let them know Claudia was in the family room.

"These are my daughters. Heather is the one with the red top and Isabella is wearing ugly purple shorts. Where did you get those, Isa?"

"From Teens Forever in the mall. Heather said the color looks good on us."

"It's a pleasure to meet you," Claudia said with a smile. "I wish I could wear that color, but I can't."

"We've seen your photograph on the cover of several magazines," Heather said. "We showed one of you in a bikini to our brother, and he thought you were hot."

"He's twelve and more interested in hanging out with his friends," Isabella said.

"I have four older brothers and grew up trying to do everything they did," Claudia said. "They are all taller than me, so that's where I get my height."

"Aunt Sloane is almost as tall as you, and she played basketball in college," Heather said. "But she's had four kids and is a lot heavier now."

"Heather!"

"Mom, I didn't say she's fat. She's not as fat as she was a year or two ago."

"What's it like to be on the cover of a magazine?" Isabella asked.

"It's a lot of work, but I get to travel the world. I won't be modeling forever. Maybe another two or three years."

"What will you do then?"

36

"I plan to finish my education and become a veterinarian. I want to buy a ranch near my hometown and raise cattle and horses."

"That sounds exciting, but totally opposite of working as a model" Isabella said.

"I'm really an Australian cowgirl at heart. I grew up on a ranch and learned to ride horses before I could walk. That's what my mother always says."

Isabella grinned at her mother. "Mom was a tomboy when she was young. That's what Grandma Colwell says."

"Can you give us some makeup tips?" Heather asked.

Claudia smiled and answered, "Yes. Don't wear any."

"Really?" Heather asked.

"I have to wear it when I'm working, but otherwise I don't bother."

"But you have one advantage over us," Isabella said. "You are beautiful. We're maybe considered cute by some of the guys, but nothing more."

Claudia looked at the twins then Emmy. "I disagree. You look like your mother, and she looks more than cute."

"Daddy always says so," Isabella replied with a giggle.

Chapter Seven

"Mom! Can me and Ben watch the construction guys start working on Mr. Bennett's new house?" Kevin asked. "Caden texted and said the machines are already there."

"Maybe you should ask your father," Emmy answered.

"He said to ask you. We promise not to get in the way, but Ben wants to video it as a school project."

"For real?" Emmy asked.

"Yeah. Like a time lapse project to show the different stages of construction."

"You guys just want to play in the dirt, but it's all right with me as long as you stay out of the way."

"It will be cool to watch the excavators working," Ben shouted as he and Kevin raced out of the house and through the woods.

Kevin jumped over a tree trunk and replied, "It would be awesome to drive one of the machines."

"Kenny, Bennett has owned that land for fifteen years, and they are just now building on it. Do you know what kind of house he plans to build? Has Brady or Mr. Robertson said anything to you?" Emmy asked as she chopped vegetables for a salad.

"They live in the Barclay Estates so he could be close to the Academy. It might be a requirement for the headmaster."

"Diane told me he plans to retire as soon as the school returns to normal. He should because their kids are grown. He wanted to retire back in December, but the trustees talked him into staying to finish the school year. Then the virus thing happened, and he felt he had to stay on."

Kenny filled a glass with ice water and sat at the island to watch her. "It's a funny story. Brady told Tony and Tony told me Bennett wanted to build a ranch. A single story home, but Marissa wouldn't allow it. She insists on a bigger house."

Emmy laughed. "She is so vain. I can see her wanting the biggest house in the city even though it's only the two of them. "

38

"Hey, Fez, how have you been?" Kenny asked as he walked out of his parents' house and spotted him leaving the carriage house. "Are you headed to work?"

Fez closed the service door. "Yes, and I've been fine. How are you, Mr. Colwell?"

Kenny shook his head. "My father is Mr. Colwell. Not me. Would you like a ride? I'm heading to Darby's to pick up something for lunch." Kenny pointed to his Jeep. "Hop in. I know it's only a couple blocks, but the humidity is high enough to make you sweat if you blink."

"Thanks." Fez climbed in and buckled up.

"Is Darby's staying busy through this mess?" Kenny asked. He started the Jeep and pulled into the alley behind the carriage house.

"We aren't open for inside dining, but we have several outdoor tables now."

"I thought most restaurants were open now. Did something change?" Kenny asked.

Fez explained why Darby's wasn't seating people inside.

"The county health department must change the guidelines more often than Tiffany Swift used to change outfits at her concerts."

Fez stared at him blankly.

Kenny laughed. "I guess you've never heard of her, huh?"

Fez shook his head.

"She was a singer who changed clothes for every song. She was popular in the early 2000s. You probably weren't even born yet."

He shrugged. "I was born in March of 2000, but I never heard of her."

"What are your plans for the fall? I've heard Olivet will start the fall semester earlier than normal to avoid the flu season."

"Yes, and I already have my housing set. I thought about switching colleges."

"Why?" Kenny asked as he waited at the traffic light. He saw Danny Darby talking to some customers across the intersection.

39

"I got a promotion at work, and I would hate to lose it. If I went to one of the local colleges, I could keep my job and still take classes."

"You told Tyler you loved Olivet." Kenny drove through the intersection, pulled in Darby's and parked. "Have you changed your mind?"

"No, but I can afford Paul Frank Junior College on what I make." Fez jumped down and headed inside. "Thanks for the ride."

Kenny waved to Danny.

"Hi, Kenny. Did you call in an order?" Danny asked.

Kenny shook his head. "No, I was visiting my parents and decided I needed a burger and fries."

"I saw Fez get out of the Jeep."

"I heard you promoted him."

"He deserved it," Danny said.

"He also mentioned changing schools. I'd hate to see him leave Olivet because of the cost."

Danny stared at Kenny for a moment. "You better not tell Emmy. You know she will want to pay everything for him."

"We can afford to pay, but I don't think Fez would let us. He's rather proud and determined to pay his way through school. Kinda like someone else we know, huh?"

"He's just like she was. Dad offered to help her through college, but she wouldn't take a cent."

Kenny laughed and said, "She wouldn't let me or Mr. Robertson help her."

"Are you going to eat here, or take it home?" Danny asked.

"Are you nuts? If I take it home without something for everyone else, I would get murdered. I'll find an empty table or else run back to my parents' house."

"Suit yourself," Danny said with a laugh.

"Mama! Mama!" Ben shouted as he raced through the kitchen to her part of the house. "There's a letter for you from Italy. It came in today's mail."

Mama sat in her rocker in the sitting room reading one of Emmy's books. "What are you hollering about, Ben?"

He held out the letter. "This came for you. I think it's from Italy. You should read it right away. It might be important."

"Let me see it." She set her book on the end table.

Ben handed her the letter. "Why would you get mail from Italy? I know you're Italian, but did you ever live there?"

"I was born in this country, but both of my parents were born in Italy."

"When did they move here?" Ben asked.

Mama looked at the envelope and smiled. "It is from Italy. My parents came to this country when they were younger than you or even Coby, but they had brothers and sisters who stayed behind. Most of the other siblings lived their entire lives in Italy."

"What part of Italy? Did they live in Rome?" He shifted his weight back and forth.

Mama shook her head. "My family lived in the northern part. The region known as Lombardy."

"Is that where your family name comes from?"

"I suppose, but Lombardi is a very common name in Italy."

Ben pointed to the envelope. "Are you going to open it? Why would you get a letter from there now?"

"I occasionally write to a cousin who lives in Milan. We are the same age, but I haven't seen her in more than fifty years. Other than in pictures."

"Does she write in Italian?"

Mama smiled and pulled out the letter. "She writes in both Italian and English, but this appears to be mostly English."

"Can you read it to me?" Ben asked.

"Have a seat, and I will read it first. Then you can read it."

Mama read the letter. She smiled at some parts. Laughed out loud at others and sighed when she got to another part. She paused and wiped her eyes.

"Are you okay, Mama? Is it sad news?"

"Yes, it's rather sad, Ben," Mama whispered.

"What happened? Did someone die?"

"Yes, someone did."

"I'm sorry. Who was it?" Ben knelt beside his grandmother and patted her hand.

41

"It was my last remaining aunt. Aunt Luciana. She was my father's youngest sister and the last sibling to pass away."

"Was she really old? Was she over a hundred?"

"She was ninety-eight." Mama looked at the letter then at the family photos on the opposite wall above the buffet. "She wasn't born before my father left home. He probably only saw her a handful of times in his entire life. She never left the Lombardy region."

"Did your father go back home very often?"

"No, but he did go back after the war a few times." Mama grinned and said, "I'll tell you about one time he visited."

"Cool! I like hearing your old stories, Mama. Even if they are kinda boring at times."

"My family owned vineyards and my father would occasionally take a trip home to take care of a business matter. This must have been in... let's see if I can remember... Yes, it was in 1984. In the summer. Papa went back home..."

"Did you call him Papa like Peter and Dotty used to call Dad Papa?"

"Yes, we called him Papa and called our mother Mama."

"Everyone calls you Mama. Even most of the adults. You're like everyone's grandmother."

"Yes, but I love my real grandkids more. Please don't tell anyone, okay?"

"It will be our secret. So what happened in 1984?"

"My parents' house burned to the ground, your grandfather passed away and Heather and Marco were sick. I didn't want Tony to catch it, so my mother and Tony lived in one of Carmen's buildings for a few weeks. Maybe not even a month."

"How old was Dad?"

"He was not quite four."

"That's old enough to miss his father," Ben said.

"Yes. He didn't understand everything." Mama smiled and patted Ben's arm as she thought about her late husband. "There was a little girl who lived in the apartment on the top floor who liked to play with your father." She paused, grinned and asked, "Do you have any idea who it might have been?"

42

Ben shrugged and said, "How would I know. I wasn't born until 2007."

"I'll show you a picture, and you can try to guess who it is. Won't take a minute because I have a copy in this drawer." Mama quickly found the photo and handed it to Ben. "Do you recognize anyone?"

Ben peered at the photograph. "That's Dad with a football. That isn't Aunt Heather, is it?"

"No, Heather was older and bigger than your father. Look again."

"The little girl is holding his hand and looking up at him. She has dark curly hair, so it's probably not Aunt Kristen. She's got blonde hair in every picture I've ever seen. It looks like she has a ponytail with a purple ribbon." He looked at Mama. "I know it can't be either of them, but it reminds me of Heather and Isabella."

"You're getting very close," Mama said with a grin.

Ben inspected the photograph closer. "Is that Aunt Emmy? Did she and Dad really know each other when they were kids? I've heard them talk about it, but always thought they meant like kids in school or something. If that really is Aunt Emmy, she was just a little girl."

"They first met in the summer of 1984. In late July. They played together every day and became best friends for a time."

"What happened? Did you see my father at all?"

"I couldn't visit him very often because I was taking care of Heather and Marco, but I did take the picture. My mother moved out of the apartment building to another house when my father returned."

"Did my grandpa live in the apartment?"

Mama shook her head.

Ben smacked his forehead. "Oh, I'm sorry, Mama. I'm such a goof. He had already passed away, huh? I should have known that."

"It's okay. We had to delay his funeral until my father returned from Italy."

"Peter and Dad have that in common. They both lost parents at a very early age."

43

"Yes, they've known hardship."

"Dotty told me once she doesn't remember Aunt Heather at all. Her mom, I mean."

"She was only a year old when her mother passed away."

Ben looked at the letter again. "Do you ever dream about going to Italy and having like a huge family reunion of all the Lombardi and Bertucci cousins and relatives?"

"I used to think about it, and we did have a couple reunions. Now the younger generation isn't interested, and us older ones are too old and set in our ways to travel."

Ben grinned and said, "It's 2020. You don't have to travel, Mama. You can use your laptop and Facetime, or have a Zoom meeting. It's so easy."

"It might be easy for you."

"I can help you learn how to do it."

"Does it cost much?"

"I think it's free to Zoom, but I'd check with Mom first," Ben replied.

"That's an excellent idea. Maybe you could help me set it up one of these days."

"Okay, I'll do it, but do you remember enough Italian to understand what they're saying?"

"If they talk slowly, I might."

Ben laughed and said, "Mama, can you picture Aunt Emmy talking slowly and holding her hands still? She's totally Italian."

Mama grinned and looked at the photo again.

Chapter Eight

"Emmy, I noticed you didn't sing again this week," Alice Kramer mentioned in the foyer after the second service. "Are you not feeling well?"

"I'm fine, Mrs. Kramer, but I'm taking time away from the worship team. I've been doing it so long, and I feel God is pointing me in a different direction."

"I can understand. I've been teaching for twenty-five years, and every summer I feel God urging me to try something new," Mrs. Kramer said with a grin. "Maybe you will feel recharged after taking time away. Everyone loves hearing you sing."

"Thank you, and it's possible I will return on a part-time basis, but my days of leading the team are finished. I'm fairly certain of that. Have you heard anything about whether or not the school will function normally when it starts?" Emmy asked.

"The last information I received was we will start online for the first couple months before we evaluate the situation. Where did you decide to send the girls for high school?"

"We are going to try The Barclay Academy for a year. Their online curriculum is more advanced than at Ronald Reagan High School or St. Raymond's."

"It's a good school if a little liberal in ways. I wish we had the resources to start a high school. Maybe we will in the future," Mrs. Kramer said then left to find her husband.

Emmy waved to more people, and several of them asked why she didn't sing on the platform. She answered politely until Kenny and the kids rescued her.

"I heard people talking about you, Em," Kenny said on the drive home.

"Was it about me not singing?"

"Yes, but one of them mentioned how nice it was to see the young people leading the service."

"I guess I'm too old to be part of the team now." She stared out the window. *I will have to be patient and answer questions for a few weeks until they get used to me not singing.*

"What are we having for lunch? Don't tell me taco salad. I'm turning into a taco," Kevin asked as they arrived home. He waited until Isabella got out then scooted past her and sprinted up the stairs to the mudroom. He burst through the door and into the kitchen. "Uncle James! I thought that was your car. Did you bring lunch? I'm starving."

Father James looked up from the book he was reading at the large island. "Sorry, Kevin Michael, but I didn't stop at Darby's."

"That's okay. I'm sure Mom can make something other than taco salad for once."

"I could make pasta." Emmy walked up to her half-brother and rubbed his back. "How are you feeling? Better?"

Father James shrugged and rolled his shoulders. "I saw my chiropractor this week and got adjusted. I feel ten years younger now."

"Mom, you used to make a cold spaghetti salad, but you haven't made it in years," Isabella said. "Could you make it today? We could have that and sandwiches."

"I think I have everything, but let me check my recipe," Emmy said.

Ninety minutes later everyone was either in the pool or sitting at one of the round, glass-topped tables under a large umbrella.

"The spaghetti salad was pretty good," Father James said. "I doubt if I've ever had that before."

"It's not something your mother would have made, huh?" Emmy teased. "Not a Russian dish."

"If it didn't contain potatoes or cabbage, my mother didn't cook it." Father James looked at Kenny and asked, "Have you given up on the girls not wearing those skimpy bikinis?"

Emmy smacked his arm. "Why are you bringing that up? You asked just to get a reaction."

"It's okay, Em. I'm getting better at knowing which battles to fight and which to avoid. They might get away with wearing those bikinis now, but wait till they are old enough to date."

46

Emmy rolled her eyes and muttered, "You are not going to lock them in a closet until they're thirty."

"No, but there are other ways to control their dating."

"Are you going to make them take Kevin along as a chaperone? My mother used to force Diane to bring me on her dates, so I could spy on her."

"I've heard that story before," Father James said. "Did you report back to your mother and spill the beans?"

"No, and eventually Mom gave up on trying to control Diane's life. She switched her focus to me."

"Mom, Peter wants to swim. Can I tell him it's okay?" Heather asked.

"It's all right with me. Ask your father," Emmy said with a grin.

"Daddy, can Peter come over?"

"Yes, but he needs to bring Dotty, Noemi and the boys. They might want to swim, too."

Heather smiled. "Thanks. I'll text him and let him know."

Emmy stared at Kenny.

"What?" he asked with a shrug.

"Do you think making all the kids come with Peter will make a difference?"

"It's worth a try." Kenny watched the girls dive into the pool and shook his head. "I love my daughters, but sons are easier..."

"In what way exactly?" Emmy asked with her arms over her chest.

"You know what I mean." Kenny squirmed in his chair.

"No, I don't. Tell me." Emmy put her elbows on the table and frowned at Kenny.

Father James chuckled and said, "This should be interesting."

"Boys can't get pregnant."

Emmy slapped the table top knocking over her glass of ice tea. "Men! Fathers can be so hypocritical. Are you saying it would be all right for Kevin Michael to become sexually active but not the girls?"

"You know better." Kenny stood the glass of tea upright. "He needs to follow the same rules."

Emmy grinned at Father James. "It's so easy to push his buttons and embarrass him. I almost feel guilty doing it, but it's so much fun."

"Maybe you should confess your sins and do the proper penance," Father James said.

"Did she tell you about quitting the worship team?" Kenny asked.

"I didn't quit," Emmy insisted. "I'm taking a break. There's a difference."

Father James nodded and replied, "She even asked for my advice. After getting over the shock, we talked about it. It's not something she chose to do without serious deliberation."

Emmy stuck out her tongue at Kenny as the Bertucci boys rode their bicycles up to the deck. Peter pulled up a moment later in his car bringing his sisters.

"Thanks for letting us swim, Aunt Emmy. Dad said thanks, too. Now he can spend the afternoon with Mom."

"You're welcome, Ben, and I think I'll call your father every ten minutes to annoy him."

"He said you might be childish enough to do that, so he turned off the phones," Ben said then cannonballed into the pool.

"I wasn't really going to pester Tony," Emmy said looking guilty.

"Of course not," Father James said.

"How are your parents coping with the virus thing?" Kenny asked a few minutes later.

Father James answered, "It hasn't changed much. They didn't go out very often before."

"None of us leave the house as often now," Emmy said.

"True. My parents use a delivery service for their groceries, and Dad hasn't put gas in the car for two months. They do go for walks, so they aren't completely lazy."

"Have you been walking?" Emmy asked.

"I get up early and walk. I like to beat the heat," Father James replied. "Plus, it's a good time to pray and meditate."

48

"Tell me," Emmy said. "If I get up at six, I have two hours to get stuff done before anyone else gets out of bed. I can be very productive during that time."

Later that afternoon Emmy was curled up on the couch in the family room watching a movie when her phone chirped.

"I hope I haven't called at the wrong time," the voice asked.

Emmy grinned and reached for the TV remote. "I'm sitting by myself watching a silly movie, Pastor Chase. You didn't interrupt anything."

"That's good to know," Chase Hillman replied. "I have a reason for calling out of the blue, but first, how is everyone?"

"We are doing great. Did you know Kenny had the virus?"

"I did. Is he okay now?"

"He's fine," Emmy explained how everyone thought she had the virus but all she had was a cold. "Tell me about the girls. How old are they now?"

"Anna is twenty-five and Jada is twenty-two. They both graduated from Mount Vernon Nazarene University."

"No way! Really? The twins are starting high school in August."

"Yes, and Anna has two daughters..."

"Wait a second!" Emmy shouted as she sat up straight. "Are you telling me you're a grandfather?"

"Yes, and Yvonne is a grandmother. That's how it works when your children become parents. She loves it, and since Anna and Lucien live three blocks away, she can spoil the girls."

"What about Jada? What is she doing?"

"She is engaged to Troy Martin. He's on my staff and also teaches a class about ancient languages at Trinity College. That's a small school here in Toledo."

"Unreal!" Emmy said. "They were little girls when I first met you. How long have you been gone? I can't remember."

"We left in February of 2013. Seven years ago."

"It seems longer."

"A lot has happened in those seven years. Did I tell you I'm no longer the worship pastor?"

"No! Why not? What are you doing?"

"I became the senior pastor two years ago. I still fill in if needed but otherwise I leave the worship team alone."

Emmy explained how she and pastor Rebecca co-led the team. "But now I'm taking time away. I feel God calling me to do something else."

"Then this is the perfect time to mention this," Chase said.

"What?"

"Our worship pastor resigned three weeks ago, and I'm looking for a replacement. Yvonne suggested I call you, but I told her you were still involved in your church."

"I couldn't move to Toledo!" Emmy exclaimed. "Why would you even ask?"

"I wouldn't, but the Holy Spirit keeps whispering your name in my ear."

"Are you sure it wasn't Yvonne?" Emmy asked.

"Perhaps it wasn't to ask you to move to Toledo, but maybe it was God telling me to call you and see how you guys are doing."

"That makes more sense. I could never leave SoHam."

"I can see why you want to take a break from the team. You've been singing at church for almost twenty years. That's a long time."

"The twins sing with the teen group now and Kevin is getting better on the drums. Maybe we will start a family band someday."

"You have someone to play keys, drums and guitar. You need a bass player," Chase said.

Emmy laughed and said, "Maybe one of the teens from church will start dating Heather and we can teach him."

"The twins aren't old enough to date."

"Not for another twenty years according to their father."

Chapter Nine

"What time are you going to start recording?" Emmy asked as she and Kenny ate breakfast Monday.

"Will and Stuart should be here by nine to get everything set up." Kenny took another bite of toast and added, "The guys should arrive by ten."

"This is the last CD on your current contract, right?" Emmy glanced out the window and saw Kevin heading to the pool. "Has Mr. Kesson talked to you about a new deal?"

"We have talked about it, but the guys aren't in a hurry to sign a new contract. The industry has changed so much. We might decide to become independent like so many other bands."

"Do you think it will take long to record this one? You said you would like to keep it simple."

"The whole band is ready to record, and we agreed not to spend more than a month in the studio. I can always add tracks after that, but we are not going to spend a year or longer on this project. It's not worth it to us now."

"Will you feel okay if the CD isn't up to past band standards?" Emmy asked. "Once it's out, you can't take it back."

"I didn't mean it like that. You know how it is. You can listen to a CD and think of so many different sounds you could use. At some point you have to say it's finished. It's like editing your books."

"Tell me. I hate reading them after they're published. I always think I should have cut lines out or added more description or whatever. I agree. You have to say it's finished at some point otherwise nothing would ever get released."

Kenny finished his toast, drained his coffee and asked, "What about your quarantine book? Is it finished? How many versions do you have?"

"Only eighteen different versions of this one. I'm sending it in today. It should be available by Wednesday. That's why I love self-publishing. I can release a book whenever I choose."

"Are you going to show me the cover? What did you end up calling it anyway?"

"You can see the cover later, and I called it *I'm Releasing the Prisoner: Two Weeks in Quarantine.* What do you think?"

"I need to see the cover before I decide," he said then stood up. "Maybe you can show me when we take a break. I better help the guys." He kissed Emmy and went downstairs.

Emmy booted up her laptop and took another look at the cover. "When you can see the cover, it makes sense." She sighed and closed the folder. *It's only a short little book. I don't expect anyone to buy it.*

"Did I tell you the quarantine book is available online now?" Emmy said as everyone sat down to eat dinner Wednesday.

"Mom, you didn't tell us it was finished," Heather said as she took a pork chop from the platter and passed it to Isabella. "Can we read it, or is it only for adults?"

"You can read it, but it might bore you since you were here for everything," Emmy said. "I hope the sauerkraut isn't too salty. I didn't add any salt as I cooked it."

Kevin took a bite. "Tastes good to me, but I like salt on my potatoes."

"I never had a chance to check out the cover," Kenny said. "We got on a roll and didn't stop working until eight o'clock."

"You could look at Amazon if you really want, or else wait until my author copies arrive," Emmy said.

"Mom, the pork chops are so tender. Did you add applesauce? I can kinda taste apples," Isabella said then took another bite.

"I thought you liked it when I add applesauce."

"I do," Isabella answered. "The combination of sweet and sour is perfect."

"Emmy, come and tell me about the cover," Kenny shouted later.

"Be right there. I'm loading the dishwasher."

She joined him in the den a few minutes later.

"What do you think? Do you like the cover?" she asked leaning over the back of his chair and looking at his laptop.

52

"I get the title now. Did you take this?"

"No, how could I? That's me in front of our bedroom doorway. I couldn't take the photo and be in it, too."

"Where did you get the yellow police tape? Who took the picture?"

"Brady took it, and I called Detective Sanders. He sent his son over with the tape. You remember Officer Sanders, right? He was the first one on the scene when I got hit by that SUV."

"I remember him." Kenny looked closely at the cover. "Okay, I like it. This is a different font than the one you use for your Claire and Ruby books, right?"

Emmy told him the names of the different fonts and other technical tricks she used for the cover.

"I didn't know you knew how to do all that," Kenny said.

"It's not difficult. I have the latest version of Photoshop and it has great features."

"Maybe we should let you do the artwork for the new CD. What do you say?"

She shook her head. "You couldn't afford me."

"Girls!" Emmy hollered. "Do you want to watch Shaun and Tinsley's wedding? It's on Facebook."

She waited for the twins to hurry downstairs before starting the video.

"Where did they get married?" Isabella asked. "Are there people watching in person?"

"They got married in the church where Tinsley works. She's one of the staff pastors," Emmy said.

"She is the children's pastor," Isabella replied. "Too bad she didn't get hired at our church. I've only talked to her a couple times, but she seems really sweet."

"She's walking down the aisle. Let's listen," Emmy said.

The twins sat on either side of their mother on the couch. Fifteen minutes later, it ended with Shaun and Tinsley kissing.

"Mom, why are you crying?" Heather asked. "It was just a video. It's not like we were really there."

"I always cry at weddings, or videos of weddings."

Heather grinned and said, "You better make sure you wear waterproof makeup when Isa and I get married."

"Will I embarrass you if I cry at your wedding?" Emmy asked after drying her eyes.

"Not unless you dance weird at the reception," Heather teased.

"I'm sorry I haven't talked to you lately, but I've been busy with the kids," Mary Galves told Emmy as they sat on the deck and drank coffee. "Jonah is watching them this morning because I needed a break, and I have a doctor appointment at ten."

Emmy looked at Mary and asked, "Are you sure you aren't having twins?"

Mary laughed. "No, I've gained more weight this time. I'm going to look more like my mother after I have this one. I may never again be the slender girl you once knew."

"Speaking of slender girls..." Emmy said then paused.

"You want to know about Dahlia, right?"

Emmy nodded then took another sip of coffee.

"She graduated from North Park. They held a ceremony of sorts. It was filmed, but no one could attend. No families, I mean. College went by so fast."

"Dany told me she found a job and moved to Indianapolis," Emmy said.

Mary listened to the birds singing before replying, "She did. Ma and Da are still upset."

"I can understand why. Dahlia is the baby of the family. Oh, you have to tell me more about Eli, too."

Mary smiled and said, "I will."

"What kind of job did Dahlia find?"

"She's working in an insurance office. Nothing special about the job. She could have found one just like it in SoHam."

"Sounds like she wanted to get away."

"She felt she needed a new start in a new city." Mary looked at Emmy for a second then added, "Dahlia changed after she lost the baby. She thought Ma and Da would never forgive her for what happened, but they did."

54

"I know," Emmy said softly. "I was there when Dahlia had a long talk with them."

"Dahlia didn't tell them she was moving until the day before she left. Ma and Da felt betrayed when she did that."

"Did she hurt them intentionally?" Emmy asked. "I can't believe the Dahlia I knew would do that."

Mary shook her head. "I don't believe she did it to hurt them, but I think she did it so they couldn't talk her out of moving, and she isn't the same Dahlia you knew as a child. She doesn't share our faith in God anymore."

"She hasn't been to our church for a long time," Emmy said. "Does she attend one in Indianapolis?"

"Not to my knowledge."

Both women sat for a time without speaking.

Emmy took a deep breath and said, "Tell me about Eli and Ashtyn. How does she spell her name? Heather told me, but I forgot."

Mary spelled the name for Emmy.

"Ashtyn McDaniels Michaelis," Emmy said slowly. "You know I've never really thought of Michaelis as an Irish name, but it is. Tell me how your brother met Ashtyn."

"Eli was in Atlanta on a business trip. A teacher's convention of some sort. Whatever. He went to a local Nazarene church and sat a few feet away from Ashtyn. He claims he heard her singing and fell in love instantly."

Emmy put her hands to her heart and sighed.

"After the service he gathered enough courage to talk to her, and she must have been insane because she liked him."

"Your brother is tall, handsome and charming," Emmy said. "I always wondered why some single young lady didn't snatch him up years ago."

"I suppose it was because God had other plans for him," Mary said with a sparkle in her eyes.

"Yeah, and that plan was Ashtyn McDaniels. I love that name. Ashtyn, I mean. Have they set a date for the wedding?"

"They want to wait until they can have a normal wedding and reception. Actually, her parents insist."

"So, he left his job at Jamie McGee Junior High and found one outside of Atlanta and is living there all by himself, huh?"

Mary laughed and pointed at Emmy. "You're wondering if Ashtyn is living with him, aren't you?"

Emmy shrugged. "I would find it difficult not to... you know... if I was in that situation."

"You made it to your wedding..."

"Only with the grace of God and lots of cold showers."

"What's this I hear about you leaving the worship team?" Lynette Jefferson asked over the phone. "When did this happen and why?"

"How did you find out?" Emmy asked.

"Paul may be the pastor of SoHam First Nazarene, but we still have friends in Crest Ridge. Tell me why you made this decision," Lynette insisted.

"I felt God telling me it was time to do something else. I've been on the team for almost twenty years."

"That's no excuse. There are pastors who preach for over fifty years."

"I needed a break. Pastor Rebecca is better equipped to lead the team..."

"Hold on, girl. Didn't you write a song about God using inadequate, ordinary people or something like that?"

Emmy rolled her eyes. "Yes, and he used me on the team, but now God is leading me in a different direction."

"Let me get this straight. You aren't touring anymore."

"No one is," Emmy said.

"Yes, but you retired from touring before the pandemic closed down the industry and the economy," Lynette said.

"Yes."

"And now you aren't even singing at church. Should I be concerned?"

"No, my faith and relationship with Jesus are stronger than ever."

"Good."

"How are the girls?" Emmy asked.

"Don't change the subject. I'm not through talking about singing yet."

"Fine," Emmy said with a sigh. "What else?"

"You could do us a favor and sing at our church once in a while. I'm not asking you to become part of our worship team."

"That didn't work out when we tried it before," Emmy said.

"Quite a few of the people who complained about the music in years past have moved away or left the church. Sometimes God's Kingdom grows by subtraction," Lynette said with a laugh.

"Tell me. We have a few members I would love to send your way."

"Thanks, but no thanks."

"Can we talk about the kids now?" Emmy asked.

"Yes, how are your kids doing? Has school started?"

"Not yet, but soon. The school decided, or maybe they didn't have a choice, but anyway, the first couple months will be online. Heather and Isabella will be taking classes online from The Barclay Academy."

"How can they be in high school already?" Lynette asked. "They were babies a couple years ago."

Emmy snorted and said, "They aren't babies now. They're bigger than me in every way you can imagine. Except maybe their butts."

"TMI, Em," Lynette said. "Ruth and Esther turned twenty last week."

"And you think my kids are getting old. Are they still going to Olivet?"

"They will be starting their third year there. Ruth changed her major and is going to be a nurse. Esther still thinks she wants to teach, but I really think she wants to be a pastor's wife."

"You can't always choose who you fall in love with," Emmy said. "You know how messed up I was when I was their age."

"And yet you turned out sorta okay," Lynette teased.

"Thanks for the endorsement."

"You're welcome," Lynette replied.

"How are things at the church? Is Paul doing okay? I heard you're meeting in person."

"He is, and we were able to open up earlier than you because we are so much smaller."

"Liz told me one of the smaller churches in the district had to close because they were so deep in debt."

"It is often a struggle for churches with fewer resources. The finances here were a concern at first, but our people have been very faithful in giving. That combined with the lower costs of running the building have enabled us to actually increase what we have in the bank. A lot of pastor's wives don't have access to finances, but Paul keeps me informed. The overall picture. Not details about who gives what. He doesn't know that."

"I wouldn't have the foggiest idea how our church is doing. Pastor Tyler never talks about money. Unless it's a special need. Sometimes we take up a collection for a certain situation, but I have the feeling the church is in good shape."

"Paul always says it's one thing for the church to be in good financial shape, but he would prefer the church be in great spiritual shape."

"I agree with him," Emmy said. "How can the pastor know. There's no way Tyler can't know everyone's spiritual condition in a church our size." Emmy laughed and added, "I'm amazed he can remember everyone's name. I sure can't."

Chapter Ten

Fez knocked on the back door of the Colwell house and waited to be let in.

"Come in, Fez," Mrs. Colwell said. "Are you all packed and ready to go?"

"Yes, ma'am." He followed her into the kitchen.

"Would you like something to eat before you leave?" she asked.

"No, thanks. I ate already."

Mr. Colwell walked into the room and asked, "Did you get the brakes fixed on your car?"

"Yes, I did. The front pads needed to be replaced, but the rear ones are good for another 30,000 miles. Give or take. Thank you for paying the mechanic. I'll pay you back," Fez said.

"I'm not worried about it." Mr. Colwell sat at the counter and peeled a banana. "I used to be allowed a donut or other pastry, but now I have to eat fruit and cereal that tastes like cardboard."

"You are allowed to eat whatever you want one day a week," Mrs. Colwell said. "Don't feel sorry for him, Fez. He ate junk for sixty years, and now he's paying for it."

Mr. Colwell waved a hand dismissively. "Are you living in a dorm? I probably asked you before, but forgot."

"I'm sharing an apartment with three other guys. The university owns the building, so it costs the same as a dorm."

"Four guys in one apartment, huh?" Mrs. Colwell grimaced. "How will you manage?"

"It can't be any worse than the roommate I had last year. He was a slob, and I'm more of a neat freak."

"Did you choose your roommates, or did the college assign you to an apartment?" Mrs. Colwell asked.

"I'm in the random housing group. I met the guys briefly, and I think we will get along okay."

"Do you have to share a bedroom?" Mr. Colwell asked.

Fez laughed and shook his head.

"Should we take that as a no?" Mrs. Colwell asked. "In my college days, it was easier for the women to share bedrooms."

"I should clarify that. It's a three bedroom apartment, but we decided to move all the beds into one room and use the other two bedrooms as offices. Rooms to study in, I mean. Some of my classes are online. Some are in-person and others are both. I have one class that's all online on Monday. Wednesday half the class is in-person and the other half online. Friday it's the opposite. It gets hard to remember which classes are online at times."

"You are welcome to stay in the carriage house any night you come back to SoHam. You said you planned to keep attending Kenny's church."

"Yes, I like it better than any of the other churches I've been to. It feels like home."

"Did you say Pastor Hammond taught one of your classes at Olivet?" Mr. Colwell asked.

"Yes, that's how I met him. I wanted to check out his church to see if he was as good a preacher as he is a professor. He's good," Fez said with a chuckle. "Thanks for everything. I should get going."

"Before you go I have something for you," Mr. Colwell said. He left the room and returned after a few minutes. He handed a check to Fez.

"What's this?" Fez asked.

"It's what was deposited in your savings account," Mr. Colwell said.

Fez laughed and shook his head. "I don't have a savings account anywhere. I don't have enough money to start one. Not after paying my tuition."

Mrs. Colwell grinned and said, "You did, but we called it rent."

"I don't understand," Fez said staring at the check. "This isn't right."

"Let me explain," Mr. Colwell said. "You paid us rent every month and we put it in an account. This is what you've paid in rent plus the little interest it earned. The banks don't pay squat anymore, but it was a few bucks. I would have invested it the market, but didn't want to take a chance."

"I can't accept this. I owed you rent..."

60

"Yeah, Kenny said you'd be reluctant to accept charity. We charged you *rent*, and you always paid it on time. Consider this... I don't know... but it's for you. Most college kids don't have much spending money. You can use it however you need. Doesn't matter to us, and you can keep living in the carriage house as long as you want. You can spend weekends here, or summer's when you aren't home in Wisconsin. We would rather have you living here than an actual renter who might trash the place."

"I would never trash it. It's kinda like a historical place. It's where Fridays At Five got its start."

"Thanks for coming in to help," Pastor Rebecca said to Emmy Monday afternoon. "I've been struggling to organize the worship team into groups. I didn't think it would be this difficult."

Emmy sat in the soft chair next to Rebecca's desk. "I'm glad we have enough people to divide into teams. Wait. I'm glad *you* have enough people. I'm not part of the team anymore."

"You might be in the future. I can't imagine you won't ever sing again," Rebecca said.

"Do you have a list of all the team members handy?" Emmy asked.

"Yes, and we added a couple new names, but we lost more than we gained."

"There have been so many families who haven't returned since the shutdown. I wonder if they're watching the livestream or not bothering with church at all."

"I don't know all the families who were here before the pandemic, but I do know some of the younger families haven't returned."

Rebecca handed a sheet of paper to Emmy. "This is an up-to-date list."

Emmy scanned the names for a couple minutes. "I can see why you're having difficulties."

Rebecca took a deep breath. "I'm glad you understand. I thought I was losing my ability to organize."

"I only see four male vocalists and that's including Adam," Emmy said.

61

"Adam is a good singer. He can harmonize so well."

Emmy laughed and added, "You should force him to sing lead. He sings lead for The Only Hope and does a great job." She checked the list again. "Isaac can sing, but you have to twist his arm. Is his sister finished with college yet?"

"Not yet, and when she finishes, she might not be living in the area. That's what I heard anyway."

"We can probably divide the group into two teams, maybe three, but no more." Emmy mentally divided the people into teams she thought would work together. "Next year should be better. This pandemic crap has to be over, and more people will return to church."

"I can only schedule the teen group once every two months for now."

"Why?" Emmy asked.

"Pastor Daryl told me it was all they wanted to do until the new year."

"Are you still going to use the Planning Control software? I found it useful."

"Yes, because it's the only way I can keep things organized." Rebecca checked the list. "There were two new volunteers, but they aren't church members. They could rehearse, but if I stick to the rules, I can't let them be on the platform on Sundays."

"I kinda wish Tyler would relax that rule. There are plenty of talented people who come to church, but never actually join."

"How can we form three teams?" Rebecca asked.

Emmy pointed at the names. "There are three drummers not counting the young man who plays with the teen band. Let's start there."

"I want to limit the number of vocalists to no more than four," Rebecca said.

"Are you including yourself?"

"Four plus me."

Thirty minutes later they checked their teams.

"Okay, you and Ryan will be scheduled every week except when the teens are scheduled. Can you handle it?"

"I should be scheduled every week since I am the worship pastor," Rebecca answered. "Ryan will switch between singing and playing the drums. He's finished with his National Guard duty. Thank God."

"I can tell you're pleased."

"Very much. I'm concerned about using Nathan and Bryce every week."

"You wouldn't need two guitars every week. It would depend on the songs," Emmy said. "Tyler could play once in a while. Maybe one Sunday a month."

"We only have two bass players," Rebecca said. "I wish we had one more."

Emmy shrugged. "Tyler and Liz can play bass in an emergency. Mason doesn't mind playing as long as he doesn't have to work. I bet Isaac could play bass if you give him a week to rehearse. He learned enough chords to play acoustic in a few days. He can play trumpet and violin, too."

"That's right! I forgot," Rebecca said.

"Remember when we talked about adding a trumpet and flute to the team? You could have a mini-orchestra."

"I've thought about it and asked a few people, but none of them seem willing to spend the time to rehearse. Will Heather and Isabella be upset if they're only scheduled once a month?"

"Not at all. They will be thrilled to be part of the team."

"I will send an email to everyone. We can always make adjustments, but this is a good start." Rebecca hugged Emmy and whispered, "You are always welcome to come back even if it's once every couple months."

"Are you coming over for lunch?" Phoebe Hammond asked Emmy after the Tuesday morning Bible study.

"Your mother invited me. Is that okay with you?"

"I don't mind. Daddy has to leave to teach at college."

Sheila Rosek approached and said, "We're going to the Dragon House for lunch. Would you like to join us?"

Emmy shook her head. "Maybe another time. Liz invited me to join them."

"It was nice to have you in our group today. Our group isn't limited to older people."

"I enjoyed the discussion," Emmy said. *And the way Tyler kept you on track. I've heard the group tends to wander.*

"Most of the time Tyler does the talking, but everyone joined in the discussion today. Some subjects are more controversial than others."

Emmy followed Liz to their house.

"I made a pasta salad. You don't mind do you?" Liz asked as she opened the fridge and brought out a large Tupperware bowl.

"Not at all," Emmy said taking the bowl from Liz. "This is like the one I use for my taco salad."

"Mom tries to copy your recipe for taco salad, but it's not the same," Natalie Hammond said as she opened the cabinet and pulled out several bowls. "We use bowls for the salad, but you can eat it off a plate if you'd prefer."

Emmy smiled at the oldest Hammond sibling, who would become a teenager on her November birthday. "A bowl works for me. You are going to be as tall as your mother soon. You're already taller than me."

"I will be taller than you one day, Miss Emmy," Phoebe said. "Did you know David turned four last week?"

"I sent him a card. He will start preschool in the fall."

"Yes, and I will start first grade."

"Do you know Conor Robertson? He's my nephew and will start first grade, too."

Phoebe giggled. "He was in my kindergarten class and sometimes we sat next to each other."

"Did you like sitting beside him, Phoebe?"

"It was all right. I taught him some songs to sing about Jesus. He doesn't come to church all the time."

"Did I tell you Jason and Michelle are moving?" Liz asked after she let the kids leave the table.

"I heard they were trying to get teaching positions in Thailand. Did they find a school?" Emmy asked as she set the bowls in the sink.

64

Liz shook her head. "They couldn't get into Thailand because of the virus, but since Michelle's family originally lived in New Zealand, they were able to find positions there."

"Is New Zealand letting people into the country?"

"Not normally, but because of Michelle's family they were able to obtain a work visa. They have to go through a quarantine period but then they will be allowed to move into their house."

"They bought a house?"

"Yes, it belonged her grandparents. They are leaving Friday. They have to come to Chicago to fly out, so I will have a chance to see them before they leave."

"How long will they be there?"

Liz shrugged and answered, "It could be years."

"You don't sound pleased about that."

"I'm not and Mom tried to convince them not to leave."

"I don't know them all that well, but I am surprised they would move so far away."

"Jason has his own way of doing things, but he doesn't make rash decisions."

"Are they ever going to start a family?" Emmy asked as Phoebe and David talked to Derby about going outside. Emmy watched Derby wagging her tail. "I suppose not everyone wants kids. Kristen's brother Derrick and Amber don't want children."

"I used to think I wanted six, but I'm happy with four," Liz said as she closed the door after Phoebe left it partially open.

"Tony and Sloane have six all together, and you've had as many when the foster kids were here."

"Yes, but our days as foster parents are over for now," Liz said with a sigh. "God is moving us in another direction, too."

Chapter Eleven

"I want to thank you all for taking the time to be here this evening to talk about the school. I will try to make this brief." Lenore Toth looked out at the people seated in the old sanctuary. "I hope you understand the school board has made their decisions based on the guidelines set in place by the different government agencies. I was hoping we would be able to start school in person."

"So was I," Tyler said. "We have four children who attend here." He chuckled and added, "Now Liz and I have to teach from home, and she has her class to teach, also."

"Starting this way doesn't mean school will be online the entire year," Mrs. Toth said. "The board will constantly evaluate the situation, and open the school as soon as possible. I have three of the school board members with me tonight, and we will answer your questions if we can."

"How are we supposed to provide for daycare? There are plenty of us who have to work, and now we have to either stay home with the kids or pay someone," Mrs. Salvina said. "We can't keep doing it."

"It's not fair," Mrs. Bindley added. "We pay tuition to send our children to this school and pay taxes for public schools, too."

"That has always been an issue," Mrs. Toth answered. "In this state public schools are supported through property taxes. Every homeowner pays regardless of whether or not they have students in the public schools."

Several other parents asked questions and voiced opinions. Lenore and the board members tried to answer as best they could.

"If there are no more questions, I will ask Pastor Tyler to pray to close," Lenore said twenty minutes later. "Oh, the coffee shop is open on a limited basis."

After the prayer Emmy joined her friends at a table.

"I wish there was something we could do to help families like the Salvinas," Liz said.

Emmy nodded. "I can sympathize with Mrs. Salvina, but her husband earns too much for them to qualify for assistance."

Diane mentioned, "Too many families fall in the cracks. They earn just enough not to qualify, but not enough to afford the tuition."

"At least the school offers scholarships for families in those situations," Kristen said.

"I can't believe how fast the kids have grown up," Sloane Bertucci said looking at Emmy. "Peter is a senior and Dotty is a junior already."

Sloane taught eighth-grade math for the church's school and knew the Colwells and Robertsons donated a large sum each year for scholarships.

Emmy opened a sealed sugar cookie and said, "Can you believe my twins, Zach, Noemi and Caden have to start high school at home? Part of high school for me was the social aspect."

"You mean the boys, right?" Kristen teased.

"I had girl friends, too," Emmy said.

"I hope we can open the school soon," Liz said. "Natty, Kevin, Ben and Grace are all in seventh grade, but won't see each other."

"The little ones like Conor and Lily can adjust," Diane said. She grinned and added, "I can teach them, but no way can I teach Caden."

"At least The Barclay Academy is equipped to teach online. They're supplying every student with a computer," Emmy said. "I suspect they raised the cost of tuition to cover it though."

At the close of the Monday morning staff meeting, Wyatt asked Tyler, "When are you taking a vacation? You usually spend two weeks in Maine every summer."

"Yeah, but I don't want to leave with everything that's going on. I want to be here in case we have to make changes."

Wyatt looked at the other staff then said, "Do you think we can't handle the church for two weeks? We aren't clueless."

"I know you aren't, but I don't like to be away in times of crisis."

"Take your vacation," Wade said. "Everyone else has taken a vacation. It's your turn. Do it before travel is restricted."

"I'll think about it," Tyler said.

"What's to think about?" Wyatt asked. "You need to take care of your family. Go on vacation soon."

Emmy entered the control room of Kenny's basement studio while the band listened to playback of a newly finished track and asked, "Kenny, since the kids have their assignments for the day, would you mind if I run down to Paul's Bookstore? I want to get out of the house."

He shrugged and replied, "Go ahead. I'd go with you, but we're trying to finish recording by Friday."

"You can keep working. I told the kids not to bother you unless the house catches fire."

"Thanks, but they better not start a fire."

Emmy drove downtown and parked in the deck behind Paul's Bookstore. She texted her editor, Denise Bartell, who agreed to meet her if she could get away from the office. She entered the five-story building located on Polk Street through the back door and saw the owner, Paul Tockstein, talking to a customer near the checkout counter. She waited until he finished his conversation and he turned around. She held up a copy of Annie Mercer O'Dell's latest book and waved.

"Would you like to buy a book? I can heartily recommend that one," he said. "Plus, I have several copies by a local author you might enjoy. It's a new release, and I've already sold one or two copies."

"Do you recommend the book?" Emmy asked with a grin.

Paul shrugged, then laughed and replied, "It's not bad for a quick read. How are you? How's everyone doing?"

She bumped his elbow and said, "We are okay. Kenny is back to normal. The guys are recording a new CD in our basement. I'm glad to see you have reopened the store. I was afraid you would close and just be online."

"I thought about it, but I like for people to be able to put their hands on a book and browse. I haven't opened the coffee shop, but I might one of these days."

"Do I have to wear my mask?" she asked.

"You can take it off as long as no one minds. I don't wear mine unless I'm talking to a customer."

"Excuse me! Excuse me!" a customer shouted rushing toward Paul and Emmy. "Are you Emmy Colasanti?"

"Yes, I am," Emmy answered with a grin.

"I bought your book. Would you sign it for me, please?" She pulled the book from the bag and held it out.

Paul handed Emmy a pen, and she signed the book. Another customer approached with one of Emmy's books.

Paul smiled and asked, "How about hanging around for a while? Do you have the time?"

"I don't have any plans for this afternoon, but I need to be home in time to cook dinner. Denise might meet me here in a little while."

Paul brought out a table and chairs for Emmy and Denise. He set copies of her books on the table and made an announcement on the store's PA.

Ten minutes later Denise Bartell burst through the door carrying her black leather briefcase. She removed her wide-brimmed burgundy-colored hat and sat next to Emmy.

"I didn't know if you'd make it," Emmy said after signing another copy of her latest book.

"I wasn't sure myself. I had to interview a person for a story coming out tomorrow and it took longer than I planned. How are you? I didn't know you had this on your schedule."

"I didn't. I popped in to get out of the house, and Mr. Tockstein talked me into hanging around for a while."

"Have you signed many books?" Denise asked picking up a copy of Emmy's new book. "I like the cover, but I haven't read it yet."

Emmy and Denise continued their conversation when Emmy had a break between customers.

"It's been steady for an impromptu event."

"Have you begun your outline for the next book?"

"Yes, and I'm almost finished with the first draft," Emmy answered. "Will you have time to read it soon?"

"I will make time. Your books are easy to edit. You don't make grammatical errors, and you've learned the craft of writing. I don't have to correct the same mistakes over and over."

Emmy told Denise the basic plot of the next book.

"It sounds interesting. Not my favorite genre, but I still enjoy reading them." Denise took a call on her cell phone. "I need to run. Another fire to extinguish at the office."

"Thanks for stopping by," Emmy said. "I'll send you the draft as soon as I can."

The next afternoon Emmy sat at the desk in the kitchen, worked on paying bills and then checked the sales numbers of her new book. "Holy cow! This is amazing."

"What's amazing?" Kevin asked as he grabbed a bottle of water from the fridge

"The new book. 'I'm Releasing the Prisoner' is selling better than any of my other books. I didn't expect anyone to buy it and it's already sold a thousand copies. I better not tell your father, or else he will get a big head."

"You better not tell him because your book might sell more copies than his new CD when it comes out. No one I know still buys CDs."

"Not all the sales of the book are physical copies. Most people buy the electronic versions now."

"I might be weird, but I like to read a real book most of the time," Kevin said. "I finished all my schoolwork, and I'm going for a swim."

Chapter Twelve

"Play the last chorus one more time," Jeff Rawlings said as the members of Fridays At Five sat in the control room Friday night.

Will Consoli played the chorus.

"It sounds better now," Jeremy Lenhart said. "Did you double the voices?"

Stuart Lederer nodded.

"We agreed not to spend the rest of the year tweaking this thing," Dave Persching said. "We've done that in the past and the CD sounded too polished. This one needs to sound raw."

"I agree," Paul Joseph said.

Kenny looked at Adam Vicini, the newest member of the band. "What do you think?"

"I've recorded CDs with The Only Hope before, but we always had a budget and could only spend a limited time in the studio. I'm used to working quickly."

Kenny said, "I will start post-production Monday morning, and unless I come across something I can't fix, I vote we're finished."

The guys high-fived each other and packed up to leave.

"I'm confident we can release it in early October."

"We will have to meet and decide if we want to re-sign with Mr. Kesson and Steward Music Group," Jeff said.

"We have to see if he still wants us," Dave added.

Jeremy paused by the door leading to the stairs. "We could do what so many other bands are doing and go independent."

"Or Mr. Kesson could decide to sell the company and retire for good," Kenny said. "He's talked about it in the past. Now might be the right time for him to finally do it."

"Does that car belong to Fez?" Kenny asked as he and his father looked out the kitchen window at the carriage house.

Mr. Colwell lifted the curtain and checked. "Yes, he must have stopped in to do laundry or maybe pick up more clothes. I know he left some stuff here."

"I'll text him, and see if he wants breakfast," Emmy said. She was helping her mother-in-law with a fry-up. "If he wants to eat with us, we should add more potatoes. He has a healthy appetite." She sent a text and received an answer within a minute. "He says he's hungry and would love to eat with us."

"How soon is breakfast going to be ready?" Mr. Colwell asked. He sat at the table and drained the last of his coffee.

"Ten minutes or so," Emmy answered. "Be patient. I added more potatoes and veggies so we'll have enough."

Kenny sat with his back to the windows and inhaled the aroma of onions, bell peppers, potatoes, sausage and chorizo sizzling on the stove. He watched his mother pour the scrambled eggs into a different pan.

Emmy opened the door for Fez a few minutes later.

"Come on in. Breakfast is about ready." She held the door, and Fez scooted his two hundred and twenty pound frame past her. "I hope you're hungry because we made enough to feed an army."

Fez smiled and ran a hand through his thick, dark hair. "All I had before I left the apartment was half a bagel." He waved to everyone and stood by the counter shifting his weight back and forth.

"Have a seat," Mr. Colwell said. "How's school going?"

Fez bumped elbows with the men and sat in the corner. "Something smells good."

"We call it a fry-up," Kenny said and explained what was in the concoction.

"We make something very similar, but we stuff it into burritos."

"That would be good," Mrs. Colwell said as she set the eggs on the table. "What would you like to drink, Fez?"

"Water is okay for me," he replied eyeing the mixture Emmy placed in the middle of the table. "That looks like something my grandmother used to make."

Emmy offered to pray before they ate.

"We serve it family-style," Mrs. Colwell said. "Take what you want, and pass it along. There's more on the stove, so don't be shy, Fez."

72

Kenny got up, moved to the fridge and returned with a bottle of Perkins Louisiana Hot Sauce. "Try this. It's probably mild compared to what you're used to, but it has a little kick to it."

Fez added it, took a bite and added more. "It's okay."

Emmy added a few drops. "It's too much for me, but I didn't grow up eating spicy food."

For a time the only sound at the table was forks scraping plates and mouths chewing food.

"You didn't tell us about your classes," Mr. Colwell said after setting his fork on his plate and pushing it away.

Fez took a drink of water then said, "It's complicated."

"Why?" Emmy asked.

"Okay, so I have classes every day, but not all of them are in-person. Some are in classrooms, but others are online and two are a combination."

"How do you keep track?" Kenny asked.

Fez pulled out his phone. "I keep my schedule on here. Oh, this is a new phone. My old one was damaged, and I replaced it."

"Do you still have your contact info?" Emmy asked.

"Not all of it," he replied.

Emmy added the missing contact information to his phone while he talked about his classes.

"So, this is really funny," he said with a grin. "I was sitting at my desk doing a Zoom class when one of my roommates walked out of the shower and stood behind me and started talking."

Emmy looked up. "Was he right out of the shower?"

"He had a towel wrapped around him, but otherwise... yeah, he was still dripping water. I told him I was on a Zoom call, and he stared at my laptop for a second before he ran out of the room."

"I'm glad Zoom and all this other stuff didn't exist when I was in college," Emmy said handing the phone back to Fez.

"Em, you never lived in a dorm or on campus. You always had your own place," Kenny said.

"Yeah, but I took showers and didn't always... never mind." She looked at Fez, but he was staring out the window. "What else has happened?"

73

"Nothing much. I see my friend every day, but we don't have any classes together."

Emmy's eyes sparkled. "What friend? Does she have a name?"

"Virginia Harwood. You might know her."

Emmy looked at Fez then at Kenny then back at Fez and asked, "Is she a friend of Liz Hammond."

Fez nodded. "The Harwoods live across the street. Virginia and her sister, Tara, both attend Olivet."

"Was there another sister? An older one. Probably closer to Liz's age."

"That would be Isla. She graduated from Olivet several years ago. She has a job close to Detroit, I think."

"Are you and Virginia dating?" Emmy asked.

Fez hesitated.

"You don't have to answer her," Kenny said. "Sometimes she can be a bit nosy."

Emmy stuck out her tongue at Kenny.

"I'm not sure exactly what our relationship is at the moment," Fez replied.

"I've seen her at church before," Emmy said. "She's smart, pretty and has a good personality."

Everyone stared at Emmy.

"What?" she asked with a shrug.

"Guys would say a girl has a good personality if they thought she was fat or not exactly a beauty queen," Kenny explained.

"Virginia is far from fat, and she would win a beauty contest if there were a thousand other entrants," Emmy said. She stood up and gathered the plates. "There's more if anyone is still hungry."

"I'm full," Fez said. "Thank you."

Mr. Colwell looked at his wife. "I am only allowed one helping, but we can save the leftovers for lunch."

"Mama, are you ready to start?" Ben asked that afternoon. "I've got the Zoom meeting all ready to go."

Mama sat in her rocking chair, patted her hair, took a deep breath and nodded. "I'm nervous, but ready. I haven't seen my cousins for an eternity."

Ben hit the icons on his laptop and set it on a stand in front of Mama. Within a few minutes several Lombardi and Bertucci cousins were jabbering away.

"Thank you for doing that for me, Benjamin," Mama said drying her eyes and holding out her arms an hour later.

Ben moved the stand and leaned down in front of her. "You're welcome, Mama." He allowed her to hug him. "We can do it again sometime if you want."

"I would like that very much, but I want to spend my time with my family here. Seeing all my cousins is nice, but it's like living in the past. I want to live in the present."

"Are you all packed?" Wyatt asked after the second service.

Tyler checked his mailbox in the church office. "We're ready to go. Do you have any questions?"

Wyatt shook his head. "We can handle the church." But then asked, "How long does it take to get there? I was in New Hampshire once when I was a kid, but I've never been to Maine. I'd like to do someday."

"Mapquest tells me I could get there in nineteen hours if I never stop, but it usually takes twenty-two or twenty-three hours because we stop often."

"Are you taking Derby?"

Tyler shook his head. "She usually goes with us, but not this time. She's staying with Dany and Darian today, and they're going to take her to Tony's house. If she can get along with Scout, she will stay there. Otherwise, Darian will take care of her."

"Have a safe trip, and enjoy your vacation."

"I will check my phone and email occasionally, but not every day," Tyler said.

"I won't bother you unless something extraordinary occurs." Wyatt shook hands with Tyler and turned off the light.

"Did you get much accomplished today?" Emmy asked as everyone sat at the table to eat dinner Monday evening.

"I made some progress. You?" Kenny asked.

Emmy looked at the kids. "I spent three hours in school." She shook her head. "I never would have survived doing school online. It's so boring."

"Mom, we don't like it either," Kevin said. "Why can't I go to Ben's house, and Aunt Sloane can teach us. She can teach more than math."

"It's not up to me, Kevin," Emmy replied. She looked at the twins. "How do you feel after a week of virtual school?"

"It sucks, but we will survive until real school starts," Heather said.

"It doesn't seem real to me," Isabella replied. "There is some interaction between students, but nothing like real life. That's part of school, too."

"Can I go to Ben's house after I eat?" Kevin asked.

"I suppose. Why?" Emmy asked.

"Darian and Dany are bringing Derby over. If Derby and Scout get along, they're going to live together while Pastor Tyler's on vacation."

"Dogs don't live together like people do," Heather said.

"Yeah, they do," Kevin insisted. He looked at his father. "Could we get a dog if it's one of those allergy-free ones?"

"I didn't know there was such a thing," Kenny answered.

"I read online about a breed that doesn't shed as much and lots of families have them even if someone's allergic."

"I don't know. You'd have to ask your mother," Kenny said avoiding eye contact with Emmy.

"Why does it have to be my choice?" Emmy asked. "I don't want to be the bad guy who says no."

"We've never had pets like other kids," Heather said.

"Would you like a dog sleeping on your bed?" Emmy asked.

"No, but it could sleep with Kevin."

"I never had a pet when I was a kid, and neither did your father," Emmy said. "Why do you want one now?"

"Other kids have pets. Most families have pets. The Osbornes have three cats, but they hide most of the time."

"Other kids wear glasses. Do you want to wear glasses just because other kids do?" Emmy asked.

Everyone stared at her.

Kevin finally asked, "What's that got to do with anything? Dad uses reading glasses sometimes, but none of us wear glasses."

Kenny looked at Emmy and scratched his ear. "Are you trying to tell us something, Em?"

She took a deep breath. "I might need glasses. I've been having trouble seeing stuff."

"Have you been to the eye doctor?" Kevin asked. "We had to go for school, remember?"

"We've seen Dr. Larson a few times," Isabella said. "He's nice and it doesn't hurt."

"I haven't been to an eye doctor for ages," Emmy said.

Kevin grinned and asked, "Are you afraid you'll have to wear thick glasses like Jarrett Bindley? His glasses are thicker than Coke bottles."

"How would you know? Have you ever seen a Coke bottle for real?" Heather asked.

"It's just an expression, but if he doesn't have his glasses on, he can't see anything."

"I'm not that bad," Emmy said.

"You could wear contacts like Aunt Sloane. Mama Bertucci wears glasses. It's not a big deal," Kevin said. "Lots of old people wear them."

"Kevin Michael! Your mother is not old," Kenny said with a frown.

"Right. I forgot," Kevin replied. "Can I go see Ben now?"

"Yes, you may go, but don't stay too late."

Kevin set his dirty plate in the sink and rushed out the door.

"If I ever need glasses, I want to wear contacts," Isabella said.

Emmy sighed and said, "I should make an appointment to see the doctor, but Diane doesn't wear glasses. Daddy never wore them, and Mom didn't until her last few years."

77

"Grandma Isabel wore them, but she was real old," Heather said. "Don't worry, mom. We won't tease you too much if you need glasses."

Emmy made a face at the girls.

"Dotty, where are Scout and Derby?" Kevin asked as he raced into the family room. "I saw a car in the driveway. Did Darian bring Derby over already?" He stood still as he saw Dany and Sloane enter the room.

"We arrived ten minutes ago," Dany said. "Scout and Derby sniffed each other for a minute then started wagging their tails. Tony and Darian took them outside to let them run."

"I'm supposed to be allergic to pets, but I might not be as bad now as when I was a kid. See you later. I'm going to find Ben." Kevin rushed out of the room and headed outside.

Sloane laughed and asked Dany, "Did you see the look on his face when he saw you?"

"Yes, he looked surprised for some reason."

"I think it's because you and Emmy are about the same size, and he must have realized how she looked when she was expecting. Boys his age are often confused about sex."

"Ben! Taylor! Where are the dogs?" Kevin hollered. "Hi, Uncle Tony. Hey, Darian."

"Hi, Kevin. Aren't you allergic to dogs?" Tony asked.

"Maybe, but not as much anymore. Do you ever wear glasses?"

"No, why?" Tony asked.

"Mom might need glasses because she's getting older. That's all." Kevin spotted Ben with the dogs and sprinted away.

Tony grinned and whispered, "Wait til I see her. I'm going to have one more thing to tease her about."

Chapter Thirteen

Kenny parked the Odyssey in the lot next to Ciao Bella and everyone got out.

"I'm going to eat until I can't breath," Kevin said. "Can we take doggy bags home?"

"Not tonight," Emmy answered.

"Em, remember when we sometimes had to park several blocks away?" Kenny asked.

"I remember," she replied.

"Why?" Kevin asked. "Couldn't you park right here?"

Kenny shook his head. "Until a few years ago there was a building here. The only parking was on the street. On busy nights you might not be able to find a spot very close."

"I remember a few times when we had to walk for ten minutes," Emmy said.

Heather heard the music coming from inside as she walked around the corner. "If they're always so busy, why are they closing the restaurant?"

"Is it because of the virus?" Isabella asked.

"Ben said they were invited, too, but I don't see them yet," Kevin said while looking up and down the street.

"The Sabatino family has operated Ciao Bella for close to forty years. Maybe longer," Kenny said. "The pandemic might be a factor, but I think they want to retire, and neither of their children are in the restaurant business."

"Are their kids old like you and Mom?" Kevin asked. "Hey! There's Ben!" Kevin waved and Ben and Taylor started running.

"Slow down!" Tony hollered.

"Did we have to dress up because this is the last night they're going to be open?" Heather asked.

"I thought it would be nice if you wore dresses," Emmy replied. "I used to wear a dress when I came here."

The children reached the door first. One of the employees opened it, and the kids waited inside.

"I love the smell of their fresh bread," Isabella said.

"Mama, do you remember what year Ciao Bella opened?" Tony asked. He held her hand as she climbed the three steps leading to the wooden, double door with stained glass inserts.

"I remember bringing you here when you were only a few months old. I think it opened in 1980, but there was a different restaurant here before that."

"Do you remember the name?" Sloane asked.

"No, but Enrico or Florentina might."

Mama paused as she entered the building. She took in a deep breath, looked around then closed her eyes for a moment.

"Are you okay, Mama?" Emmy asked.

"Yes, dear. I was imagining the way it looked a long time ago."

"Maria, you made it," Enrico said as he and Florentina approached.

Mama smiled as Enrico bowed then kissed her hand. "It's a pleasure to see you tonight."

Florentina laughed at her husband, who had always been a dramatic host, and hugged Mama. "We have a special section reserved for your family and your friends."

"The place looks lovely tonight, Florentina," Mama said.

"Please follow me," Enrico said. He held his head high as he escorted her to their private section.

Emmy grinned at Kenny, but then bit her lip.

"What is it, Em?" he asked softly.

"I don't know whether I should be happy for them because they can retire or cry because we will never eat here again."

"I'm sure you will do both before the night is over."

Enrico waited until everyone was seated and announced, "We are doing things differently tonight. You may order anything on the menu and as much as you like." He looked at Tony and smiled.

Emmy made a face at him. "Save some for the rest of us."

"Everything is on-the-house tonight, but..." He held up one finger and added, "You may tip the service staff."

"That's very generous, Mr. Sabatino." Kenny said. He looked at Tony and mouthed, "We will be generous, too."

A few minutes later Emmy placed her order and noticed several important people from SoHam. She nudged Kenny and whispered, "I'm surprised we were invited. Most of the people here are big shots."

"We were probably invited because we've been eating here since we were kids," Kenny answered.

"Why isn't Mr. Robertson here?" she asked.

Kenny checked the people seated at their tables. "Other than me and a couple others, everyone I see is Italian."

Emmy saw Fire Chief Randich. "He's not Italian, is he?"

"His father wasn't, but his mother was. He looks Italian."

Enrico and Florentina mingled with all the guests, but he took a moment to sit with Tony and Mama.

"I'm really going to miss this place," Tony said.

Enrico replied, "I will miss the people, but I am ready to retire. It's time for us to be the ones who are pampered."

"It's a shame the children aren't interested in taking over the business," Mama said. "Where do they live now?"

"Joseph and his family live in Connecticut. He works in New York City on Wall Street. He and Maria have three children. My daughter, Linda, is married to a surgeon. Dr. Nathan Moyer," he said with obvious pride. "They live in Boston and have four children. Melissa is their oldest. She was the only grandchild to ever work in the restaurant. I would have given the business to her, but she is teaching at the University of Notre Dame."

Tony smiled when he mentioned Notre Dame.

"What are you going to do with the building?" Emmy asked.

"I sold it to a man who operates a restaurant in Miami. He plans to reopen after he remodels it."

"It won't be the same," Mama said.

"Many of these people will leave after they eat and socialize for a while, but you are welcome to stay as long as you like. This is my gift to you for your support through the years."

Mama patted his hand, and he stood up and walked away with great dignity.

An hour later the kids were finished with their entrees and dessert. Many of the people had left. The staff moved their tables together so they could talk easier. The younger boys sat at the far end of the room away from the adults.

"Mama, will you tell us what is was like to come here when it first opened?" Peter asked.

"Oh, I don't know where to start," Mama answered. She rubbed a hand along the table, which was a fine piece of furniture like you would find in a home, and touched the fancy red tablecloth.

"Start with the first time you remember bringing Tony here," Emmy suggested.

"Let me think. I know we ate here when he was a baby."

"How did you first hear about Ciao Bella?" Isabella asked.

"The first time we heard about it must have been when Enrico and Florentina got married."

"Were you at their wedding?" Tony asked. "I didn't know that. How did you know each other?"

"Enrico's father and my father knew each other. They were good friends, and your grandfather helped Enrico and Florentina start Ciao Bella."

"Really?" Emmy asked. "My grandfather helped Mr. Robertson get started."

"They were generous men," Mama said. "Mr. Sabatino... I don't remember his name now. He was a prominent man in SoHam much like my father."

"Did you and Daddy ever come here on dates?" Heather asked her mother.

Emmy grinned at Kenny and answered, "I used to come here with him before we ever started dating. His parents would invite me along."

"Are you sure you didn't invite yourself?" Tony asked with a grin.

"I think she did," Kenny teased.

"Did not!" Emmy insisted.

"She used to hang around me all the time. She couldn't have been ten the first time she tagged along."

82

"Grandma and Grandpa Colasanti brought me here when I was a little girl, but I don't remember coming with my parents."

"She must have been quite a nuisance," Heather said. "Did Uncle Rory ever bring you here?"

Emmy shook her head. "Rory never took me anywhere you would consider a date, but your uncle Tony did." Emmy turned her attention to Tony and made a face at him.

Dotty grinned at her father and asked, "Did you really date Aunt Emmy? Real dates not going somewhere as friends. I've heard stories about it, but always assumed they were rumors."

"It was a long time ago, and I must have been under the influence of a concussion otherwise I wouldn't have taken the brat on a date." Tony grabbed one of the last rolls and threw it at Emmy. "I brought her here for dinner on our second date."

Emmy shook her head. "No way! It was our first date. The second one was when you took me out for breakfast at The Hungry Lion and then we went sledding on Windsor Hill. After that you brought me home to meet Mama and Heather." Emmy looked at her daughter and said, "His sister. Not you."

"I knew it wasn't me, Mom," Heather said rolling her eyes.

"Are you sure it wasn't the other way around?" Tony asked.

"Positive. We had a snowball fight and the rubberband holding my ponytail together broke, and you found that purple ribbon." *I still have the ribbon in my music box.*

Mama laughed.

"What's so funny, Mama?" Noemi asked.

"I remember that day as clear as a bell. It was snowing like a blizzard, and your father brought Emmy to the house. They played outside like they did when they were little kids." She paused and added, "You have heard that story, right?"

"Yes, that was when they first met," Isabella said. "She was four and kissed Uncle Tony."

"I told them to come inside, and he carried her over his shoulder. Heather was home from college for some reason." Mama paused and closed her eyes for a brief moment. "Emmy had her hair tucked under her stocking cap at the time, and Heather thought she was Timmy Murphy from next door."

The twins, Noemi and Dotty all asked, "She thought she was a boy?"

"Until her hair tumbled out from the stocking cap. Even then Heather thought Emmy was one of the neighborhood kids. A junior high friend."

"Why?" Isabella asked.

"Because your mother looked about your age even though she must have been... what? Seventeen at the time."

"I'm pretty sure I was seventeen, and he was still sixteen," Emmy said.

"You stayed for dinner. I remember that," Tony said.

"Where was Daddy?" Heather asked.

"I was touring with the band," Kenny said. "This was during the time we were on the road for over a year, right?"

Emmy nodded. "Your father was gone for the longest time. We hadn't really started dating because he thought I was too young. He told me to date other guys because he knew he would meet other girls." Emmy grinned then pointed at Tony. "I must have been crazy because I thought he would be a guy I would like. I know it sounds totally insane now, but at the time we thought differently."

"Not me," Tony said. "I only took you on dates because Kristen begged me to. She told me no one would date you because..." He paused.

"Why?" Isabella asked.

Emmy looked at Tony and thought, *Because everyone knew my sister, and thought I was easy like her. The guys either wanted to sleep with me, or were afraid to ask me out because they were afraid I would corrupt them. I suffered because of Diane's reputation.*

"Because your mother was so smart," Tony said. "None of the guys I knew wanted to date a girl smarter than them. So, I took her on a couple dates to please Kristen."

"Oh, is that why you brought me here with Mama that night with the ring in your pocket and were too nervous to propose?" Emmy asked with a smile.

Immediately, everyone stopped talking.

"What did you say, Mom?" Isabella asked after a moment. She looked at her mother, then her father and then at Tony.

"Ooops!" Sloane said. "Someone just put a foot in her mouth."

Noemi looked at her father and asked, "Did you ask Aunt Emmy to marry you? Please say you didn't."

"Yeah, that would be way too weird." Heather looked at Isabella and cringed. "That means they probably kissed and stuff."

"Gross!" Noemi said.

"Mom, would you care to explain?" Heather asked. "Does Daddy know about this... night?"

"Yes, I know," Kenny said.

"I didn't actually propose here," Tony replied waving a hand to encompass the whole restaurant.

"Were you here?" Dotty asked Mama. "Can you tell us what happened? Are they making up this whole incident?"

"I shouldn't," Mama said.

"Tell us," all the kids hollered.

"Okay." Mama took a deep breath. "Tony bought a ring, and planned to propose here, but he kept getting interrupted by the waiters. He was so nervous. He was dressed up in a suit and Emmy wore a nice dress. Eventually, Tony took Emmy home..."

"Without proposing?" Noemi asked.

"He didn't. He brought us back to the house Emmy shared with Kristen, and after drinking some coffee, we sat in the living room. He got on his knee, showed her the ring and proposed. I remember the look of shock on Emmy's face, and I knew Tony had made a mistake. He thought she felt differently than she did. They loved each other, but not in the way he thought." Mama stopped and looked at Emmy. "Do you want me to tell them the rest?"

"I will," Tony said. "I was both shattered and relieved. Here I had spent a small fortune on a ring and she said no. Luckily, Kenny loved her and offered to buy the ring..."

Heather slapped the table. "No way! Mom! Did Daddy propose to you with Uncle Tony's ring?"

Emmy nodded. "But let me finish."

"Please do," Heather said.

"Kristen and I had been window shopping for jewelry. She liked to wear fancy jewelry. I didn't even have my ears pierced at the time. Anyway, we were in Watson's Jewelry Shop, and I saw this ring I thought was beautiful. I pointed it out to Krissy. Later, Tony took her shopping and bought the exact ring. If he hadn't bought it, I believe someone else would have. So, you see it was God telling him to buy the ring so your father would give it to me later when he asked me to marry him."

"That's weird," Dotty said. "Romantic, but still weird."

"How did Daddy propose?" Isabella asked. "Was it so romantic you couldn't say no?"

Kenny laughed and answered, "I proposed at halftime of a football game, and she tackled me and said yes."

Heather, Isabella, Dotty and Noemi looked at each other and made faces.

"That's not nearly as romantic as Uncle Tony's proposal," Heather said. "You were at a football game, really?"

"No, the game was on TV. It was the Bears against the Vikings, right?"

Kenny nodded.

"I would expect Dad to propose during a football game," Peter said and Uncle Kenny's proposal to be very romantic."

"Did you expect Daddy to propose the way he did?" Isabella asked.

"Maybe not, but I loved your father in a very special way. That's why I said yes," Emmy replied then kissed Kenny.

Kevin Ben, Taylor and Coby walked to the other end.

"We're hungry. Can we have more dessert?" Kevin asked.

"What were you talking about?" Ben asked. "All I heard was something about Aunt Emmy tackling Uncle Kenny at a football game."

"You can have as much dessert as you want," Emmy said. "Just don't make yourself sick."

"I don't understand this one bit," Heather said. "You and Uncle Tony act more like brother and sister than anything else. You tease each other all the time, and I know he loves Aunt Sloane the way you and Daddy love each other."

86

"Did anyone else ever ask you to marry them?" Dotty asked Emmy.

"Mom, please don't tell me Uncle Rory proposed," Heather said. "I love him like a real uncle, but... never mind."

"No, Rory and I were always just friends. We hung out together, but I never kissed him. To the best of my knowledge."

"Were you and our first mother close friends?" Dotty asked. "Is it all right if I ask, Mom?" Dotty said to Sloane.

"Of course, sweetie," Sloane replied.

"Heather was away at college most of the time, but we were good friends. Kristen and I would stay at her apartment when we attended the games," Emmy answered.

"Did you go to more football games than Daddy's concerts?" Isabella asked.

"I'm sure I went to more concerts."

Kenny nodded and added, "She was only fourteen when Fridays At Five formed. She would sing with us at the local gigs, and the guys in the band loved her like a little sister."

"For a while you did, too," Emmy said. She looked at her girls then Tony and Sloane's kids. "We were best friends from the first day we met. I was seven and he was ten. He looked like a dork, but it didn't matter."

"I don't think you look like a dork, Daddy," Isabella said.

"Thank you, Isa. I always thought your mother looked pretty, and she still looks okay for her age," he teased.

Eventually, everyone was ready to leave. Enrico stopped by to say good night.

"I don't care about the rules, I'm shaking your hands." He shook the guys' hands and hugged all the ladies. Even the young ones. Florentina joined him and hugged everyone, also.

"We promise to stay in touch, Maria," Florentina said. "We will spend winters in Florida and split the rest of the year between the kids."

Emmy watched as Kenny and Tony left a tip on the table. "How much did you leave?" she asked softly.

"A thousand dollars between us."

"Good."

The kids walked outside and waited. Sloane and Kenny walked out.

"I think Emmy, Tony and Mama want to say goodbye in private," Kenny said.

"I understand," Sloane answered. "They have lifelong memories of this place. I don't, but I am sad it's closing."

"I've been coming here just as long. Longer since I'm older, but I understand her need to say goodbye without me and the kids there." Kenny heard a tugboat whistle on the river and smiled.

Tony put his hands on Emmy's shoulders and squeezed them. "Mr. Sabatino, I wish you all the best in your retirement. Think of the positive side. You won't have to put up with this brat anymore."

Emmy elbowed him in the stomach without turning around.

"Let me give you one more hug, my bambino," Enrico said to Emmy with outstretched arms.

Emmy cried as she hugged Enrico for the last time. Tony stood behind her and blinked his eyes rapidly. She rested her head on his chest and whispered, "You've always been so good to me. I will never forget you."

"I will never forget you," he whispered. "Please don't tell anyone, but you were always my favorite customer from the time you were a little girl with curls."

Tony shook his hand one more time and put an arm around Emmy's shoulders. He offered her a handkerchief, and she took it.

"I'm sorry if I embarrassed you by being a baby," she whispered.

"I would have been shocked if you hadn't cried."

Mama hugged Florentina again, looked around, took a deep breath, sighed and whispered, "This place holds so many memories. I will cherish them till the day I die."

Chapter Fourteen

"Kevin Michael, would you run down and check the mail for me?" Emmy asked Friday afternoon.

"Sure, Mom. What are we having for dinner?"

"Your father wants to order pizza. Is that okay?"

"It's okay with me." He dashed through the mudroom into the garage, grabbed his mountain bike and raced down the winding driveway. He slid to a stop by the open gate and checked the mailbox built into the brick gate support. He rode hard up the hill as though it was a mountain finish in the Tour de France. He jumped off his bike and headed inside.

"Is there anything other than junk mail?" Emmy asked as she opened the website for Kerry Lynn's Pizza and Pasta while sitting at the kitchen desk.

"It looks like mostly junk," Kevin replied as he sorted the mail. "Wait! Here's something. It looks pretty fancy like a wedding invitation or something."

"Let me see," Emmy reached out and he handed her the cream-colored envelope. "The postmark is from Newcastle."

"That's the rich city, right? Who's it from?"

Emmy checked the return address on the back. "Alejandro Santiago."

"Who's that?"

Emmy sat back in her chair, smiled at Kevin and said, "He's a good friend of a man who lived down the street when I lived in Timberline Heights."

"You mean in the house you shared with Aunt Diane?"

"Yes, and Kristen lived there with me after Diane got married and moved to Toledo."

"I've been past it. It looks like an okay house." He waited as Emmy held the envelope and stared at the ceiling. "Are you going to open it, or sit there in dreamland?"

"Oh, you want to know what's inside, huh?"

"Yeah, I'm curious. Do you know anyone who's getting married? Does Mr. Santiago have kids?" Kevin tried to snatch the envelope away, but Emmy moved her hand.

"I'm not sure if he and his wife had any children. They would be adults by now if they have any."

"Mom! Open it!"

Emmy opened the envelope and extracted the card inside, which was inside another envelope.

"It must be a wedding invitation," Kevin said. "Boring."

"Wait! It is an invitation, but not to a wedding," Emmy said.

"To what?"

Emmy finished reading the invitation, grinned at Kevin and replied, "It's a birthday celebration."

"Why would someone mail fancy invitations for a stupid birthday party?"

"Don't use that word, and it's a celebration for Fernando Ramos and Ethan Hanks."

"Who?" Kevin shrugged.

"Old friends from Timberline Heights. Ethan lived in the house across the street, and Fernando lived at the other end," she answered. "I worked with Ethan at Robertson Industries for a few years."

"Should I know these guys? Are they old?"

"They are turning sixty this month. The party is for them. They were always secretive about their age."

"Okay, I get it. It's a party for you and Dad. Let me know when the pizzas get here. I'm going to ride my bike through the woods, but I'll have my phone. Text me." He put a hand to his ear and dashed back outside.

"Have you ordered the pizzas yet?" Kenny asked as he walked into the kitchen. "I'm finished for the day. The project is almost done." He saw the invitation in Emmy's hand. "What's that?"

She explained.

"Wow! When was the last time we saw those guys? It's been a few years, I would guess."

"I used to get an occasional email, but not for a long time. I bet we haven't seen either of them in eight or nine years. I'm surprised we would get an invitation."

"So, when is this party?" he asked while looking at the website. "Make sure you get one of the Supreme Specials."

"I will, and the party is a week from tomorrow. Saturday the twelfth."

"Shoot!"

"What's the matter? We don't have plans, do we?" Emmy asked while finalizing the pizza order.

"You don't, but I do."

"What?" Emmy asked then put a hand to her mouth. "Crap! That's the day the band is doing the livestream in Nashville for musicians in need, right?"

"Yeah, and we can't cancel. Denny Dottery and Mike Rowell set it up to raise money for struggling artists. We promised to be there. Well, not exactly there in Nashville, but we will be streaming live from the basement. Maybe outside. It depends on the weather. Either way, I can't be in two places at once."

"Could you guys record your set earlier?"

"We kinda agreed it would be a live broadcast. Originally, they wanted to do the whole thing in Nashville, but the logistics didn't work out. So, they agreed to let us do our set from here. The 88s are doing their set from California."

"I almost forgot about it." She looked at the invitation. "I could reply that we can't make it."

"I bet Mr. Robertson and Mona got invited, too."

"You're probably right," Emmy said. "I'll call her and ask."

"You could go with them. Have you been to Mr. Santiago's house since that one party?"

She shook her head. "I was only there the one time. It's a beautiful home. You do know Mrs. Santiago passed away, right?"

"I remember you telling me, or else I read it somewhere. Did Mr. Santiago ever remarry?"

"I don't know. Would you mind if I skipped your livestream to attend the party?"

"No, but I wish it was another day. I'd love to see his house."

Emmy laughed and said, "Did I ever tell you how I thought the paintings were copies and Ethan told me they were real?"

"Maybe."

"He collects art. Picasso and guys like that. Mr. Robertson collects old cars, and Mr. Santiago collects old paintings," Emmy said with a grin. "You should collect old guitars."

"I do have a few guitars," he replied. "My '59 Les Paul is pretty valuable."

"I'll call Mona and see if they're going."

"Are you still eating dinner, Mona? I'm sorry to bother you if you are," Emmy said later that evening.

"We finished an hour ago."

"Did you get an invitation to Mr. Santiago's house?" Emmy asked.

"Yes, we did," Mona answered then laughed. "Bill dug his old tuxedo out of the closet and tried it on. He didn't want to buy a new one. He can be so frugal at times."

"Did it fit?" Emmy asked.

"He claims it will if he loses a couple pounds. I told him to buy a new one if he wanted me to attend with him."

"Can I go with you guys? Kenny can't go because the band is doing a livestream that night." Emmy explained everything in too much detail.

"Of course you may go with us. Bill asked Mr. Sandchek to drive that night."

Emmy giggled and said, "Are we going to ride in the armored car? Diane always says Rosco and Teresa are like Secret Service agents assigned to you guys."

Mona laughed. "Rosco is semi-retired now that Bill doesn't travel as often. Or you for that matter."

"I know now he and his wife would be part of the security for some of the tours, but I can't remember seeing them very often."

"They are very good at their job. Now, Bill and Rosco like to go fishing. They've known each other.. well... since high school at least."

"Do I have to wear a fancy gown, or can I get by with a nice dress?" Emmy asked.

92

"You could wear jeans and a t-shirt and no one would mind," Mona teased.

"I'll see if I have a dress that doesn't look old-fashioned. I rarely buy new ones anymore."

"How does this one look?" Emmy asked the girls the afternoon of the birthday party.

"Mom, it looks like it's a hundred years old," Heather said.

Emmy looked at the dress. "I bought it last year sometime."

"Mom, all these dresses look like you've worn them on tour," Isabella said. She searched through her mother's closet. "Here's one!" Isabella showed it to Heather.

"That's perfect! Is this a designer dress? Did it cost a fortune?"

Emmy looked at the dress, grinned and said, "It's a Steiner design."

"A what?" the girls asked.

"Never heard of him, or her. Is it French?" Heather asked.

Emmy shook her head. "Steiner Dress Shoppe. It's not open anymore, but it was a small store in SoHam where they sold wedding dresses, prom gowns and other formal wear. I bought this years ago, but I can't remember why. It's a simple black dress. Nothing fancy about it."

"Try it on, Mom. If it fits well, you should wear it," Isabella said.

Emmy tried on the dress and modeled it for the girls.

"What do you think, Heather?" Isabella asked as the girls walked around their mother.

Heather pressed on Emmy's hips. "It's a little tight here."

"Can you move around okay?" Isabella asked.

"I'm not going to play football," Emmy said. "Does it look okay?"

"Looks fine," Heather said. "Do you have dress shoes to match."

Emmy looked at her feet. "Can't I wear my sneakers?"

Heather and Isabella rolled their eyes.

"I'm kidding," Emmy said.

93

Isabella grabbed a pair of shoes from the closet and handed them to her mother. "Wear these."

"Isa, they're purple sneakers," Emmy said.

"Wear them and some purple ribbon in your hair. You will look beautiful."

"Mom! The limo is here!" Kevin shouted up the stairs later that evening. "Are you ready?"

Heather appeared at the top of the stairs and hollered, "Give us a minute. Go outside and tell them Mom's on her way."

Kevin raced outside and the rear passenger window of the black Mercedes rolled down.

"Hi, Mr. Robertson. Mom will be here in a second. She couldn't find shoes to wear."

"I hope she's wearing comfortable shoes because I want to dance with her," he answered.

Emmy rushed down the stairs, grabbed her purse and looked at the girls. "Do I look silly?"

"Mom, you look great," Isabella said.

"Is this dress too short?"

"It's almost to your knees, Mom," Heather replied with a roll of her eyes. "Go! They're waiting."

Emmy grinned and raced to the waiting car. Mr. Sandchek opened the door for her.

"I'm sorry I'm late, but I couldn't find a decent pair of shoes." She lifted her foot. "The girls told me to wear these."

"Are those sneakers?" Mona asked.

"Yes, but they're pretty new," Emmy said. "I've only worn them a couple times."

"They look wonderful," Mr. Robertson said. "I wish I was wearing more comfortable shoes."

Mr. Sandchek pulled up to the portico and opened the door.

Emmy got out and gazed at the large building. "It looks even bigger than the other time I was here."

She followed Mr. and Mrs. Robertson up the stairs, and grinned as the door was held open by a man dressed in a tuxedo.

"Mr. Robertson, it is a pleasure to see you tonight," Alejandro Santiago said shaking hands. "Good evening to you, Mrs. Robertson. You look lovely." He looked at Emmy and grinned. "You haven't changed at all, young lady. You look charming."

Emmy giggled and waved her foot at him. "I'd rather be comfortable than elegant. Where are the birthday boys?"

Mr. Santiago pointed to his left. "They are greeting guests in the winter garden. They will be pleased to see you."

Emmy scooted ahead of the Robertsons and stood in the reception line. She waved when there were only a few people ahead of her. *I see Fernando still dyes his hair, and Ethan has a few gray hairs left. Otherwise, they don't look much different than the last time I saw them. More wrinkles around the eyes, but not bad for their age.*

Fernando nudged Ethan's side and said, "Look who's waiting in line. Why doesn't she look any older than the last time we saw her?"

"Maybe she dyes her hair like you," Ethan teased.

"I never color my hair," Fernando insisted.

At last, it was Emmy's turn.

"Good evening, gentlemen. Have you seen those old geezers, Fernando and Ethan? It's supposed to be a party for them, but the only guys I've seen are you young bucks."

"Do you think her eyesight has been affected since we last saw her?" Fernando asked.

"Must have been," Ethan replied.

"Okay, are you really sixty, or was that just an excuse for a party? You claimed to be thirty-nine the last time I saw you."

"We jumped from thirty-nine to sixty. We want to receive all the senior citizen discounts we can," Fernando said.

"Are you here by yourself?" Ethan asked.

"Kenny and the band are doing a show tonight. I came with Mr. Robertson and Mona."

"We will talk later, young lady. Unless you have to get home for a curfew," Fernando teased.

Later, after dancing with Mr. Robertson, Emmy saw Fernando and Ethan sitting in the front parlor. She sat between them and asked, "Okay, tell the truth. Who is the oldest?"

"He is," Fernando said.

"I'm younger," Ethan claimed.

Emmy shook her head.

"You can't have been born at exactly the same time. One of you has to be older."

"That's true, Emmy, but we actually don't know," Fernando said.

"Why not?"

"Let me explain," Fernando replied. "I was born in Mexico, and my family moved to Michigan before I was a year old. They didn't have any birth certificate for me, so years later when I needed one, they made up a date. I know what year I was born and the month, but the exact day has been lost to history. So, I could be a few days older or a few days younger. I choose to be younger since I'm more handsome."

Emmy looked at Fernando then at Ethan. "Is he pulling my leg?"

"The summer before we started first grade his family moved next door to mine, and that's the story his parents told my parents. We were neighbors all through school."

"In Timberline Heights?" Emmy asked.

"Yes, but a few blocks from where I live now."

"Do you still live on Hickory Street?"

Fernando laughed and said, "He still lives in that ugly house. He is too cheap to move."

"Where are you living?" she asked Fernando.

"I split time between Michigan and Texas."

"Is my old house still there? I haven't been in the area for several years."

"It's still there, and looks pretty much the same. What year did you move to Bristol Ridge?" Ethan asked.

"We moved into the guesthouse in September of 2004. We lived there until the big house was finished. Wow! Sixteen years ago. Time flies."

"You have a good memory if you can remember the dates," Ethan said.

In the next few minutes Emmy learned both men were still single. Neither one had ever remarried after their divorces. Fernando had four grandchildren, and Ethan still worked as a consultant. Fernando was retired from the bank and split his time staying close to his grandkids.

"The girls are in high school and Kevin is in seventh grade..."

Emmy caught the men up on her situation.

"I might have to read one of your books someday," Fernando said.

"How?" Ethan asked. "You're too blind to read."

"I use reading glasses, so I can still read."

Emmy listened as the lifelong friends teased each other.

"How is Mr. Robertson?" Ethan asked after a while. "I heard he had a heart attack."

"He's all right now. He exercises and watches his diet. He's on medication, so he should be able to resume his normal life."

"We will have to stay in touch better," Emmy said as she was getting ready to leave later.

"It's his fault," Fernando said pointing to Ethan. "I would have sent a friend request on Facebook, but he convinced me not to bother you."

"You guys have never been a bother." Emmy hugged them and joined the Robertsons by the front door.

Mr. Sandchek brought the car up to the portico and opened the door.

"You missed a good party, Mr. Sandchek," Emmy said. "Mr. Robertson is still a good dancer."

"Mom! You're home already. Dad said you wouldn't be home until after midnight," Kevin said as Emmy walked into the family room where the kids and Kenny were watching a movie.

"How was the party?" Heather asked as she got up from the couch. "Did anyone comment on your shoes?"

Emmy grinned and held up her foot. "Mr. Robertson liked my purple sneakers."

Kenny paused the movie and asked, "How were the old guys? Did you recognize them?"

"They look about the same as the last time I saw them. More wrinkles maybe, but otherwise they haven't changed much."

"Was everyone dressed in gowns and tuxedos?" Isabella asked.

"A few of the ladies wore formal dresses, but I didn't feel underdressed." Emmy tilted a hand back and forth. "The guys were half and half. A couple didn't even wear ties." Emmy turned around. "Let me change into comfy clothes, and I'll tell you more."

She returned wearing pajamas and sat between the girls on the couch. "How much longer is the movie?" she asked.

"It's almost over," Kevin answered.

Kenny stopped the DVD when the credits started.

"So, tell us more about the party," Heather said.

Emmy first described the house and the artwork.

"Is it really twice as big as our house?" Kevin asked. "Did you get lost?"

"I didn't get lost, but the ballroom is bigger than the family room, den and library put together. There's one wing with a pool, gym and an indoor tennis court. I didn't go upstairs tonight, so I don't remember how many bedrooms there are, but if I had to guess, I'd say over ten."

"Dad said it was at a party at that house where you first met Mr. Robertson. Is he kidding?" Heather asked.

Emmy moved her feet underneath her and replied, "Yes and no."

"What do you mean?" Isabella asked.

"When I got a job with Robertson Industries, I didn't know... I didn't remember... that Mr. and Mrs. Robertson knew me and Diane when we were little. I was a baby. His first wife was named Lily..."

"That's why Aunt Diane gave Lily that name," Kevin said.

"I think Brady insisted on the name Lily and Diane agreed," Kenny replied.

"Anyway, the Robertsons would babysit me and Diane and he even taught me how to swim. Maybe it was Brady, but one of them did. Or both." Emmy waved. "It doesn't matter. Somewhere along the line, Mom and Dad stopped allowing them to see us."

"Why?" Isabella asked.

"I don't know the whole story, and Mr. Robertson has never told me all the details, but I think Dad was upset because Grandpa loaned Mr. Robertson some money."

"It wasn't technically a loan, Em," Kenny said.

"Right. Grandpa invested in Mr. Robertson's company, and it made a lot of money through the years."

"Your trust fund, right?" Heather asked.

"How do you know about that?" Emmy asked.

"We know more than you realize, Mom," Heather replied with a grin. "Go on with the story."

"So, for years I didn't have any contact with them. His wife passed away from cancer. Mr. Robertson promised Grandpa Colasanti he would kinda keep an eye on me and Diane. We didn't know about it, but that's how I got the job. I was a young girl and got this great job. I worked hard and got married and had you kids. End of story."

"Mom, tell us more," Heather insisted.

Kevin, who had been laying on the floor, sat up and faced her. "Yeah. Tell us about the night you met him at that party."

"Okay, but it was years ago. I started working at Robertson Industries in July of 2000. The party was April 1, 2001. I remember because it was a big night for me. The only reason I went to the party is because Ethan's lady friend had a family emergency. He didn't know who else to ask, so I kinda invited myself. Fernando told Ethan he shouldn't take me because I was a kid, and it was an event for mature adults."

"How old were you, Mom?" Kevin asked.

"Do the math," Heather told him.

He gazed at the ceiling for a moment. "You were only twenty, right?"

"I turned twenty-one that July."

"See! I know how to subtract," Kevin said.

"Anyway, I didn't know he would be there. I knew he owned the company and all, but I was intimidated to meet him. He sat by me at the dinner, and I was so scared I almost... never mind. He talked to me and we danced once or twice. He told me about the man who helped him start the business..."

"Did he mean your grandpa?" Kevin asked.

"Yes, but I didn't realize it. He was so nice to me. It wasn't until later that I learned he was talking about Grandpa. So, even though I didn't know I knew him, I did know him, and he's been kinda like a godparent or a guardian angel for me and Diane. More me than Diane, I think."

Kevin asked, "Is it true he owned all of Bristol Ridge and sold it to you guys and Uncle Tony and Aunt Kristen real cheap? Your land, I mean."

"He could have sold our properties for a lot more money, but he felt it was more important to have us live close by."

"We've heard stories that he donated a ton of money to the church to start the school," Isabella said.

"He did," Emmy admitted without revealing the donation she and Kenny made.

"Would you say he's a Christian?" Isabella asked.

Emmy took a deep breath and thought for a moment. "I like to think he is, but I'm glad we don't have to make that decision. It's not enough to earn your salvation by doing good deeds."

"We know that," Kevin said. "Some religions are like that, but it's different when you follow Jesus."

"Wow! I've never heard you explain it so eloquently, Kevin Michael," Emmy said. *I'm glad you listen to Pastor Tyler part of the time.*

"Why are we hearing crowd noise if there aren't any fans in the stadium?" Emmy asked.

"I'm not sure. It might be because of TV," Kenny answered.

"Do you think the Bears will be any good this year?"

"It depends on the new quarterback and if the defense stays healthy. They suffered too many injuries last year. That's why they finished in last place."

100

Emmy shook her head. "They might end up in the cellar again this year. They're losing to the Lions."

"Detroit might have a better team than normal."

"Do the players hear the fake fan noise, too?" she asked.

He shrugged and said, "You could ask Mr. Goldman from church. His son works in the team office. He might know."

"I'm sure it probably feels weird to the players," Kenny said.

"I'm going to ask Tony."

Tony answered his cell phone and asked, "Are you watching the game, brat?"

"Yes. Are you?"

"I have it on, but that fake crowd noise is irritating."

"Tell me," she said with a sigh as the Lions scored again. "Did you ever play without any fans watching?"

"Maybe in grade school. Why?"

"Do you think the players think it's strange?"

"I suppose, but after the game starts they try to ignore the crowd."

"Is that what you did when you were a player?"

"I tried to ignore a certain fan," he teased.

"Yeah, I had to yell at you because you sucked and were too slow."

"Yeah! That's how you run an offense," Tony hollered.

"It might be too late for the Bears to come back," Emmy said.

"Maybe, but Detroit is excellent at blowing leads late in the game. I'll talk to you later."

"Can you believe it, Kenny? They came back in the last minute to win. They played like crap, but Detroit played worse. Maybe there's hope for them this year after all."

Chapter Fifteen

"Mom! Where are you?" Heather shouted as she raced out of her bedroom and dashed toward her parents' master suite. "Mom!"

Emmy stuck her head out of the nanny suite at the opposite end of the hallway. "I'm in here. Why are you yelling?"

Heather slid to a stop on the hardwood floor and spun around. She had trouble gaining traction because of her thick socks, but eventually ran toward her mother.

"What's up?" Emmy asked. "I'm cleaning in here. We might have company one of these days."

"Grace texted me. Wyatt took Aunt Kristen to the hospital earlier. She's having the baby right now!" Heather shouted.

Isabella heard the commotion and popped her head out of her bedroom. "Did I hear you right? Aunt Kristen is having the baby today?"

"Yes!" Heather replied. "She might have already been born."

Emmy tore off her red bandana and removed her gloves. "I have to get cleaned up, so I can get to St. Bart's. Krissy might need me."

"Mom, Grace said both sets of grandparents are in town. Her real grandparents and Pastor Wyatt's parents, too. You can't all visit her."

"I know, but I'm going to see if Genna Ademilola can sneak me in. The hospital isn't allowing visitors at the moment."

Heather and Isabella grinned at each other.

Isabella whispered, "I hope hospital security doesn't catch Mom and lock her in solitary."

Emmy ran to her bedroom and emerged five minutes later in clean clothes. "Tell your father where I'm going. He's working in the studio."

Emmy gunned her 2017 white BMW X3 down the driveway heading for the hospital. On the way she called Genna, who worked in the labor and delivery ward as one of the head nurses.

"Hello, Emmy. How are you?" Genna asked.

"Are you on duty?"

"Why? You aren't having a baby, are you?" Genna teased.

"Not me, but Kristen Pearson is, and I'm on my way there now."

"She had the baby thirty or so minutes ago. She's in room 4012, and Pastor Wyatt is with her."

"Do you think you can sneak me into her room, or at least on the floor. I have to be there for Krissy. She needs me," Emmy said.

"Emmy," Genna said slowly.

"Okay, I want to see the baby and can't wait until they come home. I'm a terrible person."

Genna laughed and said, "Emmy, you know the hospital is not allowing visitors because of COVID-19. Pastor Wyatt was allowed to be with her, but now he has to stay until Kristen and the baby go home. That's the rule."

"Oh, please, Genna. Isn't there a way you can sneak me in? I desperately want to see her."

Genna glanced at her coworker, did an about-face and instructed Emmy where to go.

"Thank you so much. If I get caught I won't squeal on you. I'll tell the police I broke in on my own," Emmy said.

She parked on the third level of the deck, kept her head on a swivel as she hurried as fast as possible without running and made her way to an employee entrance. Genna appeared a few seconds later and opened the door using her security code.

Genna, wearing clean scrubs and a mask, laughed and said, "I shouldn't be doing this because I could get in trouble, but it's the most fun I've had in weeks. It's like you're a secret agent or something." She handed Emmy a white lab coat, an old ID tag and a mask. "Put these on and follow me."

Emmy put on the lab coat and giggled. "It's way too big."

"It's the smallest one I could find. Most of our doctors are not the size of a child."

Genna led the way through a maze of corridors to a lone elevator.

"I've never been in this part of St. Bart's, but my brother has told me about the secret passageways. He's a priest from St. John's who works as a chaplain here."

"I know who he is, Emmy, and because of all the additions over the years, there are parts of the building I don't even know about."

They rode the elevator to the fourth floor and the doors opened.

"Wait here a second," Genna whispered. She stepped out of the elevator and looked both ways. "Hurry! I'll take you to her room, but you can't stay long."

Emmy followed and they didn't meet anyone.

"Thanks, Genna. I won't stay longer than five... ten minutes," Emmy said.

Genna handed Emmy a clipboard with a few papers attached. "No more than five, and you have to leave using the normal elevators. I can't let you out of the door you came in. I'm working, you know."

Emmy nodded, adjusted her mask, knocked on the door and walked in like she belonged there.

"I'm here to see my patient," Emmy said trying to disguise her voice.

"Yes, doctor," Wyatt said. "We were expecting you."

"You were?" Emmy asked.

Kristen shook her head as she held the sleeping baby. "How did you get in here?"

Wyatt looked at Kristen then at the *doctor.* "I don't..."

"It's Emmy, Wyatt. Genna told me she was going to sneak her in here using a disguise."

Wyatt stared at Emmy for a split-second before laughing.

"You should roll up the sleeves or something, Em. You look as much like a doctor as I look like a.. I don't know," Wyatt said.

"I promise not to stay long, but I had to see her," Emmy said still standing by the door.

"You can come closer, but I shouldn't let you hold her," Kristen said with a smile. "My labor was easier than with the other two."

104

"Are you numb from the shots and drugs?" Emmy asked while slowly approaching the bed.

"Probably," Kristen replied. She held her baby so Emmy could see her face.

"She looks beautiful, Krissy."

Wyatt smiled and said, "Genna warned me she would be all red and wrinkly, but I think she is the most beautiful baby ever."

A few minutes later Genna entered and said, "Dr. Emmy, you need to leave before one of your colleagues arrives."

"Okay, I'm leaving." Emmy took a final look, sighed and blew Kristen a kiss. "Send me some pictures, and let me know when you get home."

Genna escorted Dr. Emmy to the bank of elevators, grinned and said, "I feel like we've done something naughty. I better ask Jesus for forgiveness."

"I'll tell him it was all my fault," Emmy said before stepping onto the elevator.

"How was your vacation?" Emmy asked Tyler Wednesday afternoon. "When did you get home?"

"A couple hours ago," he answered.

Tony, Ben and Phoebe walked into the family room with Scout and Derby on leashes.

"What are you doing here, brat?" Tony asked trying to hold back the excited dogs.

"I came to talk to Sloane about Kevin's math homework. It's been so long since I had a math class. I need help helping him," Emmy explained.

Tony let go of the dogs and they rushed toward Emmy.

Emmy got on her knees and let both dogs smother her with licks. After they settled down, Scout put a paw on Emmy's shoulder.

"You are such a good girl, Scout. Did you have a good time with your friend Derby?"

Phoebe sat on the floor next to Emmy and let Derby lick her face. "She missed me," Phoebe said. "I missed her, too, but I had so much fun in Maine. Do you want to hear what I did?"

"Yes, tell me." Emmy stood up and moved to the couch. "You can sit by me and tell me all about your vacation."

"You need to be brief, Phoebe," Tyler said. "We have to get home because I need to help your mother unpack and start working on a sermon. I haven't written a word in two weeks."

Phoebe told Emmy how she went lobster fishing in a restaurant and learned how to water ski.

"There were lots of lobsters in the tank, but I found a little one and wanted to keep it as a pet. Mom said I couldn't, so I ate it instead," Phoebe said then giggled.

Emmy looked up at Tyler. "Did she really learn to ski?"

"Yes, but the boat was only going fast enough to keep her on top of the water, and she was on a waterboard with me."

"I thought the boat was going so fast," Phoebe said. "After I did that, I went tubing with Mom and Natty. That was more fun because the boat went super fast!"

"It sounds like you had a wonderful time." Emmy looked at Tony. "What did you think of the Bears game?"

"It was weird."

"I agree. They should let some people in to watch the games." She stood up, petted Scout and Derby again and told Tyler, "Tell Liz to call me when she has a chance. I have to tell her how Genna snuck me into St. Bart's to see Krissy and Kayla."

Tyler looked at Emmy then at Tony.

Tony shrugged, held his hands up in surrender and said, "I don't know anything about it."

"Sounds like something she would do," Tyler said with a chuckle. "Come on, Derby. We need to get you home."

"Mom, Grace texted. Aunt Kristen is home with the baby. We want to see her," Heather said Thursday afternoon. "They got home two hours ago. Grace should have let us know earlier."

"Can we skip the rest of school today?" Isabella asked.

"I suppose, but you have to wear masks, and you can't hold the baby, or even get too close," Emmy insisted.

"That's okay. We just want to see her," Heather said with a smile.

Zach opened the door and let them in.

"Are they upstairs?" Emmy asked.

"Mom's in her room with Wyatt and the baby," Zach replied.

Heather rolled her eyes. "Is everyone going to call her 'the baby' forever. She has a name. Kayla Eve."

"Grandma and Grandpa should be here soon. Wyatt said visitors have to wear masks and can't hold her," Zach said.

"Did you hold her?" Isabella asked.

"Yeah, but just for a minute. Gracie held her longer."

"She is your baby sister," Heather said.

"I know, but she's so tiny. I don't remember Gracie being so little."

"You were just a toddler when Grace was born," Heather said.

"I'm only a couple weeks younger than you," Zach responded. "I might have even come home from the hospital first because you were premature."

"Doesn't matter now," Isabella scoffed.

"Are Wyatt's parents here?" Emmy asked.

"They left a little while ago to go back to the hotel," Zach answered.

"I thought they were staying here," Emmy said.

Zach shrugged and said, "Yeah, but Wyatt doesn't want anyone staying overnight until she's..."

"Kayla Eve!" Heather exclaimed.

"... older," Zach finished.

"I can understand that, but sooner or later Wyatt has to realize Kayla can't be kept in isolation her whole life," Emmy said.

Daniel and Karla Keasling arrived five minutes later.

"I should have known you would beat us here, Emmy," Karla said. "Have you seen my precious little one already?"

"Not today. We just arrived and haven't been upstairs," Emmy replied.

"Mom, you saw Kristen and Kayla at St. Bart's," Heather said.

Karla stared at Emmy. Mr. Keasling chuckled.

107

"One of the nurses goes to our church and is a friend. She snuck me in for a couple minutes. I wore a gown and mask and everything, so I didn't spread any germs," Emmy said rapidly.

"It's all right. We did get to see a video of her yesterday," Karla said giving Emmy a hug. She turned to look at the twins. "My, my. You have grown up so fast." She looked at Emmy and grinned. "They are taller than you."

"Mom is the shortest one in the family," Heather teased.

"We will let you see Kayla and Kristen first because you're the grandparents," Emmy said.

"Thank you," Karla said. "I never thought I would have another grandchild. Derrick and Amber refuse to consider having one or even adopting a child."

Emmy and the girls waited downstairs with Zach.

"Okay, now you can see her," Karla said. "She woke up for a moment, and I think she grinned at me."

Daniel laughed and shook his head. "It was probably gas."

"Mom, are you and Dad going out for dinner with the Pearsons?" Kristen asked later.

"We are meeting at seven. We thought we should get to know each other better, and since we're all in town, we decided to make plans for tonight. We didn't have much time to talk at the wedding, and we haven't seen them since," Karla said.

"They are wonderful, and they have accepted me into the family even though the divorce was an issue. They don't compare me to Evie..."

"That was his first wife, right?" Karla asked.

"Yes."

"Where do they live? I don't remember?" Daniel asked.

Ann Arbor, Michigan, and their names are Theodore and Genevieve."

"Do they use nicknames?" Karla asked.

"Ted and Ginny, but they can be rather formal at times. Play it by ear," Kristen suggested. "Where are you going, by the way? Not all restaurants are open."

"I called Larry's Diner. They are open," Karla said.

108

The grandparents were seated outside in the tent by the hostess who wore a mask with a smile on it.

"Michigan isn't as affected by the virus," Mr. Pearson said. "Most businesses never closed, and people are allowed to eat inside."

Daniel laughed and said, "Our governor closes and reopens things on a whim. I'll be glad when we get back to Florida. The restaurants where we live are open with certain restrictions."

"Kayla is your first grandchild, right?" Karla asked Genevieve.

"She is, and she might be our only one, but we do consider Zach and Grace to be ours, too. Do the children see their father often?"

"They did for a while, but they haven't seen him since March. He uses the pandemic as an excuse."

"I try not to make comparisons between Kristen and Evie, but I forget at times."

"It must have been difficult to lose your daughter-in-law at such an early age."

"It was, and more so because they moved to Pennsylvania."

"I lost a niece at an early age. Have you met Peter and Dotty?"

"At the wedding. Their mother was Heather Khryzman if I recall."

"Yes. Both parents passed away early," Karla said without revealing the drinking problem which ended Alex Khryzman's life.

"I am so grateful Kristen's pregnancy was uneventful. I cautioned them against having another child, though."

"So did I," Karla said. "She's forty and one child at that age is more than enough."

109

Chapter Sixteen

"Come on in, Kenny," Mr. Robertson said as he let Kenny in the front door. "Emmy said something about buying property in Idaho. Are you seriously looking?"

"We might be. She has been searching online, and she made me watch a movie about the state. It looks beautiful, but I don't want to spend a fortune on a place we might only use a month or two a year."

"I can understand your point. Land can be rather pricey in certain areas." He chuckled and added, "The cheap land is usually on top of a mountain peak, or inaccessible and unfit to build on."

"I wouldn't want a large ranch like yours."

"I was fortunate. I bought my ranch before the prices skyrocketed. If I sold it, I would make a tidy profit." He waved a hand. "I'd rather keep it. I don't need the money. Where are you thinking of looking?"

Kenny explained.

"I'll talk to a friend. He owns a real estate office in Ketchum Fork, and has access to all kinds of property."

"Thanks, but don't go to a lot of trouble. I'm not sure how serious she is. I can't imagine her living anywhere other than SoHam."

"Lunch will be ready in a few minutes," Emmy said as Father James walked into the kitchen and sat at the island.

"Good. I'm starving. All I had for breakfast was bread and wine."

Emmy rolled her eyes. "Were you serving communion to yourself?"

"No, I was fasting, so I skipped the wine. What are you making? It smells good."

She covered a pot on the stove and turned down the heat. "That's beef stew for tonight. We're having sandwiches and leftover potato salad for lunch."

He looked around and put a hand to his ear. "The house is quiet. Where is everyone?"

"Kenny took the kids to see his parents."

"I heard you were thinking about buying a house in Idaho. Is that true?" he asked while looking through a magazine.

"I've been thinking of buying property there for a vacation home. Why? Do you think it's a silly idea?"

"Not at all. Idaho's a beautiful state." He set the magazine aside. "Parts of it, anyway."

"Have you been there?" She opened the fridge, pulled out their lunch, fixed two plates and sat beside him.

He took a bite of the chicken salad sandwich and asked, "Is this homemade?"

"Yeah, I used a new recipe. Have you been to Idaho?"

"Yes, but it was a long time ago."

"What part?" she asked then took a bite of potato salad.

"A small town somewhere near Nampa if my memory serves me right."

She waited for him to elaborate, but he kept eating his sandwich.

"Tell me more about your trip to Idaho," she said after they finished eating. "I have a feeling there's more to the story than you're letting on."

"If I tell you, you can't use it in one of your books." He put their plates in the sink and rejoined her at the island.

"I can't make promises, but it's probably too boring for me to steal."

"I went up there during my spring break of my third year in college."

"By yourself? Why would you go to Idaho? Most college kids go to Florida to party."

"I wasn't there to party," he said, paused and added, "and I wasn't by myself."

"Did you go hunting with a bunch of your cowboy friends?" she asked with a grin.

"Nope. I took Sabrina Parkhurst with me."

She tilted her head and stared at him for a time. "Where have I heard that name before?"

He didn't reply.

111

She pounded the table than poked his side. "From your parents. That was the girl you were engaged to, right?"

"Yes."

She grinned and whispered, "Was it like a honeymoon?"

"I wouldn't know. I've never been on one."

"Never mind. I don't want to hear the sordid details of your sex life."

"Good because you aren't going to hear anything from me."

They moved outside and sat on the deck. For several minutes they talked about current events, but then were quiet.

"Do you ever hear from Sabrina? Do you know where she lives, or if she ever got married?" Emmy asked.

"I haven't heard from her in thirty years. Maybe longer. I'm pretty sure she got married, but I can't swear to it."

"Aren't you the least bit curious?"

"To be honest, I haven't thought about her for years. I wouldn't have thought of her today if you hadn't mentioned Idaho."

"You mentioned Idaho first. You could search Facebook. She might use her maiden name as part of her identity. Lots of women do that."

"No, thanks," he replied.

Emmy patted his hand and said, "It's okay. I'm sorry to pester you about her."

"It's all right. It's sad."

"Why?" she asked.

He shrugged and answered, "I don't know if she's even still alive, and I have no interest in learning the truth."

"She must have really hurt you. I've never known you to hold a grudge. I'm sorry."

"I don't hold a grudge, and I forgave her years ago for what happened." He waved a hand. "Life is too short, and hating someone for hurting you only succeeds in hurting you more."

"I should write that down, so I can use it later. It sounds so deep," she said with a grin.

"You make fun of your books, but I've read parts of them. They aren't totally frivolous."

"Just partly, huh?"

"Jonah, I called my doctor. He said I should go to St. Bart's," Mary Michaelis said as she sat on the edge of the bed.

He turned off his razor and asked, "Are you having contractions?"

"Yes, that's why I need you to take me to St. Bart's. I'd rather not have our baby at home if it can be helped."

"I'll be ready in two minutes," he said. He brushed his teeth while taking care of business. He dashed back into the bedroom. "I'm ready."

Mary handed him her small travel bag. "You won't be allowed to leave, so I put a change of underwear in the bag for you. If you want something other than your Sunday clothes, you should bring them, or change now."

"Thanks. You think of everything." He loosened his tie, threw it on the bed and grabbed his every day shoes.

Mary giggled while holding her stomach.

"What's so funny?"

"You are wearing dress clothes and old sneakers. It looks weird, but we have to go. They are getting stronger."

As they got close to St. Bart's, the sky turned black. The wind picked up in intensity.

Jonah turned a corner and Mary screamed, "Look out! There's a tree blocking the road."

"I see it," Jonah said as he slammed on the brakes and skidded across into the oncoming lane as another tree was uprooted.

They heard a scraping noise on the side of the car.

"That was close. We can't get through this way, Mary. I'll have to see if I can get through on Tana Drive."

She cringed as another contraction began. "I might have waited too long, Jonah. I'm sorry."

"Don't worry. I'll get you there if I have to carry you."

He tried three different streets before he found a clear path to the hospital.

"Madison is clear, but I'll have to park on the east side."

"It doesn't matter. I can walk," she said then closed her eyes because of the pain.

"I'll get you to the ER. I pray it's not blocked," Jonah said as the wind pushed the car across the road.

"Lord, please calm the storm until we get to St. Bart's," Mary prayed.

Jonah avoided two large branches and turned the corner. "We're almost there, and the road looks clear."

He turned onto the horseshoe ER drive, came to a stop under the canopy, threw his keys at the valet attendant, grabbed a wheelchair and rushed Mary up the ramp.

"I'm having a baby!" he hollered.

"Times are strange, but I doubt that," a nurse said calmly. She checked Mary and asked, "Do you know where to go?"

"Fourth floor. This is my third."

"I will let them know you are on your way."

When the elevator doors opened, Genna Ademilola was waiting. She smiled and said, "You are going to be okay. Dr. Walsh is ready for you."

"Mom, do I have to sit with you and Dad?" Kevin asked Sunday morning. He pointed to the rear of the sanctuary. "Ben and Taylor are back there. So is Zach."

Emmy looked and thought for a moment. "Okay, but you guys need to turn off your phones. You're old enough to pay attention to the service."

"We kinda listen to Pastor Tyler," Kevin said. "Enough to learn a few things, anyway. Thanks, Mom. I'll see you after church." He threaded his way through the people gathering for the second service. "Mom said I could sit back here," he said taking a seat next to Ben.

"Did you hear the thunder earlier?" Zach asked. "I think it's going to storm. We might have another tornado like in July."

"Are you afraid of a little storm?" Ben teased his cousin.

"No, but storms can sometimes turn into tornadoes. I read about the tornado that came through Crest Ridge back in the seventies. It destroyed a lot of houses and killed several people."

"That was a long time ago," Kevin said. "None of us were alive. We already had a tornado this year."

114

"Doesn't mean it couldn't happen again," Zach said crossing his arms over his chest and looking at the ceiling.

"I think we're pretty safe in here," Taylor said. "This is a new building and won't blow away in a storm."

"I hope you're right," Zach replied.

Seconds before Pastor Tyler was ready to end the service, the boys heard a loud crash and could hear the wind whistling. The lights went out, and the building was totally dark for a few seconds.

"What was that?" Kevin asked. He used the flashlight on his phone to look around.

The generators kicked in and most of the lights came on.

"If everyone would remain in your seat, we will check to see what caused the lights to go out," Pastor Tyler said.

Several of the men rushed out of the sanctuary to the foyer.

Tony pointed to the boys and said, "Stay there."

"What happened, Uncle Tony?" Zach asked.

"Not sure yet, but don't worry."

"Maybe it was another tornado," Ben said with a grin.

"Don't joke about that," Taylor said.

"Mom, do you know what happened?" Heather asked. "I don't remember the power ever going out like that."

"I'm sure it was just the storm." She looked at Kenny.

"Tony will let us know as soon as he knows," Kenny replied.

Tony shook his head. "We need to make sure no one walks through this glass."

Mr. Griffith called his son-in-law, who was a contractor. He told him about the damage and listened for a moment.

"Thanks. I'll let Tyler know." Mr Griffith ended the call and looked at Tony. "My son-in-law will be here soon. He said a twister set down and there's quite a bit of damage. We must have been at the edge of the storm."

An hour later Kenny finally made his way out of the parking lot and headed home. The kids stared out the window.

"Look at that tree!" Kevin hollered. "It was pulled all the way out of the ground."

The farther they got from the church, the less apparent was the storm damage. By the time they arrived home, the only evidence of a storm was a few small broken limbs across the road.

"I better check the woods to see if our fort was blown away," Kevin said.

"Be careful," Emmy yelled though she doubted he heard. "Kenny, you should check the house for damage."

Kenny parked the Odyssey in the garage and walked around the perimeter.

"How is it?" Emmy asked when he returned.

He shrugged and replied, "I can see leaves and small branches, but that's all. I guess we were spared the worst of the storm."

Emmy turned on the TV in the kitchen and watched a news bulletin.

"Where's that?" Isabella asked. "It looks like a war zone."

Emmy looked at the caption and answered, "It's a section of town west of the church, and then the tornado must have crossed the river." She pointed to what was left of a neighborhood and put a hand to her mouth.

"What is it, Mom?" Heather asked.

"That's Hampshire Glen." When the kids didn't respond, she added, "That's the retirement community where your grandparents lived. Part of it is demolished."

"I'm glad Grandma and Grandpa don't live there anymore," Isabella said.

"Me, too," Emmy said. She tilted her head and asked, "Did anyone see Mary or Jonah at church?"

Isabella shook her head. "I didn't. I saw Erin and Ewan with their grandparents, but I didn't see Mary or Pastor Jonah."

"When is she due?" Heather asked.

Emmy checked her phone, smiled and answered, "She's not due anymore. She had the baby an hour ago."

"Right in the middle of the storm," Isabella said.

"Is she okay," Heather asked.

"Pastor Jonah says everyone is doing great, but they had trouble getting to St. Bart's..."

"Did she have the baby in the car?" Kevin asked.

"No, but they cut it close."

"Does the baby have a name?" Kenny asked.

Emmy held up a hand and read a second text from Jonah. "Collin Jesse. He weighed eight pounds and two ounces. Ouch! That's a big baby for Mary."

Monday morning the members of The Only Hope gathered in Kenny's studio to begin recording a new project.

"Did you hear how many people were killed in the storm?" Bobby O'Connor asked.

Boyd Goldman held up a hand and extended all his fingers. "The latest report I heard was five people died in Hampshire Glen and eight others throughout the area."

"It could have been worse, but I heard the sirens going off ten or fifteen minutes before it hit," Perry Johnstone said. "My parent's house suffered some damage, but they're okay. A couple houses down the street were totaled."

"It's weird how the storm would destroy one house, but leave one next door completely undisturbed," Mason Williams said. "It's spooky."

Kenny, Will and Stuart sat in the control room as the band got ready to record.

"Have you listened to the demos?" Will asked.

"I listened to them last week," Kenny answered. "I think our job will be more of an advisory one. The guys know how they want the songs to sound, and they have the arrangements set. I feel bad about taking credit for producing it."

"We still have to record it," Stuart said. "They need our expertise to get it done."

"Is that what's it's called," Will said. "Here I thought we were just a couple old guys pushing buttons on this console."

Chapter Seventeen

"Mom! You're home. Did you get to hold the baby?" Heather asked as she rushed from the breakfast nook to the kitchen desk.

"Is he still all red and wrinkly?" Isabella asked as she followed.

Emmy shoved some junk mail out of the way and set her purse and keys on the desk. "Give me a second to hang up my jacket, and I will answer all your questions."

"I'll do it." Isabella hung the jacket in the mudroom for her mother.

"Did you hold him? Is she nursing him, or will we be able to feed him?" Heather asked.

Emmy grinned, sat at the island, spun around to face the girls and said, "Yes and yes, but sadly no."

"What?" Heather asked with a quizzical expression.

"I held Collin Jesse. That's his name. Yes, she is nursing him. So, no, you won't be allowed to feed him until he's old enough for real food."

"Too bad," Kevin teased. "Maybe Mary will let you change all the poopy diapers."

"You are so gross," Heather said walking back to the breakfast nook. "Mom, can we sell him to a needy family?"

"We tried, but had no offers," Emmy answered winking at Kevin.

"Hi, Heather," Peter texted. "Are you doing anything after school?"

She closed her laptop, picked up her phone and checked the message. "No. Why?"

He texted back. "Would you like to grab something to eat? I could drive to Darby's if you want."

Heather looked at the message and nudged Isabella.

Isabella removed her headphones and asked, "What? I'm almost finished with my Spanish class."

"Peter wants to take us to Darby's. Are you hungry?"

118

Isabella grinned and asked. "Are you sure he wants both of us to go? He probably wants to hang out with you."

Heather stared at the phone then looked at Isabella and giggled. "You mean like a date?"

Isabella grinned and replied, "Maybe, but you shouldn't let Mom or Dad hear you call it that. Especially Daddy. He always says we can't go out with boys until we're thirty-five."

"He won't know. He's busy in his studio helping the guys record a new CD," Heather said. "What should I do?"

"Bring me back a chocolate cake shake," Isabella answered.

"No way. Should I tell Mom where I'm going?"

Isabella shrugged then said, "You better because I won't cover for you."

Emmy walked into the library and asked, "Is school over for the day? If so, I need one of you to help me get dinner ready."

"I can help," Isabella said. She stared at Heather.

"Mom, would it be all right if I ride with Peter somewhere?" Heather asked.

"I suppose," Emmy answered as she picked up the book she was reading earlier. "Wait! Where are you going?"

"Nowhere special. He wants to go to Darby's and get a burger or something."

Emmy looked at Heather then Isabella. "Is there something going on I should know about?"

"He just wants some company, Mom," Heather said. "Isa could go too, but if you need her help..."

"I can manage on my own," Emmy said. "Did you finish your homework?"

The girls nodded.

"Okay, you can go, but try to be back before six if you want dinner."

Heather texted Peter, and he arrived ten minutes later. He watched the twins walk out together and pushed the door open for Heather.

"Hi, Peter," Isabella said from the backseat. "Mom, kinda suspected something was up, so you're stuck with both of us. I'll try not to be a pest."

"It's okay. This isn't like a real date. I'm just taking Heather out for a Coke and to talk."

"Yeah, sure," Isabella said with a grin.

"Hey, did Peter and the girls get back yet?" Emmy asked Tony on the phone.

"What are you talking about, brat?" he asked.

"Peter took Heather and Isabella to Darby's after school. Didn't you know."

"I just got home from work," he answered. "You should talk to Sloane or Mama."

Emmy heard the mudroom door open. "Never mind. They just got back. I'll talk to you later."

Tony set his phone down and walked into the family room. He saw Sloane working on her laptop, kissed her cheek and sat next to her.

"How was your day?"

"Uneventful. Liberty Manufacturing is not exactly the most challenging job in the world."

"Is Kristen coming back to work soon?" Sloane asked.

Tony shook his head. "I doubt it, but I could be wrong. If she does, it would be part-time. Hey! Do you know anything about Peter taking Heather and Isabella to Darby's?"

"Dotty mentioned something about him going on a date. Why?" Sloane asked knowing it would get a reaction from him.

"A date! He can't go on a date. He's too young."

Sloane looked at him and said, "He's seventeen and a senior in high school."

"That doesn't mean he's old enough to date," Tony said as he stood up.

"How old were you when you took Emmy out for dinner at Ciao Bella? Mama said she was the first girl you ever took on a date."

He waved a hand. "That's irrelevant, and I was a lot older."

Sloane laughed and said. "You weren't even seventeen yet. I know because Mama told me it was shortly after school started. You were sixteen, buster."

120

"I was almost seventeen, and a lot more mature than Peter."

Sloane nodded and said, "Of course you were. You're so mature for your age."

"What does that mean?"

"I think if you ask Peter, you will learn he likes the twins, but they aren't ready to date. They are friends. He probably wanted them along instead of Dotty. It's not cool to hang around with your sister at his age."

"I better talk to Emmy, and nip this thing in the bud before it escalates into something complicated. Peter can't take the twins on a date. They're family."

Sloane shook her head and resumed working on her school plans. Tony called Emmy.

"What's up? I told you the girls got back," Emmy said.

"Did you know they were going on a *date*?"

"They weren't on a date, you doofus. They were with Peter."

"Exactly!" Tony hollered. "I think he likes one of the twins, and not as a *cousin* if you know what I mean."

"You have lost your mind. I knew this would happen eventually. You played football too long. You should see a doctor before it gets worse."

"Very funny, brat. I'm serious."

"If it was a date, why would he take both of them? Answer that, doofus."

Tony shrugged and said, "What if he only wanted one of them to go, and you made him take both of them? Have you thought of that?"

"The girls are fourteen. They can't go on dates for two or three years, and Peter's too old for them anyway."

"Aha!" Tony exclaimed. "I knew you'd say that."

"How did you know what I would say? You have been hit in the head too many times."

"Are you forgetting how much older Kenny is than you?"

"What does that have to do with anything? I wasn't allowed to date until I was sixteen."

"Are you going to allow the girls to date before then?"

"Of course not," she replied. "To be honest, I haven't thought about it. They haven't expressed an interest in doing anything other than hanging out with friends. Though, Heather did watch a movie with Ian Plant."

"What would Kenny say if he knew one of them was going on a date?"

Emmy grinned and replied, "He would either laugh and pass it off as a joke, or he would explode and try to lock them in their rooms."

"Dotty is sixteen, and hasn't talked to me about boys."

"Why would she? Girls aren't going to talk about that stuff to their fathers. I would have never thought about talking to Daddy about dating or sex or..."

"Don't even go there! I don't want to hear about it."

Emmy laughed and whispered, "You do know the girls... mine and yours... have started having periods, right?"

He waved a hand and almost knocked off one of the pots hanging over the island. "Don't talk to me about that female stuff."

"You and Kenny are so alike. You like having sex, but heaven forbid you have to talk about it. What will you do when the boys are older?"

"Boys can learn all they need to know in the locker room from other guys. They don't need fathers to tell them about... you know."

Emmy rolled her eyes. "You are such a pig. Is that where you learned about sex?"

"I have to go..."

"You're afraid to talk to me about sex, aren't you?" Emmy said with a laugh.

"I can't talk to you about it. We aren't married."

"That didn't stop you from..."

"Goodbye, brat," he said and ended the call.

"Who were you talking to, Em?" Kenny asked. He opened the fridge and grabbed a bottle of water.

"Tony. Are you finished for the day?"

Kenny shook his head. "No, the guys are listening to the track we recorded this morning. What did Tony want?"

"Maybe you should ask your daughters?"

"Why? Did something happen to them? Where are they?"

"Upstairs. They just got back from Darby's."

"Did they bring something home for dinner?" He thought about it. "How did they get to Darby's? Did you take them?"

"Not me."

"Who?"

"Peter."

"Peter Bertucci?"

"Do you know any others?"

"Oh, that's okay."

"It might have been a date," Emmy said slowly so it would register.

"What do you mean? Who went on a date? Did Peter take a girl on a date?" He took a drink of water. "He's old enough and is a good looking young man. I would be proud to have him as a son."

Emmy laughed and muttered, "You might get your wish."

"What did you say?"

She put her hands on his shoulders, looked into his eyes and said slowly, "Peter took Heather and Isa to Darby's, but I think he really wanted to take Heather by herself. Do you understand?"

"No. Why would he want to take Heather to Darby's. He could take Dotty or Noemi or his brothers. He could take Carson..." Kenny paused and tilted his head to the side. "He took our babies to Darby's?"

"Now you understand," Emmy said.

Kenny sat on a barstool at the island and stared at Emmy. "He took my little angels to Darby's," he said slowly.

"Now before you get all excited..."

"I'm not going to get excited," he said. "I am calm. You are teasing me, but I don't know why. I know you wouldn't let them go on a date with a boy. They're twelve..."

"Fourteen."

"They can't go on dates for another ten years."

Emmy shook her head. "We might need to have a family discussion tonight."

123

After Isabella said the dinner prayer, Emmy asked, "How was your trip to Darby's, Heather? Did you enjoy it?"

"Mom! Please don't make it into something it wasn't."

"Did you go to Darby's?" Kevin asked. "Why did she get to go to Darby's and not me? How did you get there?"

"Isa and I went with Peter," Heather answered as she scooped some mixed vegetables onto her plate. "Could you pass the meatloaf, please?"

Kevin laughed and added a second large scoop of mashed potatoes to his plate. "Why would he take you two? Did he lose a bet? Did you go with Dotty and Noemi?"

"No, it was just Heather and myself," Isabella answered.

Kenny filled his plate, added barbecue sauce to his meatloaf and looked at Emmy.

"What? Did I put too much salt in the meatloaf?" she asked.

"No, it's fine. Do we have more sauce?"

"You already put it on your meatloaf," Kevin said. He looked at his parents then his sisters, shrugged and continued to eat. "Why is everyone acting so weird?"

"Don't talk with your mouth full," Emmy, Heather and Isabella said simultaneously.

"Why did you go to Darby's?" Kevin asked a moment later.

"Peter asked me... us... to go for a Coke," Heather replied. She looked at her father and bit her lip. "No biggie. Just friends hanging out together."

Kevin grinned and asked, "Did you kiss him? Did you forget he's our cousin?"

"I did not kiss him," Heather insisted. "Tell him, Isa."

"Kevin, you're being childish."

He shrugged and continued eating.

"How old do you think a young girl should be before she's allowed to go on group dates? Or solo dates?" Emmy asked Kenny.

Heather looked at Isabella and rolled her eyes.

"In my house, no one is allowed to go on *dates* until they are married," he replied looking at the twins.

Emmy snorted and asked, "How can they get married before they're allowed to date?"

124

"That was metaphorical. Maybe not the correct analogy," he said.

"Was it a metonymy?" Isabella asked.

Emmy looked at her.

"It was one of the vocabulary words today."

"What does it mean?" Heather asked. "I skipped over it."

Isabella explained the meaning to everyone.

"I'll have to remember it and use it in my books," Emmy said.

"Mom, your books are for kids. They won't know what it means," Kevin said.

Emmy looked at Kenny. "You didn't answer my question."

"No daughters of mine will certainly be allowed to *date* at the age of fourteen. Does that answer the question."

"Why not?" Heather asked. "And what exactly is your definition of a date? Would going to a youth group meeting at church with friends be considered a date?" Heather asked. "And I'm using lame air quotes because this entire conversation is lame. Isa and I are not interested in dates yet. What we do like is having fun with our friends. One of whom is Peter."

"Carson has taken us out for ice cream and you never complained," Isabella said.

"That's different. He's your cousin," Kenny said.

"We could get married in Kentucky," Heather said.

"We do not live in Kentucky," Emmy replied.

"Going to church with friends is exactly the kind of evening I approve of," Kenny said.

"Pastor Daryl caught Raven and Kensington kissing each other last week," Heather said.

Kevin laughed and added, "What a dorky name. Who wants to be called Kensington?"

"He's from England, and it's a family name," Heather said frowning at her brother.

"The point is they were caught doing something wrong," Emmy said. "What is Kensington's last name?"

"MacCollister," Isabella answered. "They're actually from Scotland, and he has this dreamy accent."

125

Kenny slapped the table. "That's it! I'm locking you in your closet until you're fifty."

Kevin laughed again and said using his best imitation of a brogue, "My name is Kensington MacCollister the fifth."

"Shut up, Kevin Michael!" the twins yelled.

"Kenneth Travis Robert Colwell!" Emmy yelled. "You are not locking anyone in a closet or anywhere else."

"Thank you, Mom," Heather said.

"Fine. How about we buy an invisible fence that shocks them if they leave the house."

"Yeah! That would be cool," Kevin said making a face at Heather.

Emmy shook her head at Kenny. "You have to face the fact your daughters are growing up."

"Me? My daughters? They are your daughters, too," Kenny said.

"Yes, but since it's inevitable, I am fine with them growing up," Emmy answered.

"Only because you remember how much you hated the way your mother treated you when you were growing up," he said with a bit of anger.

"You didn't hate Grandma, did you, Mom?" Isabella asked.

"Of course not, but we didn't always get along. She let Diane do whatever she wanted and treated me like a child. I resented it, and it caused friction in our relationship."

"I can understand why you would resent that, Mom," Kevin said. He grinned and asked, "When I turn sixteen, can I buy a big truck to drive through the woods?"

"No!" Kenny said. "And we will not discuss this dating issue until you graduate from college and are married with children."

Chapter Eighteen

"You need to take Scout to the vet," Sloane told Tony when he came home early Wednesday afternoon.

"Why? What's wrong with her?" he asked while he scratched behind her ears.

"Haven't you noticed she doesn't eat much lately? She's had a difficult time keeping up with Derby when she was here. Since then she's gone downhill."

"Maybe she misses Derby."

Sloane put her hands on her hips. "Don't be ridiculous. I called the vet. You can take her in today."

"Okay, but I don't think there's anything wrong with her," he said.

"Dad, where's Scout?" Coby asked when Tony returned later. "Did you forget to bring her home?"

"No, buddy, I didn't forget," Tony said softly. He looked at Sloane, who was making dinner and shook his head.

"What did the vet say?" she asked.

"Scout has... I wrote it down." He pulled the scrap of paper from his pocket and handed it to Sloane.

She read it and looked at him. "What does this mean? Osteoarthritis. Is it serious?"

"Yeah, and it's probably why she's been having accidents in the house. It hurts too much for her to get up and go outside."

"I'm going to look it up online," Sloane said. "Will you take the chicken enchiladas out of the oven when the timer goes off?"

"Yes," he said then checked the timer.

Sloane researched the disease on her laptop and then came back to the kitchen. She found Tony sitting at the island staring out the window.

"Did the vet recommend putting her down? Is that why you didn't bring her home? Did you already do it?" Sloane asked. "It might be better this way."

Tony shook his head. "No, I left her there, but she's still alive. He gave her someting to ease her pain."

127

"Couldn't we do that here at home? We could make her comfortable and you could carry her outside."

"That's not going to do anything but prolong her pain. You said she doesn't eat much anymore. You knows she's had acidents, and we always blamed the kids for not letting her outside. I haven't seen her running through the yard and woods since Derby left. She couldn't keep up with Derby."

"What are we going to do?" Sloane asked.

"The doctor suggested we bring the kids in tomorrow to say goodbye. After that, he will put her to sleep and... you know. I told him I wanted her ashes, so we could bury her here." He pointed outside. "I thought we could put her under that tree. She loved laying in the shade there. She could watch the kids playing and chase rabbits and stuff." He turned away and wiped his eyes.

Sloane put a hand on his back and gently rubbed it. "Will you explain it to the kids? I don't think I can."

"Maybe Mama could tell them."

"I think they need to hear it from you. They are old enough to understand pets don't live forever."

Tony gathered everyone in the family room.

"Is this about Scout?" Coby asked. "Is she sick? Is that why you left her at the doctor's office?"

Tony cleared his throat and looked across the room so he wouldn't make eye contact. "Yes, she is very sick, and I left her at the vets so he could make her comfortable." He paused and clenched his jaw.

"Daddy, do we have to put her to sleep?" Noemi asked. "That's what Jenny from school had to do with her dog."

"The vet suggested we put her down because she is in a lot of pain, and won't get any better. We are hurting her if we keep her alive because we don't want to lose her."

Coby snuggled closer to Mama and wiped his nose. "Is that why she doesn't come up to my room to sleep with me anymore?"

"Yes, it's too hard for her to climb stairs."

"I want to see her again before we put her to sleep," Ben said. "She is still alive, right?"

"Yes, but the vet gave her some medicine to help with the pain, and she's sleeping now."

"Sleeping how?" Coby asked.

"She's taking a nap like you used to do," Mama said squeezing the youngest member of the family.

"Scout has always been part of the family," Coby said. "She's older than me, right?"

"Yes, she's fourteen," Peter said. "I remember when you brought her home. She was just a puppy."

"How soon is the vet going to put her to sleep?" Dotty asked.

"He will do it tomorrow after we've had a chance to say goodbye," Tony answered.

"What happens to her after he puts her to sleep?" Coby asked. "Does he bury her somewhere?"

"No, we will bring her home, but she will be in a special vase," Tony said.

"How can Scout fit in a vase," Coby asked.

Tony looked at his mother.

"I will explain it to you later, Coby," she said.

"Okay, but I want to see her before she goes to sleep for good," Coby said.

"Did you notice Taylor didn't say anything or show any emotions?" Tony asked later that evening.

"Yes, but he's the one who holds his emotions inside," Sloane answered. "He's always been like that."

"I wish he would open up."

"Hey, Mom! I just got a text from Ben. They have to put Scout to sleep. Did you hear about this?"

"No! When did this happen?" Emmy asked.

Kevin walked into the den where Emmy was working on her book. "Uncle Tony took her to the vet today. She has some kind of arthritis disease."

"Oh, no," Emmy said. "Scout has been part of the family for almost as long as the girls."

"Ben said they have to see her at the vets in the morning, and then he will put her to sleep."

"I should call him. He's probably a basket case."

"I know Scout isn't my pet, but I will miss her," Kevin said.

Emmy called Tony's cell phone.

"I heard about Scout," she said before he could say hello. "When did this happen?"

"Do you mean when did she get sick, or when did I take her to the vet?"

"Kevin said you took her today. Has she been sick long?"

Tony sat in his recliner and answered, "Sloane noticed it before me. I guess she's been suffering for quite a while, but it's gotten worse since Derby left. Not that it's Derby's fault."

"I'm sorry. Is there anything I can do?"

"Well, I might need you to go with me when I pick up her ashes. I don't want to take the kids, and Sloane has to teach..."

"I can go if you want. When?"

"Probably Friday. We're going to say goodbye in the morning."

"Let me know when you need me." She paused then whispered, "Tony."

"Yeah."

"I'm sorry about Scout."

"Are we ready to go?" Tony asked after breakfast. "We're supposed to be there at nine thirty."

"Since we all can't fit in the Sienna, can I drive?" Peter asked.

"Yes," Sloane answered. "You can take Mama with you."

"I think we need to buy a vehicle that will hold all of us," Tony said.

"I hope you don't mean a motorhome," Sloane replied. "That would certainly not be an efficient method of transporting the family."

Tony shook his head and said, "They make larger vans. The Ford Transit has a capacity of fifteen."

"We don't need one that large," Sloane said.

"I'm going to check them out. I would like for everyone to be able to ride together."

Ben grinned and said, "You could trade in your truck since we don't have a camper anymore."

"No way!" Tony exclaimed. "I need my truck, and we might buy another fifth wheel someday."

"We will discuss this another day." Sloane looked at Coby. "Are you ready, little man?"

He shuffled his feet and stared at the floor. "I don't want to go."

"Why not?" Sloane asked.

"I'm afraid I will cry and everyone will make fun of me," he whispered.

Tony picked him up and hugged him. "We are all going to cry, buddy. No one will make fun of you."

Ben waited until Tony set Coby down and put an arm around his shoulders. "It's okay to cry sometimes. I know I will cry, so I can't tease you."

Coby looked up at his older brother and whispered, "Do you promise not to tease me?"

Ben raised a hand and said, "I promise not to tease you about Scout, but I will tease you for being a spoiled brat. You're the baby of the family, so everyone spoils you."

Coby frowned and smacked Ben's arm. Then he looked at his mother and asked, "I'm not spoiled, am I?"

"No more than any of your other brothers and sisters," she answered.

They arrived at the SoHam Animal Hospital and Tony opened the door. Everyone trudged inside as if walking slowly would make everything better.

The receptionist smiled and said, "I will get Dr. Reynolds for you."

The kids huddled around their mother as they waited to see Scout.

"Will we get to pet her?" Ben asked.

"Do you think she will remember us?" Coby asked.

131

"I would answer yes to both questions," Sloane said. She looked at Tony and saw he was struggling to keep his composure.

Dr. Reynolds rushed up to them. "If you come with me, Scout is waiting in one of the exam rooms." He looked at Tony and added, "I gave her an extra dose of painkiller. She had a hard night."

"She is awake, right?" Tony asked.

"Yes, but she might not do more than wag her tail. She will certainly recognize everyone by smell if nothing else. Were you aware her eyesight has deteriorated to where she only had limited sight?"

"I wondered if that might be why she didn't move much," Tony replied.

Dr. Reynolds opened the door and said, "There is enough room for everyone to step inside. Take as much time as you need. I will be waiting across the hall."

"Thank you, Dr. Reynolds," Sloane said.

Coby held his mother's hand as everyone silently entered the room.

Ben looked at his brothers and sisters sad faces and made a decision. He walked up to the exam table where Scout lay. He rubbed behind her ears and said, "Scout girl, it's Ben. Are you happy to see me?"

Scout lifted her head and her tail began to move slowly back and forth.

"You remember me, don't you, Scout," Ben whispered in her ear. He rubbed her head and the tail began moving faster.

Fifteen minutes later Sloane and Mama hugged the kids as they left the room.

"We will put you in your favorite place," Tony said softly.

Tony had his last look at her as Dr. Reynolds closed the door.

Sloane hugged her boys. Mama hugged Dotty and Noemi. Tony picked Coby up and carried him to the van. Ben rubbed Taylor's back when Taylor finally let his emotions show.

"It's okay, Tay-Tay. You don't have to be brave," Ben whispered.

132

Taylor wrapped his arms around Ben and buried his face in his chest. Ben continued to rub his brother's back.

They stood by the van for a moment.

Mama said, "I will ride in the van. Who wants to ride with Peter?"

No one volunteered at first.

"I will ride with him," Dotty said. "He needs someone with him to make sure he doesn't get lost."

Emmy was there to greet them when they arrived home.

"Hi, Aunt Emmy," Noemi said.

Emmy hugged Noemi, who was only a couple weeks younger than the twins, and whispered, "I'm so sorry about Scout. I came over to see if you needed anything. I could make lunch if anyone is hungry."

"I didn't eat breakfast," Ben said. "I was too nervous."

"What would you like, Ben?" Emmy asked.

"A sandwich would be okay. I just need something to quiet my belly. It's starting to growl."

Emmy made sandwiches to order and watched Ben try to lift everyone's mood.

"Dad, I have a suggestion," Ben said.

"What would that be?"

"I think we should talk about our favorite memories of Scout tomorrow. I know we're all sad, but we should remember the fun we had with her. What do you think?"

Tony ruffled Ben's hair, smiled and said, "I like that idea. Everyone should have a chance to tell a story about Scout."

"What if we tell the same story?" Coby asked. "I'm not good at telling stories."

"It won't matter," Tony replied. "You can think of a story today, and tomorrow we will have a memorial celebration of Scout."

"I'll think of something tonight," Coby said.

Emmy smiled at Tony. *I know you're going to lose it at some point. I probably will too.*

"What time are you going to pick up Scout?" Emmy asked the next morning. "Did you take the day off?"

"I took a couple vacation days. The company wants us to take vacation time now. Otherwise, everyone will wait until the virus thing is over." He chuckled and said, "If everyone waits, there won't be anyone working in the office."

"Do you still want me to go with you to the veterinarian?" she asked, closed her laptop then poured out the remains of her cold coffee.

"Yeah. I'm going to leave about nine thirty. Should I pick you up?" He rubbed his jaw and added, "I need to shave and shower first."

"Sure, and use soap."

"What?" he asked.

She chuckled and said, "Sorry. Force of habit. I'm always telling Kevin to use soap."

"I think I can remember on my own, brat. I'll be there soon."

"That should be deep and wide enough," Tony said as he finished digging a hole for the urn containing Scout's ashes two hours later. "Should we put the urn in the hole before we share our stories?"

Most everyone nodded.

Coby handed the rectangular-shaped, dark chocolate-colored urn to his father.

"Maybe you should set it in the... hole," Tony said.

Coby got on his knees and placed the urn in the middle.

"Maybe you should have the photo of Scout facing the house," Sloane said.

"Yeah, that would be better," Taylor said.

Sloane whispered to Emmy, "Taylor tried not to show his emotions, but he's doing better now. He told me he had a good story to tell everyone."

Emmy watched her girls holding hands with Noemi and Dotty. Kevin stood next to Ben with his hands folded in front of him.

134

"That's looks good," Tony said as Coby and Peter adjusted the urn. "Who wants to share a story first?"

"I do," Taylor said.

"Go ahead, son." Tony nodded.

"Last year I had the flu. I got sick and was in bed for like three days. The only times I got up were to throw up or have diarrhea..."

"Oh, gross," Noemi whispered to Heather. "I remember when it happened.

"... Scout stayed with me the whole time. She slept on the floor next to my bed, and every time I went to the bathroom, she went with me. Sometimes she would lay next to me on the bed. She helped me get well, and I feel sad because I couldn't help her get well." He paused and choked back his emotions before ending with, "I think God has a place for pets where they are healthy and get to run around and chase rabbits and stuff."

Tony hugged Taylor. "Okay, who wants to be next?"

"I have a story," Coby said. "Ben helped me think of it and helped write it down."

All the kids shared a story about Scout. The younger boys looked at Peter.

"I guess it's my turn," Peter said. "My favorite story is the time Carson and I were climbing a tree, and he got his foot stuck. He couldn't get it out, and I told Scout to run home and bring help. She did and Dad came, but he was too big to climb the tree." He grinned at Emmy and said, "Aunt Emmy had to climb the tree to rescue Carson."

"I could do it because I'm small and don't weigh as much as this big guy."

"Sometimes, it's an advantage to be a runt," Tony teased.

Tony let each child put a shovel of dirt into the grave. He finished filling in the spot and then pounded a wooden cross into place.

"We should plant some wildflowers here," Dotty suggested and maybe build a border around it."

"Yeah," Ben said. "We can find cool rocks. Right, Kevin?"

"Yeah! I know where we can find some."

135

"Can I help?"

"Sure, Taylor. Good story, by the way," Kevin said.

As they walked home, Kevin asked his father, "Could we get a puppy? I've never had a pet, and I want one. There must be some kind of dog that's safe for kids with allergies."

Emmy heard the request, shook her head and said, "I don't think it's a good idea. You might enjoy it at first, but puppies grow up fast."

"I promise to take care of it even after it's old like Scout," Kevin replied.

Emmy looked at Kenny.

"Maybe I can do some research and learn more about breeds that are less likely to cause a problem."

"That's fair," Emmy said. *I hope there isn't a breed that would work. I don't want to train a puppy, and I can't see the kids taking it out for a walk in the middle of winter.* She looked over her shoulder at the Bertucci house. *I suppose the real reason is because I couldn't do what they had to do. It would break my heart to lose a pet almost as much as losing a child.* She looked at her kids as they walked ahead of her and Kenny. "Well, maybe not that much."

"What did you say, Em?" Kenny asked.

"Nothing. I was just thinking out loud."

Chapter Nineteen

"Hey, Emmy, did you hear the latest news?" Kenny asked. He walked into her bathroom as she was getting ready to shower. "You aren't going to believe this."

"Believe what? What are you talking about? Couldn't it wait until later? I need to shower and meet Denise. She wants to go over the book in person for some reason."

"Dave proposed to Claudia last night, and she accepted. He's getting married," Kenny said with a smile.

"That was pretty quick. When did he meet her?" she asked turning on the water.

"I don't remember exactly," he replied with a shrug. "It wasn't too long ago."

"Isn't she like half his age?" Emmy asked checking the water temp and then walking into her shower.

Kenny thought about it for a moment. "Yeah, Dave is forty-seven now, and she's in her twenties."

"Can we continue this after I get dressed?" she asked. "I don't want to be late."

"Sure," he answered. "Too bad I already showered."

"You are insatiable. Go away."

"Mom, I don't understand this assignment," Kevin said when Emmy came downstairs for breakfast. "Can you explain it to me, please?"

"Let me see it."

Kevin handed her the laptop, and she read the instructions.

"Am I supposed to go outside and write an essay about what I see?" he asked. "How would she know what I see? I could pretend I'm seeing the pyramids of Egypt or Niagara Falls."

"I think she knows we don't live in Egypt. I'm pretty sure she wants you to learn to express in writing what your eyes see. Don't over complicate it."

He rolled his eyes and said, "I will see a bunch of trees."

"Do your best," she said.

He sighed and headed outside.

137

"Do I have time to tell you about Dave and Claudia?" Kenny asked.

Emmy checked the time as she grabbed a blueberry bagel and whipped cream cheese from the fridge. "Make it quick."

The twins, sitting in the breakfast nook, looked up from their laptops.

"What's going on with Dave and Claudia?" Heather asked.

"They are engaged to be married," Kenny answered.

"Get out!" Heather hollered.

"No way!" Isabella shouted.

"Why not?" Kenny asked.

"For one thing, he's an old man, and she's only twenty-three. He's like ten times older than her," Heather said. "She's a gorgeous supermodel. He's okay, but not exactly a ten if you know what I mean."

Isabella asked, "Do his kids know? They might not be too pleased with their father marrying such a young woman."

Kenny shrugged and answered, "I'm not sure. They will know sooner or later."

"You better not leave Mom for a younger woman," Heather warned. "I'll shoot you if you do."

Kenny laughed and replied, "I would be crazy to leave your mother."

Emmy made a face at him. "No one else would put up with you."

"I love *you*, Emmy," Kenny said.

"You better. I need to go. Let me know how this ends up."

Isabella picked up her phone and after a few minutes, she informed everyone, "Deborah knows. I texted Dotty, who texted a friend who texted one of her friends who lives close to Dave's house, and she texted Deborah. We're on a group text now. All the kids know, and they are pissed off. Big time upset!"

"How can you do that?" Kenny asked.

"Dad," Heather said slowly. "Don't you know anything?"

"I know how to text, but I've never been involved with a group text. Us old guys use conference calls, or we meet in person."

138

Kevin walked in shaking his head. "This is stupid. All I wrote is that I see trees and bushes and stuff. I didn't see any animals. I give up."

Kenny looked out the window, laughed and said, "I can help you for a few minutes, son, but then I will be working with Adam and the guys. Do I need to tell you to stay in school?"

"Dad, we know we're in school even if we're sitting at home. We won't play hooky," Isabella said.

"Speak for yourself, Isa," Kevin smirked.

Emmy arrived at the Starbucks and saw Denise Bartell sitting outside talking on her phone.

"Give me a minute to handle this fiasco, and I'll be right with you," Denise said. She talked excitedly for another couple minutes before ending the call. "I apologize for that, but no one knows how to make a decision." She took a deep breath, laughed and asked, "How are you? Can you believe the governor closed restaurants again. I'm not going to drink my coffee outside when it's snowing," she said with a hearty laugh.

"I agree and we are all well. You?"

Denise waved her hands and replied, "My life is total chaos, but I thrive on it. Work is almost impossible. My kids are driving me up a wall even though none of them live at home anymore." She paused to take a sip of her coffee. "So, I read your chapter about the dog, and I wasn't impressed. It didn't move me to tears like it probably did you."

"How can I change it?" Emmy asked. "I cried like a baby when I wrote it."

"I want to see more emotions from those kids. I bet they were rather emotional in real life. This is based on a true story, right?"

Emmy nodded.

Denise waved a hand. "How did they react? Try to get in their heads. I'm sure not all of them reacted the same. Make me see the differences."

"I will rewrite it and send it back today. You did like the rest of the book, right?"

139

Denise nodded and said, "I thoroughly enjoyed it. You have a real knack for writing dialogue in the voice of these teenagers." She smacked the table, laughed and said, "I laughed until my sides hurt when I read about them trying to explain to the principal why they needed to be excused from English class for the rest of the semester."

Denise's phone rang again. She checked the caller ID and said, "I'm sorry, but I have to take this. It's a phone interview with a person who works in the governor's office. He's canceled five times."

"I'll work on the chapter and get it back to you."

"This is much better!" Denise texted later that evening. "I almost cried, and that takes a lot. I'd say you are ready to release the book."

Emmy texted back, "I worked on it all afternoon. I'm glad I almost made you cry."

Kenny saw Emmy pumping her fist and asked, "Are you watching football?"

"No, I had to rewrite a chapter and I almost made Denise cry. I'm so happy."

Kenny stared at her for a moment, then shook his head and walked away.

"Kenny, could you give me your honest opinion about the cover for my new book?" Emmy asked as he walked past the den.

He retraced his steps and entered. He stood behind her as she sat at the desk. "Show me."

She pointed to the monitor. "It's that one."

"Did you change it?"

"Yes."

"Show me the other one," he said.

She opened her previous cover. "Can you see the difference?"

"Yes, I love the expression on her face." He pointed to the girl on the left. "I can hear her saying 'this is a secret', or whatever your title is."

"It's 'You Can't Tell a Soul.'" She flipped back and forth between the covers. "Okay. I'll go with the new one. I'm going to send in the files and it should be ready by tomorrow night."

"Emmy, did you see the news?" Kristen asked.

"What news? How is Kayla feeling? Grace told Isa she was running a fever."

"Kayla is fine. We gave her some baby Tylenol. It was only a slight fever, but I called the doctor anyway."

"That's good. What news are you talking about?"

"I know you don't follow politics..."

"Sorry, but it doesn't interest me."

"President Rhodes tested positive for COVID-19. He is in the hospital."

"That's not good. Is he going to be okay? He's not exactly a young man."

"He is sixty-two. If I had to guess, I would say his doctor is being very cautious."

"I suppose the guy running against him will use this as another reason to vote against Rhodes."

"That might backfire, but time will tell." Kristen chuckled and asked, "Do you know who is running against the president? I bet you don't."

"I do so," Emmy insisted.

"Who? What is his name?"

"It's the guy who was vice-president a few years ago. His name is Joe something, and he's from Indiana."

"You have no clue. I hope you learn something about the candidates before you vote."

"Finally. I didn't think school would ever end today. Fridays suck," Kevin said. He closed his laptop, removed his earbuds and took a deep breath. "I'm going outside. I need to get out of the house."

Heather looked out the window and laughed. "It's pouring."

Kevin checked and slapped the table. "Crap! Is it going to rain forever? I don't remember what sunshine looks like."

"Dad said we need the rain," Isabella said.

"Why can't it stop when we're done with school?"

"Why can't what stop?" Emmy asked as she walked into the room.

"The stupid rain," Kevin answered pointing outside. "I wanted some fresh air."

"I should ground you for using that word, but I kinda feel the same way," Emmy said. "We need sunshine, Lord."

"Dad said your new book is done. You didn't let us read it and give our opinion like you usually do," Isabella said.

"I let you read most of it," Emmy answered. "I added a chapter at the last minute."

"What about?" Heather asked.

"It was about a family that lost their pet."

Kevin turned away from the window. "Is it about Scout?"

"For the most part, but I changed a few facts."

"Will it make us cry when we read it?" Isabella asked.

"I hope so," Emmy answered. She pulled up her website and showed them the new book.

"I like the cover," Heather said. "Ruby and Claire look like they've done something naughty, and are trying to keep it a secret."

"What did they do?" Isabella asked.

Emmy grinned and answered, "You will have to read the book. You can order the Kindle version if you want."

"I might do that," Isabella said. "It looks like this will be a rainy weekend."

Chapter Twenty

"Did you listen to the news this morning, Emmy?" Kristen asked. "Why do I even ask? You never do."

"Kenny told me President Rhodes is out of the hospital and doing a lot better."

"He gave a speech as he was leaving the hospital. He assured everyone his health is not an issue."

"The guy running against him probably thinks it is." Emmy heard the doorbell and saw a UPS truck leave a moment later. "Wasn't there a president a long time ago who caught pneumonia at his inauguration and died like a week later?"

"I don't think it was that quick, but I do recall it happening."

"Don't you remember his name?" Emmy asked with a chuckle.

"Sorry, but I was not born yet."

"I'm glad the president is doing better. I pray every day for the leadership of our country."

"Emmy, I told you not to bring anything," Frances Rawlings said when Emmy walked into her kitchen with a bowl of taco salad.

"I had to make something, and this is easy. How have you been? Is your arthritis getting better?"

Frances rubbed her elbow and said, "The medication helps, but my joints hurt when I wake up, or when it rains."

"Where is the birthday boy?" Emmy asked. "Sebastian let us in. He's almost as tall as his brothers. How old is he now?"

"He turned twelve the last day of September," Frances answered. She took the taco salad and set it on the crowded counter. "Frank is seventeen and Trent fifteen. They are all taller than me and will pass Jeff up soon if they keep growing. They eat more than I would have thought possible." She shrugged and added, "But they are boys."

"Kevin Michael eats a lot, but the girls are getting more conscious of their looks, so they don't eat as much."

"I saw them singing at your church. They look so grown up."

"I didn't know you watch our livestream," Emmy said. "Did you like it?"

"I catch it once in a while. We don't always make it to our church," she said then admitted, "Actually, we haven't been there since March when this virus mess started."

"A lot of people are staying home and watching online."

Jeff walked into the room behind Emmy and put his hands on her shoulders. "Thanks for coming."

She did an about-face, grinned and said, "You don't look any older than the last time I saw you. You actually look pretty good for a seventy-year-old rock star."

"And you look all right for an old lady of forty," he teased back.

Eventually, the other members of Fridays At Five and their spouses arrived.

"Where's Dave?" Jeremy asked. "Is he still in Australia?"

Jeff nodded and said, "Yeah. Haven't you heard the news? He's engaged to Claudia."

"I heard, but I didn't know if it was serious, or simply a rumor."

"Joshua talked to Danny, and learned the older kids haven't talked to Dave in months," Amanda Lenhart said.

Teresa Joseph scoffed, "She's barely older than Tommy's girlfriend, Sabrina."

Emmy giggled then said, "But she's almost a foot taller. Sabrina's only an inch or two taller than me."

Jeremy grinned at Emmy and teased, "Everyone's kids are taller than you except for Kinsey and Alex."

Emmy made a face at him. "Alex is one and Kinsey's only seven. It should be a few years before they're taller than me.

"I think I'm going to leave all the food on the counter and table," Frances said. "Everyone can take what they like and sit wherever they find a place."

"Are we going to sing first?" Emmy asked.

144

"I'm a little old for a birthday cake and candles," Jeff said. He looked at Paul Joseph and added, "P.J. didn't make a big deal about turning fifty last year. He's the old man of the band."

P.J. smiled and said, "You need to remember that and respect your elders."

"If we aren't going to sing, I will say a quick prayer, and we can eat," Emmy said.

"The CD is officially available now," Kenny said the next morning. "I don't know how well it will sell, but it's out."

"What is it called?" Isabella asked.

"*When Light Flashes*," Kenny answered. "Do you like the title?"

"I've heard better," Heather said.

Isabella answered, "I like it. It's short but catchy."

"It's like the first CD of new songs you've put out in forever," Kevin said as he sat through a boring class on his laptop. "Kids will think you're a new band."

"The last CD of new material came out in early 2017," Kenny replied. "That wasn't ages ago. Plus, we released that live set in 2018."

"How did it sell?"

Kenny shrugged and answered, "About as well as we expected."

"No one buys CDs anymore," Heather said. "They are like cassette tapes. If we want new music, we either download it or listen on a streaming service."

Kevin laughed and said, "I once saw an eight-track tape. Maybe you should release your music on that format. It might make a comeback."

"Ha! Ha! At least we are in a position where we don't have to rely on future CD sales for our income," Kenny said.

"The pandemic won't last forever," Isabella said. "One of these days you will go on tour again."

"I hope it's before we are too old to travel."

"Has the band talked about doing another virtual concert?" Emmy asked. "That might boost sales."

"We did discuss it, and we're going to do one the sixteenth of November."

"What day of the week is that?" Emmy asked.

"It's a Monday."

Emmy made a face. "Why do it on a Monday? You guys rarely did shows on Mondays because it was a slow day."

Kenny shrugged and said, "That's the day the guys chose. A few people might watch."

"It's still possible you could do a short fall tour," Emmy said.

Kenny shook his head. "We talked about it last week."

"What did you decide?"

"Jeff and Frances bought another house to restore. He's going to be busy with that. Jeremy is doing another movie score and won't have time. Adam is busy with The Only Hope's latest project."

"Are they going to do some livestream concerts?" Emmy asked.

"I think so," he answered. "They've been filming some of their sessions with the hope of making a movie out of them."

"I wondered what they were doing."

"Dave is spending most of his time with Claudia. They are planning their wedding. P.J. is the only one who has the time to tour."

"Certainly by the start of 2021 bands will be allowed to tour. They have to earn a living somehow."

"I sure hope so," Kenny responded.

"Where are you going, Mom?" Isabella asked shortly before noon the next day.

"I made an appointment to see Dr. Larson," she replied.

"Why? Do you need glasses?" Kevin teased.

Emmy shrugged and said, "Maybe. I've been having trouble reading."

"Lots of old people need glasses, Mom," Kevin said. "You should take Dad with you."

"I heard that, Kevin," Kenny hollered.

"I am not an old person, young man," she retorted making a face. "Make sure you pay attention and do your assignments. I'll be back later to make lunch."

"Could you bring something home from Darby's?"

"No, I'm not going to be close, and we have food in the fridge that needs to be eaten."

Emmy arrived at the doctor's office and checked in with his receptionist. She answered all the questions pertaining to COVID-19 and explained about Kenny's positive test.

"He wasn't sick, and I suspect his result was a false positive."

"He hasn't tested positive lately, has he?"

"No, he's good to go," she answered.

"Come on back," Dr. Larson said. "I haven't seen you since the last time the kids needed an exam. How is everyone doing during this crazy period?"

"The kids are bored because they can't see their school friends." She told him about Kenny and their experience with quarantine.

"My daughter-in-law tested positive back in March, but she didn't exhibit any symptoms either."

He checked her eyes and had her read the chart.

"Your eyes are okay, but you might need glasses at some point in the future. For now, you could buy some reading glasses at the drugstore or any of the box stores. Even Amazon. Try the different magnifications, but you shouldn't need anything stronger than one and a half times."

"Thanks, Dr. Larson. I was worried I might need a prescription."

"You could try contacts when it comes to that."

"My friend, Kristen, wears contacts, but I don't know if I could stick something in my eye. I don't even like to use mascara for that reason."

He chuckled and said, "It's easier than people think."

"What did the doctor say?" Kevin asked when Emmy returned. "Do you need bifocals or thick glasses?"

"No, I just need cheap reading glasses for now. You can make fun, but one of these days you might need glasses. Your father probably needs glasses, but he's too vain to admit it."

"I saw him borrow Mr. Consoli's glasses last week. He said he needed them to see the fine print on a studio printout," Kevin said.

"See? I told you he was vain."

"I don't see the big deal. There are a bunch of kids at school who wear glasses. Lendahl Dromberek's glasses are real thick. Some kids tease him and call him Coke, but I don't."

"Bennett just called Brady," Diane said as she and Emmy sat in the family room drinking tea. "Mackenna had a boy."

"How is she doing? Is Spencer happy to be a father?" Emmy asked.

"I think he's thrilled, but Marissa refuses to be referred to as a grandmother. She thinks by ignoring the baby, she will not appear any older."

"I'm sure she will change her mind when she gets to hold the baby."

Diane laughed and said, "She vows to never change a diaper or feed him."

"What did they name him?" Emmy asked. "Did Grandma Marissa insist on a formal southern name, or did they name him Billy or Joey? Something like that."

"That would really piss off Marissa," Diane said with a grin. "Brady, what did Spencer name his son? Do you know?"

Brady looked up from his book and said, "Edward William, and they want to call him Eddie, but I'm sure Marissa will put a stop to that."

"I'm going to call him Eddie Billy when I see her just to tick her off," Diane said.

"Have you heard anything about Abigail lately?" Emmy asked. "She must be through with college by now."

"She finished and moved to Houston. She works for an aerospace company. How old is Abigail now?" Diane asked Brady. "She must be close to thirty, right?"

"No, Spencer's older. He's twenty-eight or nine, and she's three years younger."

"Did she ever get married?" Emmy asked.

Diane shook her head and answered, "No, but she lived with her boyfriend for a year or so. Marissa wanted to disown her, but Bennett liked the guy. She broke it off, and I don't know what her status is now."

"I hope Spencer and Mackenna don't decide to move closer to their parents. Denver is a good place to raise a child. Especially when the grandparents are like Marissa," Emmy said. "I need to get home. I have to make sure Kevin doesn't skip his afternoon classes.

"Talk to you later, Emmy."

She returned home and asked Kevin if he needed help with anything.

"I'm good, Mom. Where did you go?"

"I went to see Diane. She has a new nephew."

"Who had a kid?"

"Spencer and Mackenna. That's Bennett's son. They had a boy."

"Ben and I checked out the new house he's building," Kevin said.

"Please tell me you didn't go inside."

"No, we walked around the outside. It looks bigger than our house, and maybe even bigger than Grandpa Robertson's house."

Emmy grinned and said, "That's because Marissa wants to own the biggest house in the city. She thinks it shows how important she is."

"Whatever," Kevin said. "Someone has to clean it."

Emmy chuckled and pictured Marissa cleaning a toilet.

Chapter Twenty-One

"Hey, Ben, you'll never guess what I just heard from Jamiel Ramel," Kevin said. He laughed and added, "This will make your day."

Ben jumped up the steps onto the rear deck and asked, "What did you hear? I heard your mom decided you could have a puppy."

"Yeah, Dad did some research and they've been thinking about letting me have one. If we get one, you can play with it, too," Kevin said.

"What was the other thing you wanted to tell me?"

"Jamiel lives by the Osbornes and Plants. His parents are doctors like Dr. Plant. They know each other. Anyway, Jamiel told me Ian Plant got caught selling drugs, and would have been arrested and thrown in jail except his father knew the police officer and got Ian out of trouble."

"Drugs? What kind of drugs?" Ben asked.

"Some kind of pill stuff. Not the kind of drugs you smoke or stick up your nose," Kevin waved a hand. "Apparently, he stole them using his father's name or something. I'm not sure how he got them, but he was selling them to people."

"Do our parents know? Your mom will freak out. Heather used to like Ian before she started liking Peter."

"They haven't said anything, so I don't think they've heard. It takes parents longer to learn stuff than us kids, but eventually they will hear about it."

"Are you going to tell Heather or Isa?"

Kevin thought about it for a moment. "I suppose I should. I don't think Heather talks to Ian anymore, but she should know what he did."

"What do you want to do this afternoon? I'm glad it's the weekend. I'm sick of online school. Mom makes sure all of us pay attention to the teachers even though she has to teach her classes," Ben said as the boys headed into the woods.

"We could see if we can expand our fort. I found a pile of scrap lumber where they're building Mr. Robertson's new house."

He pointed and added, "Not Grandpa Robertson. Bennett. His other son."

"I know who you mean," Ben said. "How do you know it's scrap? I don't want to take anything they might need."

Kevin waved and answered, "I talked to one of the workers, and he said it was going into one of the dumpsters. I don't think anyone will care if we use some of it."

"Okay, but maybe we should ask someone in charge."

"Yeah, you're right."

They rode their bikes to the site and saw someone come out of the construction trailer.

"Let's ask him," Kevin said. "He looks important."

The boys stopped in front of the man and Kevin told him who they were and asked about the scraps of lumber.

He removed his hardhat and asked, "Are you really a Bertucci?"

Ben nodded, pointed and said, "My father's name is Tony, and I live over there."

"I used to work for Bertucci & Keasling Construction. My father's name is Posey. He retired, but he built your house. Not by himself. But he was one of the foremen. My name's Blake." He offered a fist and the boys bumped it. "Where did you find this scrap lumber?"

Kevin pointed. "Over there."

They walked to the pile of lumber. Blake looked at it.

"I don't see any nails." He removed his hardhat again and scratched his forehead. "I reckon it's okay with me if you take it. What do you need it for?"

"We built a fort in the woods and wanted to use it to make a floor," Kevin explained.

"Does your father know about this fort?" Blake asked Ben.

Ben nodded and said, "He helped us a little, but we've done most of the work ourselves. It's not fancy, but it's a place to hangout and the roof doesn't leak."

"Maybe I'll stop by and check it out. I might be able to give you some pointers."

"Thanks, Mr. Posey!" Ben said.

151

"Could we use our wagon to load up the scraps?" Kevin asked. "It would be easier than carrying it by hand."

"Go ahead, but please be careful."

They returned with Kevin's old wagon, loaded it and hauled their prize to the fort.

"Do you think he will really stop to see our fort?" Kevin asked.

Ben shrugged. "Maybe."

"Blake Posey, I haven't seen you since we sold the company," Tony said over the phone. "How are you?"

"Doing good," Blake answered. He told Tony about the boys and the scraps of lumber.

"Are you sure it's okay?" Tony asked.

"Yeah, it was just bits and pieces. I told them I would check out their fort. Do you have time to show me the location?"

"Sure. How soon?"

"I'm finished at the site for the day. I could pick you up."

"Sounds good. I'll text Emmy and let her know we're coming. She might wonder why there's a strange truck in their driveway."

Blake picked up Tony and drove to Kenny's house.

"Nice place," Blake said as he parked the truck.

Emmy walked out of the garage and waved. "Blake, I haven't seen you in ages. How are your parents?"

"Enjoying their retirement. Dad keeps busy working on different projects around the house, and Mom runs the local senior citizen clubhouse. She still loves being in charge."

Tony chuckled and said, "She was the person who really ran Bertucci & Keasling. Uncle Daniel always referred to her as his boss."

"Their retirement package was more than generous," Blake said.

"They deserved it," Tony said patting Blake on the back. They headed toward the woods.

"Can I go with you guys to check out the fort?" Emmy asked.

Tony stopped, looked at her and said, "It's a boys only fort. Girls aren't allowed."

"I'm not a girl," she responded with hands on hips. "I'm his mother."

Tony shrugged and said, "Okay, but don't blame me if they start shooting at you."

"Do they have guns?" Blake asked.

"The latest in nerf guns," Emmy explained. She grinned and added, "And they can knock the wings off a mosquito at a hundred feet."

Blake laughed and said, "Good thing I have my hardhat."

"It should be over this hill," Tony said. "I'm sure we're close."

"Are we lost?" Emmy asked. "I hope we don't get stranded out here for days."

"How many acres do you own?" Blake asked.

Emmy looked around and replied, "Twenty. Maybe twenty-five." She shrugged and said, "Kenny might know, but all I know is most of it's woods. We won't ever have to buy firewood."

"Wait!" Tony said. "Stop."

They froze.

"What is it? Did you see a snake?" Blake asked.

"I thought I heard someone hammering or something," Tony said.

They listened.

"I hear it, too. It sounds like it's coming from that direction," Emmy said as she pointed back toward the house. "We went past the fort somehow."

They backtracked and found the fort.

"We were on the other side of that hill," Tony said. "It's easier to get lost back here than I thought. Your woods are thicker than mine."

The boys saw them approaching and ran to meet them.

"Mom! What are you doing here?" Kevin asked.

"I realize this is a private refuge for young men, but won't you make an exception for your mother?"

Kevin looked at Ben.

153

"It's okay with me, Kevin," Ben said. He looked at Emmy and said, "As long as you promise never to reveal this location to another mom or girl."

Emmy giggled, held up a hand and said, "I promise. But you have to promise not to bring girls back here when you get older, okay?"

"Mom!" Kevin said rolling his eyes. "We didn't build it for that."

Tony and Blake inspected the fort.

"Pretty solid," Blake said. "It should last ten years or so, but it might be hard to heat."

"We could always buy a kerosene heater if we want to camp out in the winter," Kevin said.

"Maybe a propane heater," Tony suggested. "They make them for camping. I had a portable one in the fifth wheel."

The boys showed the men, and Emmy, how they planned to use the scrap lumber.

"What do you think, Mr. Posey?"

"It should work, and it will keep out some of the varmints that roam this wilderness."

"Yeah, we want to keep out the snakes and stuff," Ben said. "Spiders are okay, but I hate snakes."

"He got caught doing what?" Heather asked later that day.

"Not so loud," Kevin said. "Do you want Mom or Dad to hear?"

Heather closed her bedroom door and pulled Kevin to her bed. "When did this happen? How did you find out?"

"A few days ago, and Jamiel Ramel told me. You know him, right?"

"I know him by sight, but not as a friend."

"Did you know he was doing this?" Kevin asked.

"No way! I haven't even talked to him in close to a year," Heather said.

Isabella walked in and asked, "What are you guys talking about? I could hear you, but not understand."

Kevin told her everything he knew.

"He should know better, and he doesn't need the money. His parents are rich," she said.

"Maybe he doesn't get an allowance," Heather said.

"I'm sure he does. We get one. Not a lot, but enough to get by," Kevin said.

They jumped when they heard a knock on the door.

"Come in," Kevin said.

Emmy opened the door, and did a double take when she saw all three kids sitting together on the bed and looking guilty.

"What's up, Mom?" Kevin asked and was rewarded with an elbow to the ribs from Heather.

"I got a text from Mrs. Ramel. Dr. Ramel. You know who I mean," she said with a wave. "Ian Plant was caught selling drugs to one of the neighbors. Do you know anything about this?"

"I heard about it earlier," Kevin admitted.

Emmy looked at Heather. "Did you know?"

Heather shook her head. "Like I was telling Kevin, I haven't talked to Ian in almost a year. We don't text or anything."

"So you had no idea he was doing this, right?"

They nodded.

Emmy sighed and said, "I'm glad. I don't understand why he would do such a thing. His parents make tons of money..."

"Mom! Money doesn't solve problems," Heather said. "Well, it solves some like paying the bills and stuff, but just because a person has money doesn't mean they don't do stupid things."

"It was pretty stupid, right?" Emmy said. "I hope he learns a lesson."

"Yeah, he will probably learn how not to get caught," Heather said.

"Why are we having a family meeting?" Kevin asked after dinner Tuesday night. "Am I in trouble? I swear I didn't do anything."

Kenny paced in front of them in the family room. "You aren't in trouble. I called this meeting..."

Emmy and the girls rolled their eyes.

155

"... to discuss the possibility of buying a puppy." He held up a finger and added, "And the responsibilities you will be tasked with if we indeed proceed with this... whatever."

"Are we seriously getting a puppy?" Isabella asked. "I want a girl puppy, so we can have more puppies later."

"I thought it was going to be my puppy," Kevin said. "You never wanted a pet before."

"If we find a puppy, it will belong to all of us," Kenny said. "That means we will all share the duties involved in bringing up a puppy." He stopped in front of the fireplace, rubbed his jaw and said, "We should buy a book about puppies because I don't have any idea what they require."

"You raised us, Daddy, and we survived," Heather said with a grin.

"A puppy is different. You wore diapers. We can't put a diaper on a puppy," he said then looked at Emmy. "Can we?"

"I saw a movie about a chimpanzee, and it wore a diaper," Kevin said.

Emmy glared at him. "No diapers. Someone either took Scout out for a walk or let her run through the woods. She was trained to stay pretty close to home. She didn't cross the road to come over here unless someone was with her."

"Sometimes she came over here," Kevin said. "I think she was looking for Ben and Taylor, though."

The family meeting lasted close to an hour.

"So, we are all agreed and committed to do our best to make this puppy experience as pleasant and painless as possible, right?" Kenny asked.

"Yes, do we have to join hands and do a cheer like basketball teams?" Emmy asked.

"No, but this is a new member of the family we might be bringing into the house," Kenny said.

Heather raised a hand. "Did we have a choice about bringing him into the family?" she asked then pointed at her brother.

"Hey! I'm not a family pet," he replied.

"Kevin, are you ready to pick up the puppy?" Kenny asked the next morning.

"Can I skip school?"

"Yes, this will be like a field trip," Kenny said.

"Where do we have to go?"

"The same place Tony and Sloane found Scout," Kenny answered.

"I thought we were looking for a labradoodle. Scout was a black lab."

"The people raise several different breeds," Kenny said.

The trip to the Mills' farm outside of Fort Orville took close to an hour because Kenny got lost. They finally arrived and jumped out of the Jeep.

Mrs. Mills saw them from her spot on a swing on the front porch.

"Are you Mr. Colwell?" she asked. "I'm Terri Mills."

"I'm Kenny and this is Kevin. We live across the road from the Bertuccis. They bought a black lab from you many years ago."

"I remember. He played football."

"Scout just died," Kevin said. "She was sick and they had to put her to sleep."

"I'm sorry to hear that. I remember when they came to buy a puppy. I believe the puppy chose them, if memory serves," Mrs. Mills said.

She talked to Kenny while Kevin waited shifting his weight back and forth.

"Where are the puppies?" Kevin asked after the adults finished talking.

"Follow me, and I'll show you." Mrs. Mills waved and led the way.

They talked while walking to a building behind the house.

Once around the side Kevin saw three puppies in a large enclosure.

"Which one is the girl? I can't tell," Kevin said.

Mrs. Mills opened the gate and brought out the female and set her down. She immediately ran to Kevin and began to wag her tail and jump on him.

"I think she likes you, Kevin." Kenny stood next to Mrs. Mills as they watched Kevin and the puppy.

Kevin sat on the ground and let the puppy lick his face. "The feeling is mutual. I like her, too."

"Mom! We're home!" Kevin hollered. "We have the puppy. She's in the back of the Jeep in her cage. Come and see her. Where are you, Mom?"

"I'm coming," Emmy said.

The girls raced past her and sprinted for the Jeep.

"Oh, she's so cute," Isabella said.

Heather looked at her and said, "She's so little. I thought she would be bigger."

Emmy watched as Kenny opened the gate.

"She's on a leash so she won't run away," Kevin explained. "We need to train her not to run into the road."

"What are you going to name her?" Emmy asked.

The kids all shouted, "Lassie!"

Emmy looked at Kenny.

He shrugged and said, "What can I say? We watched that old Elizabeth Taylor movie last week."

"We are going to have so much fun, Lassie girl," Kevin said. "Do you want to hold her, Mom?"

Emmy shook her head. "You can hold her for now."

"Mom, why does Lassie like you more than me?" Kevin asked Friday afternoon. "She follows you all over the house, and ignores me. I thought she was supposed to be my puppy. She's sleeping next to you now."

"She likes you, too, but she belongs to all of us, Kevin."

"Okay, but I'm kinda jealous because you get to hold her more than me."

"We probably hold her too much. She's going to be more spoiled than you kids." Emmy smiled as Lassie wagged her tail and licked Emmy's face. "Yes, you are going to be so spoiled, aren't you?"

Chapter Twenty-Two

"Did you know Tommy was getting married?" Emmy asked Kenny as they drove to the reception at the Joseph's house.

"P.J. told us a week ago," Kenny answered. "And before you ask, she is not pregnant. Tommy told both sets of parents that was not the reason they decided to get married at the courthouse."

"Why didn't they get married at the church then?" Isabella asked. "It seems kinda peculiar to get married at the courthouse."

Heather said, "Pastor Tyler didn't know it, but Erin Kendle was expecting when she and Nathan Doss finally got married. They went through the counseling and everything. Then she got pregnant like a week before the wedding."

"How could you tell? How did she even know?" Kevin asked. "She wasn't big and fat like Aunt Sloane when she had Coby."

"Kevin Michael! Sloane was not big and fat, and don't you ever say that again," Emmy warned.

"I didn't mean fat like Mrs. Abraham. Just big because she was pregnant."

"How old is Sabrina?" Heather asked.

Emmy looked at Kenny. "Do you know?"

"She's a little younger than Tommy, and he's twenty-two now. I think."

"Should we stop calling him Tommy?" Emmy asked. "If he's old enough to get married, he's old enough to be called Tom or Thomas."

"Actually, Em, his real name is Tommy. Not Thomas."

"Why would they do that?" Kevin asked. "How will he feel when he's ninety years old and people call him Tommy?"

Emmy grinned and said, "By then he won't care."

"Is Sabrina going to be wearing a wedding dress?" Isabella asked then giggled.

"Not a typical wedding dress," Emmy answered. "She will probably wear a dress today, and it might even be the one she wore to get married."

"Did they take pictures at least?" Heather asked.

"Teresa said she took some and so did Sabrina's grandparents," Kenny said.

"Weren't her parents there?" Kevin asked.

Kenny shook his head. "No they were both killed in a car crash several years ago. Sabrina and her younger brother were raised by her maternal grandparents."

"I didn't know that," Emmy said. "But then why would I? I didn't know her before she started dating Tommy."

"Does he have a real job, or does he just play his guitar?" Isabella asked.

"He works for the SoHam street department, I think," Kenny answered. "He makes decent money, and it's pretty secure."

"I'm going to get on his case for not playing his guitar at church anymore," Emmy said.

"Mom!" Isabella said.

"What?"

"How can you get after him when you aren't singing with the worship team?"

Kenny chuckled. "She's got you there, Em."

She made a face at Kenny. "Hush. I plan to return one day."

Tommy and Sabrina were greeting the guests in the living room when Kenny and his family arrived.

Kenny shook his hand and said, "Congratulations. I hope you have a lifetime of happiness."

After Emmy talked to them, she whispered to Kenny, "That was dorky."

"I couldn't think of anything to say. They're just kids."

They waited across the room as the girls and Kevin talked to the newlyweds. Isabella nudged Heather and said, "We need to move on so other people can talk to them.

The twins rejoined their parents. Kevin saw Sebastian Rawlings, waved and followed him outside.

"I was only twenty-two when we got married, and I wanted to marry you several years earlier," Emmy said with a smile.

"Mom, that's just because you wanted to sleep with Daddy," Heather whispered.

160

"Partly, but I did love him before… never mind." Emmy turned away and waved to Teresa Joseph.

"Dad, are you blushing?" Isabella asked with a grin.

"I will never get used to the idea you know about sex."

"There's a difference between knowing about it and having it," Heather said knowing it would embarrass her father.

"You better remember that, young lady," he said then walked away.

"Heather, why did you say that?" Isabella asked. "You made Daddy mad."

"I thought he would be embarrassed."

After eating a slice of wedding cake, Emmy bumped into Tommy as she had her head turned while walking around a corner.

"Sorry, Emmy. I didn't see you," Tommy said with a grin.

"You're silly. I wasn't watching where I was going." She pushed him in the chest then pointed at him and said, "Why aren't you playing your guitar?"

"In church?"

"There, but I heard you aren't playing at all. Why? Don't you realize you have a God-given talent? You need to use it."

"Even if I play in a rock band?"

"Any kind of band," she said, grinned and added, "Not a polka band."

"Aw, that was my dream. I've always wanted to play polkas for old people."

"After you and Sabrina get settled, you should pick up your guitar. You need to practice even if you aren't in a band."

"I'll try to make it a priority, Emmy."

"Good. By the way, I really like Sabrina. She reminds me of myself a little."

"How's that? You don't look like each other at all."

"She loves you. I can see it in her eyes, and I bet she will love… never mind."

Tommy grinned and whispered, "I think I know what you mean, and you're right. Our wedding night was fantastic."

161

Kenny walked into the kitchen Friday evening, saw Emmy and pumped his fist.

"Does this mean the guys are finished recording?" she asked as she pulled the lasagna out of the oven. "Lassie, this is people food. It's not for you. Your food is in your dish."

"Yes! They're satisfied. It shouldn't take too long to get it mixed, mastered and released."

"Are you still happy it's being released on Bristol Woods Records?" Emmy carried Lassie to the mudroom and set her down in front of her food tray. "This is your food, Lassie."

"It might have meant more a few years ago," Kenny said. He watched as the puppy ate.

"Aren't you going to press it on vinyl?" Emmy asked sticking a fork into the lasagna. "This is done. I need to make a salad and we can eat."

"Did you make garlic bread?" Kenny asked.

"I will."

"The guys want to release it on vinyl, but it will take a while. It has to be remixed and mastered because the CD mix won't sound the same on vinyl."

"I'll buy one. I won't play it, but I might hang it on the wall as a piece of artwork."

"You're funny," Kenny said as he sniffed the lasagna.

"You should take her for a walk before dinner."

"Shouldn't one of the kids do that?" he asked.

"You are right. I'm going to print out a schedule of who has to take her for walks. They need to share the responsibility, but for now, please take her outside and make sure she does her business."

"Yes, Em. Come here, Lassie. It's time to go outside."

"I get first dibs on the leftover pizza!" Kevin hollered as he raced into the kitchen. He came to a sudden stop and pointed. "Lassie, how did you escape?" He looked past the island and saw a surprise. "Ooops! You aren't supposed to do that. Bad puppy."

Kenny and Emmy entered and saw Kevin pointing at something on the floor.

"What happened?" Kenny asked.

162

"Lassie escaped and left a... surprise."

Emmy walked past Kenny and sighed. "At least it's only poop."

Heather and Isabella were in conversation as they emerged from the mudroom. They stopped and froze.

"What is that smell?" Heather asked pinching her nose.

"Lassie escaped from her cage and made a mess," Kevin said.

Emmy asked, "Who was responsible for taking her outside this morning?"

"I took her around six," Isabella said.

Kevin picked Lassie up and said, "I took her out before we left for church. I put her back in her cage, but maybe I didn't secure it right."

"Ya think!" Heather said.

"Evidently, you either didn't secure it, or she's smart enough to open it herself," Emmy said. She looked at Kenny. "I won't let a puppy ruin the hardwood floor."

"Kevin, please clean up the mess," Kenny said.

"I didn't make it!"

Emmy rolled her eyes. "No kidding, but you were supposed to put her in her cage."

"I can't clean it up. It's poop," Kevin said.

Isabella grabbed some paper towels. "I'll clean it up. It's no worse than changing a diaper."

"Thank you, Isa," Kenny said.

"She didn't ruin the floor, Mom," Kevin said. "Look! You can't even tell where she pooped."

Emmy scowled at him.

"Kevin, you are grounded for a week," Kenny said. "No electronics except for school."

"Why? What did I do?"

"It's what you didn't do. You should have made sure the cage was secure," Emmy said. She looked at the kids. "Accidents will happen, but we all need to help take care of the baby. We need to share the responsibilities."

Chapter Twenty-Three

"Where's Lassie?" Kevin asked.

"She was sleeping by Mom earlier," Isabella said.

Kevin hustled downstairs and into the family room. He saw his mother sitting on the couch watching football. "Where's Lassie? Isa said she was with you."

Emmy groaned as the Steelers turned the ball over again. She patted the spot next to her then looked around. "She was here, but I don't know where she went. Ask Heather."

"Where's Dad?" Kevin asked.

"He's in the basement. The guys are getting ready to do their concert. Don't bother him."

"I won't, but I need to check if Lassie is down there," he hollered over his shoulder as he clomped down the stairs to the basement.

"Come on, you guys! You can play better defense than that," Emmy hollered at the TV. "Why do I even watch football anymore? I just get frustrated."

Kevin looked around the open area of the basement, but didn't see Lassie.

"Lassie girl, are you down here?" He heard a bark and Lassie bounded toward him. He dropped to his knees and let her lick his face. "There you are. I thought you got lost. It's a big house, and you know where to hide."

Lassie licked him and then raced up the stairs with Kevin chasing.

"Mom, is the game almost over?" Heather asked after checking the time. "Dad's concert is supposed to start at three thirty."

"There's only a few seconds left. The Steelers are winning, but only by six points. We'll watch the show as soon as the game ends." Emmy turned her attention back to the TV in time to see the Steelers put the game away with a long field goal. "Okay, we can turn on Facebook now."

"Are you ready to rock?" Kenny asked. "Thank you for joining us. It's been a while since we did a virtual show. Today we are going to play our new CD *When Light Flashes* and hopefully have time for a few extra songs. Please, leave a comment and let us know how you are doing."

Dave counted off and the show began.

"This is the title song," Kenny said. "It's called 'When Light Flashes' and it goes like this."

Forty-five minutes later the band played the last chorus of the final track.

"We have time for three or four songs," Kenny said. He looked at the guys and asked, "Do we still want to end the show with cover songs?"

"Yeah! Let's do it," Jeff shouted.

P.J. played the intro to 'Smoke on the Water' and the guys mashed four covers together to end the show.

"Thanks for tuning in. We will see you soon," Kenny said.

The guys waved to the cameras and the show was over.

"I liked the songs at the end, but I don't think I've heard them before," Isabella said.

Emmy explained, "They were songs from the seventies. They came out before I was born and maybe before your father, too."

"They sounded good, but I'm not sure about the new songs," Heather said. "They sound old-fashioned in a way."

"I'm going to take Lassie for a walk," Kevin said as he stood up. "Lassie, come on. Let's go for a walk." He looked at the couch across the family room where Lassie had been sleeping during the virtual concert. "Where did you go, girl?"

"The new songs are good, but since you've never heard them as much, they're less familiar," Emmy said.

"I know that, Mom," Heather said. "I'll go with you, Kevin. I haven't taken Lassie for a walk all week."

"We have to find her first," Kevin said.

"She might be downstairs," Isabella said. "The basement door is open."

Kevin and Heather searched for Lassie in the basement to no avail.

"Where could she be?" Kevin asked.

Heather shrugged.

They walked into the family room outside of the studio and Heather pointed. "Someone left the door into the garage open.

"She's probably in there."

They dashed up the stairs into the garage.

"Oh, crap! The service door's open," Kevin hollered. "She might have escaped!"

"I'll tell everyone. Try to find her," Heather said.

She sprinted up the stairs, ran through the mudroom and into the house while Kevin went outside and called for Lassie.

"Mom! Isabella! Daddy! Lassie's escaped. She got out through the garage. We need to find her."

Everyone jumped up and followed Heather outside. They searched for ten minutes without seeing or hearing Lassie.

"I'll call Tony. She might have gone over there." Emmy pulled her phone from her back pocket and let Tony know what had happened.

"The kids and I and will look on this side of the road."

"Thanks, Tony."

"I hope we don't find her splattered on the road," Taylor said.

"Don't be gross," Noemi scolded smacking his arm.

An hour passed without any luck.

"Have you heard her barking or anything?" Emmy asked when she and Tony met at the entrance gate to her house.

"Ben thought he heard a dog barking, but couldn't see anything. I've walked all the way to the corner. She's not... around."

"You were thinking she might have been hit by a car, huh?"

"It happens, Em."

"At least this isn't a heavily traveled road."

"Hold it! Did you hear that?" Tony asked.

He and Emmy stood still.

"I can hear something in the brush," Emmy said.

They walked slowly from the entrance gate and followed the fence line north. It wasn't easy because of all the undergrowth.

"Stop!" Tony said grabbing her arm. "I heard a bark then a growl."

"I did, too."

Tony lifted the lowest branch of a spruce tree. "There you are, Lassie. Have you been hunting?" He grabbed Lassie with one hand and picked her up.

"You bad, bad little girl," Emmy said when Tony handed Lassie over. "You scared us so much. We were afraid you would run away and..."

"She's safe now," Tony said.

Within a few minutes the searchers were gathered on the back deck and Lassie was safely leashed to the deck railing.

"Kenny, we have to build a fence," Emmy said.

"I guess we should," he replied.

Tony pointed to the north side of the deck. "You could extend a fence from the northeast corner of the house. Run it along the yard around the north side until it was west of the pool. You could go south until you could connect it to the corner of the house by the breakfast nook."

"That would give her a large area to roam," Kevin said. "And do her business."

"What about the driveway?" Kenny asked.

Emmy pointed and said, "Put the fence along the edge of it."

"What if we want to build a road or another guesthouse on that side of the property?" Kenny asked.

"You could put a large gate in the fence," Tony suggested.

"Would she learn to dig under the fence?" Ben asked.

"Derby never tried digging her way out," Emmy said.

"Their backyard was a lot smaller," Kenny said. "We would have a lot more fence to patrol."

Kevin grinned and said, "It will be like out West. Ben and me could be cowboys and ride the fence line on our mountain bikes to check for broken areas and cattle rustlers. We could build campfires and eat beans and biscuits."

167

"It will cost a fortune to build that much fence," Kenny said.

Emmy let Lassie jump onto her lap and said, "Isn't our little girl worth it?"

Kenny called the company that built the perimeter fence, and a representative came to the house that afternoon. Kenny showed him where he thought the fence should go.

"I have a better idea." The representative showed Kenny a line where the fence wouldn't have to follow the contours of the hilly land as much.

"That would make it easier," Kenny said. "It would extend into the trees in places, too. She will love exploring the woods."

"We could use an invisible fence if you'd rather."

"Is it possible to do both?" Kenny asked.

The sales rep smiled. "Yes, but that would increase the cost quite a bit."

Kenny waved a hand. "It doesn't matter. My wife loves our puppy, and I will do anything to protect her."

"The puppy or your wife?" he asked with a grin."

"Both," Kenny said.

By Friday afternoon the new fences were completely installed. Lassie was getting accustomed to her new collar.

"We should take her for a walk along the fence," Kenny said. "She needs to get used to it."

"Does the collar hurt her if she crosses the invisible fence," Isabella asked.

"It sends a mild charge to her collar. It's more like a tingle, I think," Emmy said.

"There are flags along the fence she can see," Kenny said. "And the invisible fence is about a foot inside the wooden fence. She will learn not to get any closer to the fence than that."

"She won't get close enough to the fence to dig under it," Kevin said. "But I still think me and Ben should inspect it on our bikes."

Within a few days Lassie became acclimated to the fence and allowed to roam free.

"Now she can poop and pee in the woods, and we don't have to clean up her messes," Kevin said.

Heather rolled her eyes. "I'm never going for a walk in the woods again."

"We have to let her out the French doors onto the deck, but she will learn not to run out through the mudroom pretty fast," Isabella said.

"If it works out, we could extend the invisible fence along the driveway and that part of the property," Kenny said. "She could have an even larger area to explore."

Emmy looked at the invoice and shook her head. "Let's not get carried away. This project has already cost more than we planned. Kids, your father might need to find a real job to pay for more fencing."

Chapter Twenty-Four

"Happy birthday, Brady," Diane said as he turned over in bed to face her.

"That's right! It is my birthday. Did you plan a surprise party for me?" He used his elbow for support and raised up. "It's a special birthday."

"Why?" Diane asked.

"I'm fifty-five. Isn't that special?"

"You're special all right, and no, you don't deserve a surprise party. I heard you talking to Bennett about starting a consulting firm. You promised no more companies," Diane said as she turned away from Brady.

He put a hand on her shoulder and said, "Okay, I thought about it for a few days, but I decided it would not be worth the time away from my lovely wife and precious children."

She turned onto her back, looked into his eyes and asked, "Are you sure?"

"Yes. I want to enjoy retirement for a few years."

"So, when you're seventy you want to go back to work, huh?"

He chuckled and replied, "By then the kids will be grown and won't need me as much."

"You will have grandchildren to spoil."

"You hope," he said then kissed her.

"Caden! I don't know the answer," Diane yelled. She put a hand to her forehead and swore under her breath. "I never signed up to be a teacher. I wish this stupid pandemic would go away."

"I didn't cause it," he replied.

"Teachers go to school and learn how to teach. I barely made it through high school. I have no clue what the diameter of a circle has to do with the radius or whatever you said of a square. Leave me alone. Ask your father to help you." Diane waved her hands and marched away. "I am finished."

Brady heard the commotion and walked into the family room. "What's going on?"

"Mom blew a gasket because I asked for help with my math. Can you help me?"

"Let me take a look. I know a little bit."

"Daddy! Mom said you have a doctor degree," Lily said. "That means you are smart."

"I have a PHD, but I'm not a medical doctor," Brady said.

After lunch Brady approached his wife, who was in her recliner in Brady's study with a wet cloth covering her eyes.

"Is it safe to talk to you?"

Diane sat up and removed the cloth. "I'm not mad at you. I got upset because of the school being closed. How are parents who have to work coping with this? What do they do if they can't work from home? Childcare costs a fortune if you can even find it. Are teachers still getting paid even if they teach from home?"

"I don't know the answers, but I will help the kids with school. I may have to take a refresher course on spelling and story time, but I will manage somehow."

Diane grinned and said, "I can handle first and second grade, but Caden is in high school." She waved a hand. "Thankfully, Carson is smarter than me. He is breezing through his college classes."

"We can work together. I'll help Caden, and you can work with Lily and Conor. Sound like a plan?"

"Yes, but I can't wait for the schools to open. I'm a mom, not a teacher."

Brady walked to the bar and checked his bottle of Glenlivet 15. "Have you been sipping this?"

"Not really. I've been drinking it. There's a difference."

"I opened this two weeks ago, and it's two-thirds gone. I only had a few..."

"I said I've been drinking it. Sorry. I'll buy you another bottle."

"You don't need to. I thought you liked wine better," he said sitting in his recliner. He looked at the fireplace and asked, "I found a bottle of pills in the medicine cabinet. There was no label on it. Is it yours?"

"It's just Xanax."

"Why isn't it labeled?"

Diane sighed and said, "Because my stupid doctor won't renew my prescription."

"Then where did you get it?"

"If you must know, I got it from Ian Plant. Happy? I bought it illegally because I need it for anxiety."

"Why are you anxious?"

"I just am, okay?"

"Are you taking it because it gets you high?" he asked with a shrug.

"No! If I wanted to get high, I would buy pot."

"Does this kid sell pot, too?"

Diane scowled. "Why? Do you want some?"

"No, but I did use it in college..."

"I bet you didn't inhale," Diane interrupted then laughed.

"This is not something to joke about, Diane. If you suffer from anxiety, you should see your doctor."

"I have."

"I meant a different one."

"You think I need to see a shrink, huh?"

She stood up and walked out of the room. Brady followed.

"Lots of people seek therapy. It doesn't have a stigma attached..."

"Maybe not to you, but it does to me. I don't want Emmy to know I need a shrink." She entered the kitchen and filled a glass with ice water from the fridge.

Brady waited until she set the glass down and said, "How would she know? Why does it matter?"

"She would find out somehow. One of the kids might tell her without realizing it was private information."

"If you think your sister would gossip to her friends about you seeking help, then you are nuts." He realized what he said and grinned. "I didn't mean it like that."

"I know she wouldn't. I guess the real reason I don't want her to know is because her life is so perfect and I am a total mess."

"Thanks a lot."

172

She pointed at Brady and added, "Don't you dare tell me it's because she goes to church."

"I have never been a particularly religious person, but even I can tell Emmy's faith makes a difference."

"So it works for her. Doesn't mean it will work for me." Diane turned her back to Brady.

He moved right behind her, put his hands on her shoulders and whispered, "I have heard her say on multiple occasions that being a Christian doesn't mean your life will be all honey and roses. She has faced crisis in her life. Do you remember her accident?"

"Of course."

"She gives God the credit for her recovery."

"There is a basic difference in our personalities, Emmy is all happy and bubbly," Diane said as she waved her hands and did a little dance. "I'm gloomy and dark and pessimistic. That's not going to change because of religion."

"Who knows? It might," Brady said as he held her in his arms. "I love you no matter what."

"Hi, Diane, I wanted to wish Brady a happy birthday," Emmy said. "How old is he?"

"You know he's fifty-five."

Emmy giggled and asked, "Is he sad because he's so old?"

"Why don't you ask him and let him tell you?"

"I'm kidding. He looks pretty good for a man his age."

"Are you ever going to grow up?" Diane asked shaking her head.

"I don't plan on it. Hey! Did you see the English assignment the kids have?"

"Yes, and I want to strangle that teacher. How are freshmen suppose to do it. I tried to help Caden, and I got frustrated which made him frustrated. I had to ask Carson to help him."

"I was able to help the girls, but I'm lost in math. Kenny will have to help them with it."

"Brady is almost a math genius. He should teach all the kids."

Emmy grinned and said, "Maybe he should start his own school to compete with Bennett."

After more talk about school, Diane said, "I need a favor, but I'm not sure you can help."

"What's up?"

"Does your church pray for people who don't go there regularly?"

"Are you serious?" Emmy asked raising her voice to a higher pitch than normal.

"Well, yeah, kinda."

"We do that all the time. Don't you know anything?"

"Don't start on me."

"Sorry. Do you want me to add your name to the church's prayer list? I can do that."

"Could you kinda do it anonymously, so no one knows it's me?"

"Yeah. Some people do that." Emmy paused then asked, "Is there something I can pray about? Something specific? You don't have to tell me what, but God knows. I will just kinda remind him."

"Or her," Diane said.

"Whatever."

"If I tell you, will you promise not to get on my case about it?"

"You didn't murder Brady or one of the kids or rob a bank or..."

"Of course not, you goof."

"Good."

"I have a problem with anxiety."

"Yes, I knew that," Emmy said.

Diane took a deep breath and blurted out, "I bought some pills from a kid in the neighborhood."

"Ian Plant?"

Diane stared at the phone for a second. "Yes. How did you know?"

"God told me," she answered.

"Be serious."

174

"He got caught by his father. I guess the whole development knows by now. What did you buy? Why did you buy it from him?"

"My doctor wouldn't give me more Xanax. I need it, so I bought some from that kid. I'm not a drug addict. I need something to take the edge off."

"Sounds like a junky to me," Emmy said.

"How would you know? You've never taken an aspirin unless your doctor made you."

"I take medicine," Emmy said softly.

"What?"

"Vitamins."

Diane laughed. "You are such a baby, and I love you for it."

"I love you, too. I won't tell anyone about the pills, and I will email Kate Cordell. She coordinates the prayer list. I will tell her I have an unspoken request."

"What the hell is that?" Diane asked.

Emmy explained, "Some people are more private than others. Other people don't care who knows what ails them, or what addictions they have. If I have a special request, I don't always give specifics. God knows. That's the important thing."

"Em," Diane whispered.

"Yeah?"

"Will you pray for me, too?"

Emmy choked back the tears and nodded.

"Thanks. I know you're crying. Sorry."

Chapter Twenty-Five

"I don't imagine anyone else will be coming," Richard Cornejo said as he looked at the five other men and two ladies gathered in the small room now used as a prayer chapel in the old sanctuary. He yawned and said, "I have to admit, it was not easy to get out of bed this morning."

"Six o'clock is early for most people, but I was raised on a farm and we got up before the chickens," Jim Rosek said then chuckled.

"In the Philippines where I grew up, we didn't sleep late either," Genna Ademilola replied.

Pastor Tyler looked at the rest of the people.

Tony Bertucci stretched his shoulders and said, "If I don't get up before the kids, I never get anything done. I can't wait until schools reopen."

"Same with me," Tanya Paduchik said.

Jess and Joe Zawaski nodded.

The twin brothers, now in their early sixties, had recently returned to SoHam after spending two years working with missionaries in Eastern Europe.

Tyler Hammond took a deep breath and said, "Before we get started, I have something to tell you."

"Yes," Jim Rosek said slowly.

"This isn't easy to say, but I will be resigning as senior pastor."

Everyone froze and stared at Tyler.

"Several people in the church know I have been approached with offers from other churches over the years. Until now none of them have felt right. I have never felt the Holy Spirit telling me to move on. To really consider the offers."

"I take it this has changed," Richard said.

"If you allow, I will share the details."

Everyone agreed.

"Before the pandemic hit, I was approached by one of the more senior board members of a large church in Michigan. Their pastor was resigning, and they were in the process of finding his replacement. This offer was different from all the others. I could feel something in my soul telling me to listen. Then the virus thing happened and the world changed."

"Are you saying had the pandemic not occurred when it did, you would have accepted the offer and already be gone?" Richard asked.

Tyler chuckled and said, "Most likely. But once everything changed because of the virus, I decided I could not leave the church in the midst of..." He shrugged and said, "Chaos really. Churches were closed and... Well, I could not leave under those circumstances."

"Where is this church?" Tony asked.

"Alexandria Rapids, Michigan. It's about halfway between Grand Falls and New Preston. Forty miles west of Bartonsville."

"How large is the church?" Genna asked. "How big is the town?"

"The church building is comparable to here, but the town itself is less than half the size. The church draws from all the surrounding towns and cities."

"Is this a done deal?" Jim asked. "Could we persuade you to stay?"

Tyler shook his head. "I'm afraid the Holy Spirit overrules you, Jim."

"It would be closer to family," Tony said. "That's a benefit, I suppose."

"Yes, but we've had other offers close to home and not even considered them." Tyler looked at Jess and Joe. "You are always quiet, but what are your thoughts?"

Jess looked at Joe for a moment. Then at everyone else. "I do not have opinions until the Holy Spirit gives me one," he said slowly.

Joe nodded.

The next hour was spent praying not only for Tyler, but for the church also.

"We are visiting our families this week. In fact, we are leaving after church tonight."

"Not for good, I hope," Jim said.

177

"No. We will spend Thanksgiving with family, but I will be preaching in Alexandria Rapids this Sunday. The church board has unanimously voted to offer the position to me. The congregation is voting after the services, and we will give them our answer as soon as it becomes clear to us."

"How many people know about this?" Tony asked. "I'm guessing not many."

"Dr. Schofield knows, and of course Liz, and the new church knows." He thought for a moment. "I would ask you not to mention this to anyone until I have talked to the board. We are meeting Monday, but they do not know about the offer."

"No one?" Jim asked.

"I did tell Wyatt and Kristen because I sought his advice. The staff will need to resign because the manual requires it."

"Are you planning to take anyone from the staff with you?" Richard asked.

"I haven't decided. Until the new church actually votes on me, I didn't want to think about it."

"You and Wyatt are close friends," Tony said. "I can understand you might want him to go with you, but Kristen has strong ties to SoHam. I can't see her moving."

"It's too early to think about anything like that. If the church votes to accept me, I will give the board my resignation Monday night."

"It sounds like you've already decided to accept the position." Jim chuckled and added, "No sane church is going to go against a unanimous vote of their church board."

"It has happened, but I feel the Holy Spirit has already chosen me." Tyler gestured and added, "That sounds egotistical, and I didn't mean it to come across in that way."

"We understood what you meant," Richard said. "The Holy Spirit already knows who the next pastor will be here, and the one after that and so on."

"It won't be easy to keep this a secret," Genna said. She sighed and zipped her mouth. "It is zipped closed. I will say nothing."

"Have you told the kids?" Tony asked.

178

Tyler shook his head. "I hate not telling them or anyone in the church, but Dr. Schofield and Dr. Behren suggested I not reveal anything yet."

"I don't understand it, but I will respect your wishes."

Tyler looked at Tony for a moment then whispered, "You should tell Emmy."

"How much longer before we eat?" Kevin asked. "It's almost two, and I haven't had anything to eat since breakfast."

Emmy wiped her forehead with her hand, checked the time and looked in the oven. "Thirty minutes is the best I can do."

"Okay, I'll eat a banana or something. When are Grandma and Grandpa supposed to get here?"

"They should be here by now. Tell your father to text them and see where they are. He's in the studio."

Kevin grabbed a banana and headed downstairs.

She heard a knock, turned and saw her brother standing in the mudroom doorway.

"Can I come in?"

"Why are you here?" Emmy asked. "I thought you were helping in the food kitchen today."

"I did, but I was relieved of duty. Will you have enough food for me?" Father James asked as he sat at the island. "All I need is a slice of moldy bread and some unfiltered water."

"We will have plenty because Tony's eating at his house."

"Are you okay? You seem tense. Can I help with something?"

She took a deep breath. "I yelled at Kevin Michael last night because he forgot to let Lassie out, and she had an accident."

"Are you regretting the decision to get a puppy?"

"No, but I get frustrated because the kids have to be told to check the schedule..."

"What schedule?"

She pointed to the fridge. "I made a schedule for taking care of Lassie. She has to be fed and let outside to pee and poop. Cats can use a litter box, but apparently dogs won't."

"Didn't you ever have a pet growing up?"

179

"Not even a goldfish. I wanted one, but Mom refused. Now I can see why. Did you have pets?"

"We always had one or two dogs and assorted cats. Some of them lived outdoors and never came inside. Others would go in and out all the time." He looked around, saw the empty cage and asked, "Where is she now?"

"Kenny took her for a long walk. I want her to sleep while we eat."

Father James laughed and said, "Emmy, you do know Lassie is a dog and not your new baby, right?"

"Hush! I know she's a dog. I haven't tried to nurse her, or make her wear a diaper."

"I bet you let her sleep in your bed."

"Not all night. She sleeps in her cage. She has to be trained to sleep in her house..."

"Her house?"

"The vet said Lassie will think of the cage as her house. So she won't go to the bathroom in it unless we leave her there all day."

"Do you pick up her poop?"

"Yeah. Why wouldn't we?"

"We never did when I was a kid. Dogs made messes outside. It was normal. No one cleaned it up."

"Gross! I wouldn't want the yard to get covered in poop."

"Did Tony or the kids clean up after Scout?"

"No, she learned to do her business in the woods. Kenny hired a company to put up a fence around the north and west sides of the yard. Lassie can run around without being chained up or on a leash."

"I hate seeing a dog chained up. They should be allowed to run free. Have you ever thought of extending your fence all the way around the property?"

"Yes and no."

"Are you a politician now?"

"We have the fence along the road, and there is that noise fence, or whatever it's called that runs along Hough St. That's not ours, but our property ends pretty close to it."

"The city or county probably has a right-of-way on the back side of the fence."

"Whatever." She shrugged then said, "It would cost too much to totally fence in everything. It's not worth it. The kids like to play in the woods."

He looked out the window and asked, "How many acres are actually yard? I know most of your property is woods. You don't have a pond or a river, do you?"

"Not us. Tony and Kristen have a creek that runs through their land. Kenny said the yard is maybe three acres. Maybe two. I don't know. I'm glad we have guys to mow it."

"If I owned this much land, I would want a lake for fishing."

"There are three retention ponds in the neighborhood. Three or is it four? Whatever. There's one at the back of Andy's property. Another one on the corner by Bristol Parkway, and the other two are somewhere on the west end. You can't see them from the road."

"Thanks for the geography lesson," he said with a grin.

"Oh, hush. If you want to help, you could check the potatoes. They're in the oven."

"Which one?" he asked getting up.

"The one on the left. The turkey's in the other one."

"Don't you usually make a ham, too?"

"It's in with the potatoes. It's one of those fully cooked ones. I only need to heat it up."

"Mom! How much longer?" Kevin asked as he rubbed his belly.

Emmy looked at James.

He nodded and put an arm around Kevin's shoulders. "Kevin, would you like to show me your collection of model cars?"

Kevin stared at him. "I don't have a collection... Oh, I get it. Mom wants me out of the kitchen."

"You're such a bright boy."

"Yeah, but I'm still hungry."

181

"What are you doing here so early?" Emmy asked Tony Friday morning. "Did you want to check the fridge for leftovers? I have cranberries left."

"You know I can't stand them. I did text you. You saw my text, right?" he asked.

"I saw it, but I let you in the house anyway."

"Is everyone else still sleeping?"

"It's seven fifteen the day after Thanksgiving. Of course they're sleeping. I only got up because I use this time to write and do my devotions. What is so important you couldn't wait till later?"

"Can we sit in the breakfast nook?" he asked.

"Okay," she replied slowly. She looked into his eyes. "Something's up. Are you and Sloane having issues? Is Mama okay?"

He guided her to the table, and they sat across from each other. Tony stared out the window and gathered his thought.

"Tell me before I smack you," she said with a frown.

"Tyler is resigning," Tony said without elaborating.

"Resigning what? His teaching position at Olivet?"

Tony reached across the table and took her hand in his.

"Tony, you're scaring me," she whispered.

"Tyler is resigning to take another church," he said. "He told us Wednesday morning and we aren't supposed to tell anyone, but I know how close you and Liz are, so I didn't want you to be blindsided like everyone else."

She jerked her hand away and folded her arms over her chest. "If this is a joke, I will murder you dead."

"I wish it was."

"They aren't here now. They went home for Thanksgiving and won't be back for church."

"He's also preaching at the new church Sunday. Their board voted unanimously to offer him the position, and the members are voting after the service."

"Maybe they won't vote for him," she said fighting back tears.

"Would you vote against him?"

"Of course not. Crap! This sucks big-time."

182

"You can't tell anyone. Not Kenny. Not the kids. I haven't told Sloane or Mama or anyone except you."

"Thanks so much for ruining my day. My whole weekend." She smacked his hand.

"There's a board meeting Monday. He will officially give us his resignation then."

"Did he say when his last Sunday will be? This couldn't come at a worse time. Tell me they will be here through the holidays."

"He mentioned staying through December, taking a month off and starting at the new church in February."

"Wait a second, buster," she said forcefully. "When the senior pastor resigns, the whole staff has to resign. That means Wyatt and everyone else. Does he know?"

"Tyler talked to Wyatt, but not the other staff. He will tell them after the board meeting, or maybe before. I don't remember."

Emmy looked out the window for moment. "Krissy knows, doesn't she?"

"Yes, and she knows I know. We talked yesterday before they left to visit Wyatt's parents. She feels terrible because she can't tell you."

"Is that why you're telling me now?"

"Partly. Tyler said he was told to keep the whole thing secret..."

"Like it's top-secret spy stuff?"

"I don't understand the reasoning, but that's what he was told."

"Ordered?"

Tony shrugged.

"That's a load of..."

"Emmy! You need to allow God to..." Tony paused.

"To what? This is going to really hurt some families. I went through it when Pastor Ausland retired. That wasn't such a shock because he had been talking about retiring for a couple years." She stopped and took a deep breath. "It was a shock when Dr. Behren left. That happened really quick, but there were mitigating circumstances."

183

"Did you really think Tyler would be at Crest Ridge United his whole career?"

"Yeah," she replied. "There aren't many Nazarene churches in the country bigger than ours. I guess I thought if they ever left it would be to take a job like Dr. Schofield or a college president like Dr. Behren."

"I can picture Tyler being a District Superintendent one of these days. He could become the president of Olivet or some other university. He's a smart guy, Em, with unlimited potential."

"Are you his press agent now or what?"

"Just sayin'," Tony answered. "You can't tell Kristen I told you."

"I won't see her until Sunday. How is Wyatt going to preach knowing what he knows?"

"You got me. He must feel sick inside because he can't say anything."

Emmy stood up. "Can anyone come to the board meetings, or do you need security clearance?"

"Anyone can come to the meeting, but only board members can vote on stuff. Are you going to crash the meeting?"

"Probably not, but you better tell me how everyone reacts."

Chapter Twenty-Six

"You don't need to lockup, do you?" Kristen asked Wyatt outside the church office.

"No, Reed will take care of it," Wyatt replied. "Did you talk to Emmy earlier?"

"I saw her from a distance, but I can't face her knowing I am keeping a secret this important. I don't understand why Tyler was told not to mention it to anyone."

"I can see both sides, but Tyler said if he ever has to do it again, he will tell certain trusted church members."

"Is he going to text you with the results of the vote?"

Wyatt checked the time. "Michigan is an hour ahead of us. He probably knows by now."

Tyler texted a few minutes later as Wyatt, Kristen and the kids were in the car heading home.

"Was that Tyler?" Kristen asked.

"Yes, and the congregation voted unanimously for him."

"Wow! That is amazing. I doubt he would get a unanimous vote here. There are too many people in the church who complain about every little thing."

"Tyler isn't perfect, and there have been families who left the church because of him," Wyatt said.

"What are you whispering about?" Grace asked. "I heard you say something about Pastor Tyler."

Zach looked up from his phone. "What's going on? Why didn't you talk to Aunt Emmy?"

"Tyler and Liz have some news to tell us, but it has to wait for a couple days," Wyatt explained.

Grace shrugged and told Zach, "Miss Liz is probably expecting again. She wants to have six babies."

Zach returned his attention to his phone and the matter was dropped.

"Why is there a board meeting tonight?" Sloane asked. "You had one earlier this month. Is this an early meeting for December or something?"

185

Tony grabbed his wallet and keys. He walked toward the garage door, stopped and came back to the kitchen where Sloane was loading the dishwasher. "I suppose it won't hurt to tell you now."

She closed the dishwasher and stared at him. "Tell me what?"

"Pastor Tyler is resigning to take a church in Michigan."

"Get out! Are you kidding? Why would he do that? Ours is one of the biggest churches in the state."

"He said this was where God was leading him." He glanced at the time. "I gotta run. I'll tell you more tonight, but you can't share this with anyone yet."

"I won't, but something like this won't be a secret for long."

After letting everyone socialize for a few minutes, Tyler said, "Thank you for taking time to be here this evening. Let's get started, and if you don't mind I have something to read."

Carol Wisnewski, the board secretary, glanced at Tyler. His expression didn't give anything away. She turned to her right and looked at Roger Goldman. He shook his head and shrugged. She pushed her laptop away and sat back to listen.

Tyler placed a piece of paper on the podium in front of him. He took a deep breath and looked at the whiteboard on the back wall to avoid making eye contact with anyone.

"I began my career at Crest Ridge United Nazarene as an intern in September of 2005. In November of 2011 the church hired me as your senior pastor in spite of my young age and inexperience. I was twenty-seven and fortunate to have Dr. Ausland as my mentor and a very understanding church and church board. I had no real idea of what it meant to be a pastor, and I was extremely grateful that any church would choose to give a guy like me the chance to shepherd them, and lead them, and most importantly learn from them. And what a crazy start it was. From the funerals and the flooded sanctuary to the friendships and witnessing God's work in our midst, it truly was a great start to ministry." He paused to keep his composure then continued, "There is no easy way to say or write what comes next. It is our

186

faith in God that allows us to walk through these days confidently, trusting that He knows exactly what He is doing, and that His plan is perfect at all times and all circumstances. I hope you can rest in that faith as well. With that being said, Liz and I have accepted the call to be the Senior Pastor at Alexandria Rapids Church of the Nazarene in Alexandria Rapids, Michigan." He blinked several times before continuing, "We did not pursue this position. We had no reason to. We believe that God is at work in Crest Ridge, and because of that, there was no reason for us to be looking for anything anywhere else. When the phone call came from the District Superintendent on the Michigan District, however, it landed a little differently than the other similar phone calls I had received. There was an immediate tug in my heart by the Holy Spirit telling me I had to at least enter into a process of discernment to know whether God was working to move us to a new place.

"Over the course of the last few months, amid COVID-19, live streaming, and the general strange state of our world, we gave ourselves to praying and discerning what God was up to. After a Skype interview with the board at Alexandria Rapids, they unanimously voted to proceed to an in-person interview to see what God might have in store. Through these times, it became abundantly clear we were being moved, and God was calling us to go to Alexandria Rapids.

"I am very grateful this is such a hard thing to do. I am not running from any fires. I am not looking to escape any hardship. It is not because of any kind of financial strain. You guys made this hard because of your love and care for us. There really is nothing we are looking to escape. We are simply responding to where God is leading us, and we are doing our best to be faithful to the God who is our salvation.

"I believe if God is moving us somewhere else, He is already at work preparing someone else to be the pastor of Crest Ridge. Since this is God's doing, all of us on both ends can be confident in his faithfulness and in His leadership. It is our hope and prayer that our story will be one of God's Lordship of our lives as we respond faithfully to him.

"While we may not be in South Hampshire, we are bonded together by something so much greater than simple proximity. As fellow members of the Body of Christ, we are bonded together in an eternal fellowship with a promised reunion in the presence of Christ. We will both continue on in the work of bringing about God's Kingdom on earth as it is in heaven as we remain faithful to whatever He calls us to do and be.

"Thank you, Crest Ridge. Thank you for taking a risk on a young pastor. Thank you for showing grace when I had no idea what I was doing. Thank you for giving of yourselves and partnering with us to seek Christ's Kingdom and His righteousness. Thank you for loving us and taking care of us. You will always have a special place in our hearts.

"I urge you, just as Paul wrote to the Philippians, 'Therefore, my beloved, as you have always obeyed, so now, not only as in my presence but much more in my absence, work out your own salvation with fear and trembling, for it is God who works in you both to will and to work for his good pleasure.'" He finished, wiped his eyes and said, "Wow! That was tougher than any funeral I've ever done."

The board members silently glanced at each other.

"Did you know?" Carol asked Roger.

"Not a hint," he responded.

"I will need a copy of your letter for the minutes," Carol said.

After a few seconds of silence, which felt longer than an eternity, Dylan Michaelis said, "I can't speak for anyone else, but this is a surprise to me. I had no idea you were even looking for another church. To be completely honest, I am rather upset. How soon are you leaving?"

"My final Sunday at Crest Ridge will be January third," Tyler answered. "As I wrote in my letter, I wasn't looking, I've had offers in the past, and never really considered them. I didn't approach Alexandria Rapids. Their DS contacted me. This time I knew it was different."

Roger Goldman said, "I won't insult your integrity by offering a raise, but..."

"It's not an issue of salary or anything like that. The church attendance is actually several hundred lower than here."

"This isn't a joke, is it?" LaShae Mabry asked.

Tyler chuckled and shook his head. "It's most definitely not a joke."

"Is this why Pastor Wyatt preached yesterday?" Mike Fisker asked.

"In addition to seeing family this week, I also preached at the new church. The congregation voted to accept me as their new senior pastor."

"Did you give them an answer?" Bill Griffith asked.

"We did. The vote was unanimous, so we accepted the position immediately." He waved a hand and added, "That doesn't mean we haven't been praying about this. We have ever since I was offered the position."

Carol Wisnewski looked at the other board members and said, "It has been a while since we changed pastors, but several of us on the board have been through the process."

"Dr. Schofield will be here this Sunday to talk to the board."

"He won't preach?" Jim Rosek asked.

Tyler chuckled and said, "Not this time. He will talk to you after the service."

"Are we supposed to keep this under our hats until then?" Martin Stackhouse asked.

"I request you not divulge this information to anyone. I will read this letter to the congregation Sunday morning."

"My wife will be madder than a nest of angry hornets when she learns I knew about this and didn't tell her," Jim Rosek said. "I will respect your wish, Pastor Tyler, but I don't think I will sit by her on Sunday."

Carol got everyone's attention. "When Dr. Behren resigned suddenly, the board wanted to replace him quickly. You probably aren't aware of this, Pastor Tyler, but when the board hired you to be the senior pastor, we thought you might not be qualified for the job, and we would need to replace you after a short time."

"I thought that might be the case," he said.

189

"I'm happy to admit we were wrong. You might have been too young and certainly too inexperienced, but you were the right person for the church. I'm sure God already knows who will replace you. It is up to us to listen to the Holy Spirit and be united as a board." She grinned and said, "That might not be easy, but it will happen."

After taking care of a few new items of business, the meeting was adjourned. Tony headed home and tried to avoid Sloane, but she heard him and walked into the kitchen.

"How was the meeting?"

"Okay, but some board members were upset," he answered.

She looked at him and saw the seriousness in his eyes. "I suppose Tyler will announce it on Sunday, huh?"

"Yes, and I'm sorry, but I can't say anything."

"It's okay. I remember when the pastor left the church in Troy. It took the church months to find a replacement, and when they did, some of the people didn't like him."

"Why? What did he do?"

"Nothing really. Some people didn't like the way he preached, so they left the church."

"You can't say anything," Tony said.

"I won't but... never mind. I'm sure God will provide."

"Hi, Tommy, what are you guys doing here?" Timothy Joseph asked. "Hey, Sabrina. How's work going?"

"I'm not getting many shifts. Where are your parents?"

Tim hooked a thumb over his shoulder. "In the family room. Why?"

"We need to talk to them," Tommy replied.

Tim looked at his brother then grinned at his sister-in-law. "Are you knocked up?"

Sabrina poked him in the ribs. "You have such a special way of getting right to the point."

"Are you?"

"Yes, and we told my grandparents earlier and now we need to tell yours. Parents, I mean."

"I'm happy for you guys, but how far along are you?"

190

Sabrina frowned and replied, "Not that it's any of your business, but I wasn't pregnant when we got married."

"I'm glad," Tim said giving her a hug. "Mom and Dad will be so happy."

"My grandparents were pleased, but they have five grandkids already."

"Your baby will be their first great-grandchild," Tim said.

"That's right," Tommy replied.

"I knew that," Sabrina added.

"I'm so happy for you," Teresa said after hearing the news.

P.J. shook hands with Tommy and added, "You guys are so young to be having a baby, but we will support you in every way we can."

"Thanks, Dad. We weren't expecting it to happen so fast, but we didn't do anything to prevent it."

"That's a little too much info there, Tommy," Tim said. "We don't need to hear about your sex life."

"I did not want to wait until I was in my thirties to start a family," Sabrina said. "My siblings waited, but they are making up for lost time."

Chapter Twenty-Seven

Kenny touched Emmy's arm and asked, "Did you know Dr. Schofield would be here today?"

"No, I didn't. Is he going to preach?" she asked. "Kristen didn't say anything about it to me."

"Something's going on, Em. I can sense it," he whispered. "I haven't talked to Tony all week which is rather unusual."

"Kristen's been avoiding me, but I kinda know why," Emmy admitted.

"Mom, can I sit with Ben and Taylor?" Kevin asked.

"Yes, but stay off your phone. You need to pay attention. Especially this week," she answered.

Kevin sat with his friends, and Kenny, Emmy and the girls sat in their usual area.

After the worship team left the platform, Tyler took his place behind the recently purchased metal podium. He grabbed the edges, leaned forward and said, "Let me open with prayer." He prayed like a normal Sunday, but then he paused. "Before I get into this week's message, I need to read something."

Kenny looked at Emmy. She took his hand and whispered, "It will be okay."

Tyler focused his attention on the clock at the back of the sanctuary and spoke softly, "I began my career at Crest Ridge United Nazarene as an intern in September of 2005. In November of 2011 the church hired me as your Senior Pastor in spite of my young age and inexperience. I was twenty-seven and fortunate to have Dr. Ausland as my mentor and a very understanding church and church board. I had no real idea of what it meant to be a pastor, and I was extremely grateful that any church would choose to give a guy like me the chance to shepherd them, and lead them, and most importantly learn from them. And what a crazy start it was. From the funerals and the flooded sanctuary to the friendships and witnessing God's work in our midst, it truly was a great start to ministry." He paused to keep his composure then continued, "There is no easy way to say or write what comes next. It is our faith in God that allows us to walk through these days confidently, trusting that He knows exactly what He is doing, and that His plan is perfect at all times and all circumstances. I hope you can rest in that faith as well. With that being said, Liz and I have accepted the call to be the Senior Pastor at Alexandria Rapids Church of the Nazarene in Alexandria Rapids, Michigan." He heard several gasps from the congregation. "I leave you with a great deal of regret because we love this church, but I must go where God wants me..."

Kenny looked at Emmy, who was weeping openly by now, and asked, "You knew about this, right?"

"Tony told me Friday, but he swore me to secrecy. I couldn't tell you or anyone, and he couldn't even tell Sloane. I felt like I was in the CIA."

"This is going to upset a lot of the younger couples. They are more attached to Tyler and Liz than the church."

"I know, and I wish he wouldn't leave, but he has to obey God." Emmy looked at the girls.

"Mom, why are they leaving?" Heather asked.

"I will explain later," Emmy said putting an arm around Heather.

Tyler read the rest of his letter then looked around the sanctuary. "I am not leaving because of unresolved issues or problems. One of the things I have always tried to remind you is to listen to the Holy Spirit. That goes for me, and Liz, too. I have spent countless hours in prayer over this, and I have always gotten the same response. I need to be in Alexandria Rapids. I don't know why, but God wants me there."

The message was a little shorter this Sunday, and afterward, not many people were in a hurry to leave. The board members met in the chapel with Dr. Schofield.

"You have had a week to process this information, but the congregation has not. You will be faced with many questions, and I will do my best to guide this church through the transition period..."

Emmy saw Kristen waiting with her children as Wyatt talked to some of the older members. She walked up to Kristen and put an arm around her waist.

"I'm sorry I couldn't tell you, Emmy, but Wyatt told me not to share the news."

"It's okay. Tony told me last Friday. He said Tyler told him to tell me, but I couldn't tell anyone either. I don't understand why the secrecy was necessary. It's not like Tyler's a spy or a secret agent."

"Wyatt explained it, but I agree with you, Em. Maybe he couldn't tell everyone, but he could have told a few key members of the board. The staff didn't know until last Monday."

"Didn't Wyatt know?"

"Tyler talked to him about it, but more like as a friend asking another friend for an opinion."

Sloane joined them. "The secrecy has been bugging Tony all week. I'm glad everyone knows now."

"I remember when Dr. Behren left. Everyone was shocked, but they understood the reason for the quick change. Oh, shoot! I just remembered something. Does the whole staff have to resign?"

"Wyatt said it was in the church manual, but the board will probably ask everyone to stay through the transition period."

"Do you think there's a chance Tyler will ask Wyatt to go to Michigan with him?"

Kristen squeezed Emmy's hand and replied, "There is a good chance he will ask. I am not sure how he will answer."

"You can't move to Michigan, Krissy. I won't let you."

"I need to support my husband, Em, and I don't mean financially."

"I know, but I will die if you leave." Emmy saw Liz talking to several people. "Have you talked to Liz about this?"

Kristen glanced over her shoulder at Liz then said, "We did, but I couldn't tell you. We both felt terrible because we know how much you love them."

"I guess Michigan isn't too far away. We can always visit them."

When Liz finished talking to a new couple, she hurried to Emmy and Kristen.

Emmy hugged her and said, "I knew, but I couldn't tell you I knew. We are going to miss you so much. Our kids are so close."

194

"I know and this was the hardest decision we've ever had to make," Liz said.

Emmy sighed and said, "At least you will be here through the holidays. I'm sure you will be busy with packing and trying to see as many people as you can before you have to leave."

"We are going to try to visit with as many people as we can. The packing will have to wait. Tyler said he would do it at night if necessary."

"What are your plans for the house?" Kristen asked. "Are you going to sell it?"

"We have talked about allowing the church to buy it for the next pastor. If the board is interested."

"I think whoever the board hires would want to purchase their own home," Sloane said.

"I would think so," Liz said.

"I'm surprised Dr. Schofield didn't preach today," Emmy said. "He never passes up a chance to do that."

"Tyler thought it might be weird if he read his resignation letter and then Dr. Schofield preached."

"I hope he can find us a replacement within a few months," Sloane said. "I remember when I was a kid and our church didn't have a pastor for over a year."

"It's more important to find the right one," Emmy said. "They must be finished because here comes Tony."

"Maybe he can tell us what Dr. Schofield told them since it's not a secret anymore," Kristen said.

Liz shook her head and said, "There will still be some secrecy regarding candidates. It's just the way it has to be, I guess."

Chapter Twenty-Eight

"Would you like to see my collection?" Mr. Robertson asked after lunch. "I added a 1950 Packard Super Deluxe Eight to the list. It's a cream-colored convertible and has been fully restored."

"I'd love to see it," Galen Easton answered. "Should we ask the ladies to join us?"

Mona shook her head. "I've seen his old cars plenty of times. I want to stay here and talk to Freida about the ranch. We need to plan a visit to Hawaii after the holidays."

"The ranch hasn't changed much since the last time you visited, but I did paint the pergola on the east side of the house," Galen said.

Galen had managed the Robertson ranch on the island of Maui for over twenty years. A lifelong bachelor, he married Freida Williams five years prior after a six month courtship.

"I can't wait to get back there," Mona said. "You have fun checking out the cars. Freida and I will enjoy a cup of tea while we gossip."

Mr. Robertson led Galen along the tree-lined asphalt path to his building and opened the service door. They stepped inside and Mr. Robertson used his phone to bring up all the lights.

"That's pretty handy," Galen said.

"Yes. I can control everything from my phone. I can adjust the lights. temperature, set the alarm and even access the cameras. I turned off the alarm as we walked over here. All from this handy little..." He didn't finish.

"What is it, Bill?"

Mr. Robertson put a hand to his chest. "My..." He slumped to the floor.

Galen picked up the phone Mr. Robertson had dropped. "I sure hope I can figure this out." He looked at the phone for a moment then dialed 9-1-1 and explained the situation.

"A unit is two minutes away," the dispatcher said.

"They need to hurry."

"They are."

"Hang in there, Mr. Robertson, help is on the way" he said as he knelt beside him. He put a finger to Mr. Robertson's neck and swore. "Come on. You can't die now." He started CPR and worked on him until her felt a hand on his shoulder.

"We'll take over now," the paramedic said.

"Is that an ambulance?" Mona asked. "It sounds pretty close."

She and Freida glanced out the window and watched the ambulance pull into the driveway and speed toward the building which held the car collection.

"Something's happened!" Freida screamed.

"Bill!" Mona shouted.

"Come on, Mona. Let's see what happened."

Freida took Mona's hand and led her out of the house. They dashed to the oversized garage and entered.

"My God!" Mona said putting a hand to her heart. "Please, God, no. Not again."

"When did it happen?" Brady asked. He sighed and put a hand to his eyes. He clenched his jaw and nodded as he listened. "Where is he? I mean, where's Mona?"

Galen Easton replied, "She's here at St. Bart's with me. I followed the ambulance. Probably a bit too closely, but... anyway. I'm not sure exactly where we are now. We came in the ER section. They wouldn't let us in the room where they took him. The doctors were in there for thirty minutes or more. One of them came out a few minutes ago and told Mona. I'm so sorry, Brady. I tried to revive him before the paramedics arrived, but I could never get a pulse."

"I'm sure you did everything you could, Galen. We almost lost him in July, but he pulled through. He never told Mona, but he never did fully recover. He put on a front and pretended everything was all right."

"I will stay with Mona, and bring her home as soon as we can. Freida's with me. Did I already tell you?"

"Maybe."

"Is there anything else I can do right now?" Galen asked. He looked at Freida, who was sitting with Mona and doing her best to console her.

"Nothing I can think of. I suppose I should tell Diane, and call Bennett." Brady ran a hand through his hair. "We kind of expected this to happen sometime, but not this soon. Before his first heart attack, I always figured he'd live to be a hundred. His father lived to ninety-five and his grandfather reached ninety. Dad's brother and sister died a few years ago." Brady clenched his jaw again. "I better let you go. I need to compose myself and tell Diane."

"Mona told them they could do an autopsy. She said Dames-Blackburn would handle the arrangements. She mentioned they had talked to them after his first attack."

"Dad told me they paid for everything in advance. He wrote out specific instructions for when it happened."

"I will call you back when we're on the way home."

"Thanks, Galen." Brady ended the call and put a hand to his eyes.

"Who was on the phone?" Diane asked.

He turned to face her.

"Are you crying?"

He nodded.

"What's going on?"

"Dad is gone."

"Okay, I've called Bennett, Mr. Sandchek, the attorney. Who else should I call?" Diane asked.

"You have to call your sister," Brady said.

"Crap! Crap! Crap! I don't want to be the one to tell her. You know how she will react."

"Yes, but if you wait, she might hear it on the news. This will be an important news story. It might already be on social media."

"Would it be all right if I make Kenny tell her?"

"That might be best. Call him now."

Diane looked up Kenny's cell number. "It's ringing."

"Hey, Diane. Did you mean to call Emmy? My phone started ringing. I'm downstairs in my studio. Do you want to try calling her again?"

Diane took a deep breath. Then another. She squeezed Brady's hand and whispered, "No, I need to talk to you."

"Okay," he said slowly.

"It is horrible news."

Kenny sagged to the couch.

"Tell me."

"Mr. Robertson suffered another heart attack," she paused and added, "He's gone, Kenny. Will you tell her for me. I just can't."

Kenny stared at the phone for a moment. He answered without remembering.

"Are you still there, Kenny. It's Brady."

The sound of a different voice brought Kenny back.

"I'm here."

"Will you tell Emmy, please?"

Kenny coughed to clear his throat. "Yes, of course. She will want to know details after she stops crying. What should I tell her?"

"We're at home. She can come here. Diane would like that."

"Okay. It might be a while."

He sat on the couch with his head in his hands. For several minutes he thought of what he would say. His mind was flooded with memories of Mr. Robertson. He got on his knees and put his elbows on the couch. "Lord, please give me something to say. I know this is going to shatter her regardless of what I say, but maybe there's something to help her." He stopped praying and waited. In seconds these words from 2 Corinthians 1:3-4 were as clear as if they were spoken out loud. "Praise be to the God and Father of our Lord Jesus Christ, the Father of compassion and the God of all comfort, who comforts us in all our troubles, so that we can comfort those in any trouble with the comfort we ourselves receive from God."

He took a deep breath, stood up and said, "Thank you, Lord."

"Kevin Michael! I told you to stop texting Ben and listen to your teacher," Emmy hollered.

"Sorry, Mom, but he texted me first."

"I don't care. You are in school. Pay attention." She walked out of the kitchen toward the family room. She almost collided with Kenny as he emerged from the basement stairs.

"Sorry, Em. I didn't mean to knock you over."

"You didn't. Kevin is..."

"It doesn't matter. Come with me."

She looked at him. "You look so serious. What is it? You can tell me."

He took her hand and they walked into the library together. He sat in the large brown leather recliner and pulled her onto his lap.

"Something tells me you didn't bring me in here to kiss me," she said with a grin. When he didn't respond with something funny, she whispered, "Just tell me."

He pulled her close and whispered, "He's gone, Em. Mr. Robertson is gone."

She didn't ask what he meant. She didn't ask how or when. She sat in his lap without moving.

"I tried to think of something to say to make this easier, but I know there's nothing to ease this hurt. A verse from Corinthians came to mind. It was..."

"Praise be to the God and Father of our Lord Jesus Christ, the Father of compassion and the God of all comfort, who comforts us in all our troubles, so that we can comfort those in any trouble with the comfort we ourselves receive from God," she said before he could finish.

"How did you know?"

She shrugged and replied, "It popped into my head a few minutes ago. I kinda disregarded it and yelled at Kevin. Now I know why it came to me."

He squeezed her tighter. "You can cry now. I will hold you."

She bit her lip and cried softly for a shorter time than he expected.

"Let it all out, Em," he whispered.

She jumped out of his arms, stood up and said, "I need to go to Diane. Will you tell the kids, or should we tell them together?"

"I will tell them," he said. "If you want, you could go to the garage through the basement. I left my keys in the Jeep. You can use it."

"No, I will take my car," she said.

"Mom! Mom!"

They heard Kevin scream.

"Mommy! Come here!" Isabella hollered.

She and Kenny dashed out of the library and raced toward the kitchen. The kids scrambled out of the breakfast nook and ran into their parents just outside the kitchen. Emmy noticed the tears flowing down their faces and gathered them all in her arms.

"Is it true?" Heather asked. "I saw it on Instagram."

"Yes, sweetie. It's true."

"No! It can't be!" Kevin screamed. "He's getting better. I talked to him Sunday afternoon. Ben and I talked to him in his garage. He showed us his cars and even let me sit in one. It's not true, It's not!" Kevin broke away and ran upstairs."

"I need to go and be with Diane, but I can't leave him like this," Emmy said.

"Diane can wait, Em. Be with Kevin."

She kissed the girls and flew up the stairs.

Kenny hugged the girls and let them cry as long as they needed.

"Kevin, I'm sorry for yelling at you," Emmy said as she sat on the edge of his bed. She put a hand on his back and rubbed it as he sobbed into his pillow.

A moment later he sat up suddenly and wiped his eyes and nose with his hand. "This must be awful for you, Mom. He was your godfather, right?"

She scooted beside him and they sat together.

"Yes, he was. He's been like a real father to me."

"I'm mad because I thought he was over the heart problem. I should have said something nicer than thanks to him."

"We never know when will be the last time we see someone, or talk to them for the final time."

"You always tell us to be nice and thoughtful and not say nasty stuff to each other or about someone. Is this like a real crappy lesson for us because we didn't take you seriously?"

Emmy shook her head. "No, I think it was the time God chose for Mr. Robertson."

"Will he go to heaven? He didn't always go to church, but I've heard him pray when he didn't know I was there."

"We aren't the ones who decide. You know that."

"I sure hope he's going to heaven."

"Me, too."

They held each other without speaking.

Emmy kissed the top of his head and asked, "Do you feel better now?"

He sighed and said, "I'm okay."

"I need to see Diane."

"Go ahead. Lily and Conor might need you to hug them. He was their real grandfather."

She kissed him again and left the room.

"Is Kevin okay?" Isabella asked.

"He's all right. It was quite a shock to him."

"It was a shock to us, too," Heather said. "Poor Mona. Didn't her first husband die when he was pretty young?"

"I believe so. I never knew him. She was a widow when I met her."

Isabella said, "Our teacher said school was canceled for the rest of the day." She looked at Emmy and added, "Mr. Robertson was an important man, right?"

"He was more important than we realized."

"I always thought of him as our other grandpa. He was kinda normal to us. Not a big shot or anything."

"I thought of him as my father at times. He actually was my godfather when I was christened."

Isabella checked her phone. "I have over a hundred missed calls and texts. This is a much bigger event than we realize, huh?"

"I'm afraid it is, Isa. Much bigger."

202

"I will stay here with the kids," Kenny said. "You should go to Diane. I'll answer the phone. I'm sure we will be getting a ton of calls."

Before she could leave, Tyler called.

"Thanks for calling. It is quite a shock," Emmy said.

"What can I do to help?" Tyler asked.

"I'm not sure yet. I was heading to Diane's house. There will be a lot of people calling, and I can help take care of the kids."

"Hang on a second, Emmy. Liz is trying to tell me something," Tyler said. He put a hand over the phone and listened to his wife. "Okay. I will leave right away." He asked, "Are you still there, Emmy?"

"Yes."

"Liz called Diane, and was able to talk to the lady with Mona. She said they are still at St. Bart's. Mona wants to see Bill before she lets them bring her home. I can't see her at the hospital, so I'm going to come to Brady and Diane's house."

"Okay, I'll be there in a few minutes."

"Have you talked to Tony?" Tyler asked.

"I haven't, but Kenny called him and Kristen. Wyatt might be here when you arrive."

"Good. I'll be there soon."

Emmy walked in the front door and heard Diane talking on the phone. She turned to enter the living room and Diane emerged at the same time.

"I'll talk to you later, Mama. Emmy just walked in."

Emmy looked up at her sister and Diane opened her arms. "I know you're hurting, but we have to be strong for Mona and the kids. His family is going to need us to get through the next week. The media will turn this into a circus if they have their way."

Emmy buried her face in Diane's chest and sobbed for a moment. Then she straightened up and asked, "Has anyone talked to Mr. Sandchek? He will know how to deal with the media."

Diane nodded. I called him after Bennett. He and his wife will be at the house when Galen and Frieda bring Mona back."

"Where are the kids?"

Diane pointed up. "In Carson's room. He's been so strong. He's taking care of the little ones."

"How is Caden doing? Kevin was rather shaken up. He won't want anyone to know, but he cried like a baby."

"So did Caden. Lily and Conor cried, but that's understandable. They lost their grandpa."

"We lost our godfather," Emmy said.

Diane replied, "He was your godfather, Em. It's no secret you were closer to him than me."

"He loved us both," Emmy said.

"Yes, but he loved you more, and that's okay." Diane hugged Emmy again. "You should see the kids. They will appreciate it."

Tyler arrived with Wyatt and Brady let them in.

"We are so sorry for your loss, Mr. Robertson," Tyler said.

Brady nodded and led them into the living room. His phone rang. "Sorry, but I need to take this." He walked down the hall to his den. "Where are you, Rosco?"

"At the house with Teresa. I talked to the security company. They have already assigned extra men to the gate and have a car stationed at the secondary entrance. They will check anyone trying to enter. There will be one car patrolling the neighborhood and a car at the house. Would you like one to watch your house?"

"We should be okay."

"I talked to the mayor, and he assured me the city will do whatever is needed. Chief Sanders called me, and promised the full cooperation of his department."

"We might need them for security at the service," Brady said.

"I got a call from a contact in the Secret Service."

"Really?" Brady asked.

"The President cannot attend, but he will send a representative."

"Unreal. I forget Dad was more connected than we realized."

"Call me anytime, Brady. I will do whatever is needed."

"Who was on the phone?" Diane asked.

"Rosco," Brady said without needing to elaborate.

"I need to let Emmy know Tyler is here."

"We are on our way home," Mona said later. "Is everyone okay?"

Brady cleared his throat and answered, "We are holding down the fort."

"Galen and Freida convinced me to leave."

"Rosco and Teresa are at the house. They will screen the phone calls."

"Has everyone been notified?" Mona asked.

"I called everyone I could think of. Most people are learning about it on social media."

Mona put a hand to her mouth. "Oh my. Is Emmy all right? She will be shattered."

"She is upstairs with the kids. What can we do for you, Mona?"

She took a deep breath. "Nothing now. I should call my kids. They probably already know, but I need to talk to them."

"Diane called, but there was no answer. She didn't want to leave a message."

"That was thoughtful of her. Please tell her thanks for me."

"I will. Please call if you need anything, or tell Rosco and Teresa. They will take care of everything."

"Did Mona get home yet?" Emmy asked when she came downstairs with Tyler.

"She called a few minutes ago. They should be back soon," Diane answered. She smiled at Tyler and said, "Thank you for coming."

"I had a great deal of respect for Mr. Robertson."

Diane thought about it for a moment, then asked, "Would you stop at the house and pray with Mona? I hate to ask, but it would be helpful."

"Certainly," he replied.

"I'll go with him," Emmy said.

205

Galen opened the door for Emmy and Tyler and whispered, "She's in the parlor. She talked to her children and grandchildren already."

"Thanks, Mr. Easton. This is Pastor Tyler from our church. He knows Bill and Mona."

Galen shook his hand and let them into the parlor.

"Mrs. Robertson, I am so sorry for your loss. I talked to Mr. Robertson on the phone last week."

"Thank you, Pastor Tyler. Bill told me he asked you to do his service when the time came. I am sure he didn't expect it to be this soon. Are you still willing?" Mona asked.

"I would be honored."

"He has a service planned, but you may change it if necessary."

"We talked briefly about his wishes. I will follow them to the letter."

Mona looked at Emmy, stood up and opened her arms. Emmy hugged her but didn't cry.

"I hate to remind you, but you promised to sing for him."

"I know, but I thought it would be years from now."

"I will understand if..."

"God will give me the strength I need. That's one of my favorite verses, and Kenny will be with me. Mr. Robertson made him promise to sing with me in case I start bawling."

"Did you eat anything for dinner?" Emmy asked when she returned later that night.

"The kids weren't real hungry, but we had tacos. They're in bed already," Kenny said. "Did you eat?"

"No, I forgot and I'm not hungry now."

"You should eat something, Em. How about some soup?"

"Could you make me a grilled cheese sandwich? Or a BLT?"

"Which one?"

"A BLT would hit the spot. Toasted bread, please."

She sat at the island while Kenny fixed the sandwich.

"Did you remember we have to sing?" she asked.

206

"You have to sing. I'm there for moral support," he answered while washing the lettuce.

"Do you think our church is big enough to hold everyone?" she asked as she checked the missed calls on her phone. "I have a feeling a lot of people will attend the funeral."

"More will stop by the funeral home for the wake."

"I hope Mona doesn't overdo it."

"Here's your sandwich, Em. Would you like some tea or something?"

"Water, please."

Kenny sat next to her with an arm around her waist as she ate.

"That was good. I should check on the kids and then I'm going to bed. I may not get much sleep, but I need the rest."

"I will be up soon. I need to check my email and lock up," he said giving her a kiss.

"Don't stay up too late. I might need to cuddle."

Chapter Twenty-Nine

"Mom, the collar is tight enough to choke me," Kevin said as he got ready to leave for the funeral home. "I will suffer because it's for Mr. Robertson, but as soon as I can, I'm going to undo the collar so I can breath."

Emmy straightened his tie and brushed the shoulders of his suit coat. "Thank you for being a man. You look very handsome, son."

"You look good, too. Are you nervous about meeting the big shots?"

"Maybe, but your father will be next to me. I'll let him do all the talking."

Kevin grinned and said, "Mr. Rosco showed me his gun and the earpiece he has to wear to talk to the security people. There's even going to be lady secret agents there."

"Mr. Robertson was a very influential man. He knew a lot of important people in politics and business."

"Ben tried to tell me the president was coming. He's not is he?"

Emmy shook her head. "He can't be here, but he sent someone. I think it's one of his staff members who help run the White House." She shrugged. "Someone kinda important if not real well known by the public."

"Kinda like Mr. Robertson. He did a lot of stuff no one ever knew about, right?"

"Yes."

"But if you saw him on the street, he would say hi and be like a regular guy."

"He was rather modest in many ways, and he never liked to be the center of attention like your father," Emmy said as Kenny entered Kevin's room.

"Em, is this tie straight? I can't tell."

She straightened his tie and touched the tip of his nose. "You look almost as handsome as your son."

Kenny looked at Kevin. "We're wearing matching suits. We could be twins."

Heather and Isabella laughed from their place outside the door.

"They are both dorks," Heather said.

Kevin made a face at his sisters. "Just because you're wearing new black dresses doesn't mean you're all grown-up."

"I need all of you to be on your best behavior today," Emmy said as she inspected the girls appearance. "Heather, are you wearing lipstick?"

"Just a little. Please don't make me wash it off."

"It looks okay, but don't make a habit of it." She looked at Isabella. "The same goes for you."

Kenny checked the time. "We should get going. We need to be there early in order to find a place to park."

"Some people might have to park by the football stadium," Kevin said later as they arrived at the North Park College campus.

"It's a good thing the college was willing to let us use their auditorium," Emmy said. She saw groups of people talking while they waited to get into the building. "Make sure you wear your mask if you're around someone you don't know."

"I brought my black pirate mask," Kevin said.

His sisters rolled their eyes.

Kenny showed an officer his *invitation* and followed the directions of the off-duty officers and was allowed to park in a VIP section close to the Barclay Center.

"There's Mr. Rosco by the door," Kevin shouted.

"Kevin Michael! Please do not disturb him. I'm sure he has enough on his mind without you and Ben pestering him," Emmy warned.

"Can I wave?"

"Yes," Kenny answered.

Kevin waved and was rewarded with a salute.

"Where are we supposed to go?" Kenny asked as they entered the building. "I've been backstage for concerts, but it's been a few years."

They were escorted to the floor of the auditorium by a Dames-Blackburn employee.

Diane lowered her mask and said, "I'm glad you made it early. It's going to be a zoo later. There have already been a few politicians arrive."

"I'm sure they want to beat the crowds," Emmy said. "How's Mona doing?"

"She didn't get much sleep the last three days, but who can blame her. Teresa and Freida have been taking all the calls and only allowing friends and family to talk to her."

Emmy looked around. "Where are Lily and Conor?"

"They were here earlier, but I let them go home. Tomorrow will be difficult enough."

"Who took them? Brady didn't because he's talking to Bennett."

"Rosco arranged for them to get home. He's been like the Rock of Gibraltar. I don't know what we would have done without him. Galen and Freida extended their vacation."

"Who are the people sitting on the couch by Mona?" Emmy asked.

"Her son and daughter, their spouses and her grandchildren. They flew in early this morning. I guess they had trouble leaving California because of the virus. Something like that anyway."

"Have you met them before?"

"A couple times. Should I introduce you?"

Emmy waved. "Maybe later."

"I'll talk to you later, Em. I need to pay my respects to Marissa and her parents."

"Good luck with that. Are they trying to make this about them?"

"They tried earlier. Mona and Teresa shot them down like a dive bomber in flames," Diane answered with a smile.

Kevin tugged on Emmy's arm and asked, "Does everyone get to talk to Mrs. Robertson?"

Emmy shook her head. "Diane told me the general public will not be allowed to talk to family and friends."

"That's good. Mona doesn't need to be talking to everyone," Kenny said.

"Does that mean I can't talk to Ben?" Kevin asked.

Emmy straightened his tie again. "Tony will be here soon. You can talk to Ben, but you need to be respectful."

"Geez, Mom. I know this is a wake. We aren't going to play games."

"I know, but I'm a mom. I have to remind you."

"Mom," Heather whispered, grabbed Emmy's hand and pointed.

Emmy saw who had attracted Heather's attention. "That's the mayor and Chief Sanders. You've met him before."

"He came to the house when you had your accident," Isabella said.

"He grew up in Raynor Park like me and your father. He's older than us."

Kenny whispered, "I should talk to him. I'll be back soon."

"Can I go with you?" Kevin asked.

"Sure. Are you going to tell him you want to be a detective?"

"No, I want to talk to the officer with him."

"That's his son, Eric. He was the first officer on the scene of your mother's accident."

"Did he save Mom's life?" Kevin asked.

"He might have."

"Mom, can we talk to Grandma Mona now?" Heather asked.

Emmy looked and didn't see anyone by Mona. "Go ahead, but make it quick."

The twins hurried to Mona's side. She saw them coming and opened her arms to hug them.

Isabella whispered, "We're so sorry about Grandpa Robertson."

"I know you are, dear. He loved you girls so much. You look so pretty today. Are those new dresses?"

"Mom made us buy new ones because the only black ones we had didn't fit right anymore," Heather answered.

"I need to talk to your mother," Mona said. "Would you tell her, please?"

"Of course," Isabella said.

211

Heather waved at Emmy and motioned for her to join them. Emmy was talking to Sloane, who had just arrived, and didn't see Heather's wave.

"It looks like you're wanted," Tony said as he put his hands on her shoulders and turned her toward Mona and the girls.

"I'll talk to you later." Emmy made her way to Mona.

"Emmy, I need to introduce my children and grandchildren before everything gets crazy." Mona took Emmy's hand and urged her to follow. "Now don't be shy. The kids want to meet you. They've heard about you all their lives."

"Heard about me? Why?" Emmy asked.

"Because Bill liked to brag about you." Mona stopped in front of her children. "This is Emmy Colasanti-Colwell. You can introduce yourselves because I need to talk to the mayor."

"It's a pleasure to meet you. I am Reid Moneywell. This is my wife, Helena, and the three munchkins are our children. You need to forgive them. They won't talk while wearing their masks."

"I can understand that." Emmy adjusted her own mask.

"Hello, I'm Mona's daughter, Janet, and this is my husband, Ellery. My kids are not as shy. This is Elias and Jessie."

Emmy bumped elbows with everyone including the kids. "I am so sorry for your loss."

Ellery used his cane to help get to his feet and replied, "We should be consoling you. You were Bill's favorite. He talked about you every time we saw him or talked on the phone. He was your godfather, right?"

"Yes," Emmy said softly.

Reid smiled and said, "Mom has told us the story of how your grandfather helped Bill start his company and that you used to work for him."

"Yes, and that's how I met your mother." Emmy bit her lip and looked for Kenny because Chief Sanders, the mayor of SoHam and another man in a black suit were approaching.

"Emmy, I need to introduce you to Mayor Trumbetti, and this is Nash Robinson." Chief Sanders hugged Emmy and whispered, "Mr. Robinson works in the White House. He wants to talk to you."

212

Emmy greeted the mayor, who then moved on to other people. She looked up at Mr. Robinson and grinned because his navy blue tie wasn't straight.

"When my children learned I was coming to South Hampshire to represent the President, they insisted I meet you and ask for an autograph. Would you oblige me? If I fail in their request, I will be banished and ostracized from my home."

"Why would they want my autograph?" she asked. "You work for President Rhodes. You're an important man."

He dismissed her remark with a wave. "To them I am just another father who works long hours. They read every book you publish and I believe they have several of your CDs."

Emmy grinned and said, "I want them back."

He stared at her with a blank expression.

Chief Sanders laughed. "Emmy is referring to the CDs."

"Aha! I understand. I doubt they would be willing to surrender the CDs or the books."

Chief Sanders produced a pen and paper for Emmy to sign. She asked for the names and wrote a brief note to them.

"Thank you very much. I talked to Mrs. Robertson for a moment and extended President Rhodes' condolences. I met Bill in 1985 at an informal gathering in Houston, and we talked several times throughout the years. We took out our wallets and showed each other photos of our children. He showed me a photo of a young girl with dark, curly hair and beamed with pride because she had learned to swim and something about learning to read earlier than other children." Mr. Robinson grinned and said, "He told me her name was Emily, but everyone called her Emmy. Whenever we met over the years, we would catch each other up on our children and their accomplishments. He always included you as though you were his daughter."

Emmy bit her lip and Chief Sanders put an arm around her and squeezed her shoulders.

"Dear me. I have caused you emotional stress."

Chief Sanders answered, "It okay, Mr. Robinson, Emmy has always been unable to hide her emotions."

"I can't help it. It's just the way I'm wired."

"I've known her since she was a child and she's always been shy and.. well... as pretty as could be. But she could be tough, too. I remember she beat up my younger brother once because he tried to steal a kiss," Sanders said.

Emmy turned red. "I just smacked his arm."

Mr. Robinson said. "Please accept my personal condolences as well as those of President Rhodes." He checked his watch and nodded to the two men in black suits hovering nearby. "I must return to the city. My duties never cease."

Emmy watch him walk away. She turned to Chief Sanders and asked, "Did I really ask him to return my CDs?"

"Yes, but I doubt he will remember."

"I wonder how he knew so much about me."

"I had to brief him about you. Oh, the part about he and Mr. Robertson talking about you and the kids was totally true. He told me that story when we picked him up at the airport."

"Did he fly in on Air Force One?"

Chief Sanders laughed. "No, a regular business jet."

Kenny and Tony watched as the crowd filed past the casket.

"The whole city might turn up," Tony said.

"I heard there was a delegation coming from Europe."

"I wouldn't be surprised."

Kenny pointed to Mona. "Mama and Mona are talking. I wonder what it could be."

Tony cleared his throat. "They have become close friends the last few years. Now they have something else to talk about."

"Mom, do we have to stay here all day?" Kevin asked shortly after four.

Emmy checked the crowd. "We can leave as soon as I say goodbye to Mona."

"I'm not sure you can get close enough, Em," Kenny said.

"I suppose you're right. I hope she doesn't stand all day. She should sit down and take a break once in a while." Emmy looked at the crowd once again and grabbed Kenny's arm. "We can't leave yet. There's Principal O'Dell. I have to talk to him."

214

"Would you mind if I take the kids home and come back for you?" Kenny asked.

"Go ahead. I can get a ride home with Tony or Kristen. She's here now, and they won't stay too long."

Kenny kissed her and gathered the kids.

"We'll see you at home, Mom," Kevin said.

Emmy made her way through the crowd and walked up to Liam O'Dell."

"Ms. Colasanti, have you been behaving, or do I need to give you a detention?" He frowned but a smile slowly emerged.

"I've been good. How are you? I heard you were in the hospital for a few days."

"Ba, that was the end of last year. My blood count was low, so Keith and Elisabeth took me to St. Bart's. I saw your brother when I was there. He told me how you met."

"It was pretty amazing. He looks so much like Daddy."

"I noticed."

"I haven't talked to Annie or Matt in forever. I should get together with her soon."

Liam chuckled and said, "You will have to go to Vermont if you want to see her."

"Why? Did they move?" Emmy asked.

"In April. They bought a bed and breakfast."

"I didn't know."

"It was rather sudden. One of Matt's relatives passed away and the house became available. They figured Annie could write her books in Vermont just as easily as in SoHam. She and Matt are homeschooling the kids now."

"Do you get to see them very often?"

"Only on the computer. I haven't been able to travel to Vermont, but Keith and Elisabeth have."

"It's a beautiful state."

"They stayed for a week so there would be a paying guest in the place."

"Please tell her I said hello when you talk to her again."

"Will do. You take care."

Chief Sanders put a hand on Tony's arm to get his attention.

"Hello, Chief Sanders. How are things going during the shutdown?"

"Boring. All I do is try to please politicians. I liked it better when I was a detective. Do you have a minute?"

"Sure. What's up?"

"You probably haven't heard and might not remember him, but Ronald Delaney was paroled a few months ago."

"I remember him. Should we be concerned?"

Sanders shook his head. "He's in Texas. I talked to the chief in San Antonio, and had him picked up two days ago and charged with jaywalking so we could account for his whereabouts."

"Has he made threats against Emmy again?"

"No, but I like to keep informed about his location."

"Thanks for letting me know. Should I tell Emmy?"

Sanders shook his head. "No need. Mr. Sandchek is aware of his situation. I doubt he could even find SoHam anymore. His time in prison was not beneficial to his health. Physical or mental."

Emmy spotted Kristen and Wyatt and made her way through the crowd.

"Emmy, did you already talk to Mrs. Robertson?"

"Yes. Kenny took the kids home. Could I catch a ride with you?"

"Of course. We can't stay too long."

"Can I hold Kayla?"

"Okay, but she might wake up soon and start screaming."

"I can feed her if you have her bottle," Emmy said taking the sleeping baby from Kristen.

"We saw Liz and Tyler a while ago, but I think they left already," Kristen said. "I don't envy him."

"Why?" Emmy asked.

"He has to do the service in front of all the big shots."

"I think he will handle it like any other funeral," Emmy said.

216

Chapter Thirty

"Why do we need tickets to get into church?" Kevin asked to annoy his sisters.

"Haven't you ever been to a concert?" Heather asked. "You need a ticket to get in. How dumb are you?"

"This isn't a concert, Heather. It's Mr. Robertson's funeral. There's a difference."

"Yes, but there were so many people wanting to attend the service the funeral home had to do something to limit the amount of people inside the sanctuary," Isabella explained.

Kenny waited for the red light to change. He looked at Emmy and asked, "Are you okay? You look preoccupied."

"Sorry. Were you talking to me?" she asked. "I was thinking about the day Mr. Robertson told me and Diane about the house."

"The one on Hickory?"

"What about it, Mom?" Isabella asked.

"He bought it and gave it to us. He did so many generous things over the years that no one knows about."

Kenny parked behind the old sanctuary. They entered through the back doors and walked down the hall past the church offices to the foyer of the new building and stopped.

"Why is everyone milling about?" Kenny asked.

Kevin squirmed close enough to see why there was such a long line. "They're checking for invitations," he said when he returned.

"I have ours," Kenny said.

"Good. We need to be inside if we're going to sing," Emmy said with a grin.

They made it inside the sanctuary and were ushered to reserved seats near the front. Kenny saw Diane waving from the door leading behind the platform.

"Em, I think Diane wants you."

Emmy noticed and said, "I think she wants me to join the family. She said they would have one final chance to see him before they close the casket. I better go."

Emmy edged through the crowd checking out the floral arrangements and made her way to the side room where the family had gathered.

"Emmy, you are as much a part of the family as anyone," Diane said. "Didn't you want to see him one last time?"

"Yes, but I'm not really a part of the family."

Mona heard the conversation and put an arm around Emmy. "Yes, you are. Don't let anyone ever tell you differently."

After a final viewing, the family began making their way to their seats at the front. Brady and Bennett whispered their goodbyes to their father and walked away with heads held high.

"Mrs. Robertson, you may take as much time as you need," Clement Dames Armstrong whispered with his hands clasped together.

"Thank you," Mona answered pulling Emmy with her.

Mr. Armstrong nodded and backed away.

Emmy held Mona's hand as they approached the casket.

"I've lost two husbands, but I cherish them both." Mona ran her hand along the suit he wore, turned to Emmy and said, "You were always his favorite, but he tried not to spoil you too much. Lily made sure."

Emmy squeezed Mona's hand and tried to blink away the tears. "I don't remember much about her. I was rather young when she passed."

"I said my goodbyes to him earlier. I'm ready now. I don't want everyone to have to wait too long." She touched the lapel of his jacket and whispered, "Goodbye, Bill, I will be strong for you."

She turned away and took Emmy's hand. Emmy clenched her jaw as she took a final look over her shoulder.

"Thank you, Clement," Mona said.

He nodded with his hands still clasped together.

Emmy guided Mona to her seat then joined Kenny and the kids.

"You okay?" Kenny asked as he squeezed her hand.

"Yes and no," she answered.

The people from Dames-Blackburn closed the casket and moved it in front of the platform. They quickly reorganized some of the floral arrangements before walking quietly out of the sanctuary.

Tyler sighed, blinked his eyes a few times, rose from the front row and made his way to the podium, "I would ask you to rise as we begin this memorial service with a prayer."

Kevin read the program and looked at his mother. "Was that his favorite song?"

"It was one of them," she replied.

"Don't sweat it, Mom. You always do a great job at funerals."

"Thanks, I think."

Tyler cleared his throat and began by going through some biographical information. He paused and said, "You can read all this in the program or online. I want to talk about the real William Richard Robertson..."

"I never knew his middle name," Emmy whispered. "I just realized that."

"I didn't either," Kenny said.

"I knew it started with an R, but I never heard anyone use it."

Heather frowned at her parents and whispered, "I want to hear Pastor Tyler."

"He was a man driven to succeed but not driven by success if that makes any sense. He once told me he would be happy if he could provide for his family and maybe help others in a small way." Tyler paused, looked up at the ceiling and waved a hand. "He succeeded in that beyond anyone's knowledge..."

"Did Mr. Robertson pay for the school and new church?" Kevin asked Heather.

"I don't know. Probably. Now hush and listen," Heather responded.

"He often did things behind the scenes because he shunned the spotlight whenever possible. He influenced people by his actions and not his words..."

"Are you ready, Em?" Kenny asked.

She nodded, wiped her eyes, took his hand and they made their way to the platform. She looked up at the tech booth and Bruce Sutherland started the backing track to 'Amazing Grace (My Chains Are Gone)'. He brought up the level and Emmy closed her eyes and began to sing the words though her mind raced through memories of Mr. Robertson.

Kenny sang the second verse and their voices blended together for the chorus and rest of the song.

"Don't they sound so good together," Mona whispered to Brady.

"They do," he answered wiping his eyes and handing a tissue to Mona.

As Emmy and Kenny finished someone in the back started to clap. Soon everyone joined in.

"Are we supposed to clap at a funeral?" Ben Bertucci asked his father.

"Not usually, but it's okay now."

"Is Mom really going to talk in front of all these people?" Kevin asked.

Isabella answered, "Yes. She wrote a poem, remember?"

Emmy made her way to the podium holding her wireless mic. "Mona asked me to say something... I'm Emmy Colasanti-Colwell, by the way and Mr. Robertson and Lily were my godparents. Diane's too." She nodded at her sister. "You would think I would be used to being on this platform because of all the times I've sang at this church, but I'm scared. I had to pray and ask for God's help to even walk over here." She glanced at Mama Bertucci who smiled at her. "A while back I wrote a song called 'Inadequate Ordinary People' and it kinda fits Mr. Robertson. I tweaked the lyrics slightly, but here it is..."

"She made it through without crying," Tony said to Sloane. "That's amazing."

Sloane handed him a tissue. "Too bad I can't say the same for you."

Mama smiled at Emmy as she and Kenny made their way back to their seats.

Tyler waited a moment before returning to the podium. "Thank you Kenny and Emmy. Mr. Robertson would be so proud of you." He opened his Bible and held it up. "I would like to read one of Mr. Robertson's favorite scriptures. It can be found in John 14:27. Please allow me to read this short verse. 'Peace I leave with you; my peace I give you. I do not give to you as the world gives. Do not let your hearts be troubled and do not be afraid.' Mr. Robertson understood you would grieve for him, and he knew it would not be easy for some of you, but be assured God provides for our every need..."

The men from the funeral home returned after Tyler prayed and took his seat. They moved the floral arrangements and wheeled the casket out the center aisle. The pall bearers followed.

"We're ready now, Mrs. Robertson," Mr. Armstrong said.

"Thank you, Mr. Armstrong," Brady said. He helped Mona to her feet, and she patted his hand as she wiped her eyes.

Mr. Armstrong then nodded to his assistants. He ran a hand through his white hair, adjusted his tie, smoothed out his black suit jacket and escorted the family out of the sanctuary. The rest of the staff ushered the remaining guests out of the sanctuary.

"Where do we go now, Mom?" Kevin asked. "Are we going to eat later?"

"We are going with the family to the cemetery. There is a dinner this afternoon at The Barclay Country Club for family and close friends."

"Do I have to keep my tie on until after we eat?"

"Would you do it for me?" Emmy asked.

"Sure, but I'm really doing it for Grandpa Robertson."

Chapter Thirty-One

"What kind of cake did you make for Uncle James?" Kevin asked as he used a finger to swipe some frosting.

"Stop that!" Emmy said as she swatted his butt. "It's a chocolate cake with chocolate icing."

"Did he ask for that?"

"Yes, and he chose the menu for dinner."

Kevin checked the stove. "Chili, huh?"

"And homemade cornbread."

"Is the chili hot?" Kevin asked as he sniffed it.

"It won't melt your stomach, but I added a few slices of jalapeno peppers. Don't breath on it," she scolded.

"Text me when dinner's ready. I'm going to hang out with Ben at the fort. I have my phone." He raced out the door.

"Wear a coat. It's cold out," Emmy said but doubted he heard.

"Knock, knock. Can I come in?" Father James asked.

"You don't have to knock, Uncle James," Isabella said. "Dinner is almost ready."

He walked past the island to the stove and sniffed the chili. "It smells spicy."

"It's not firehouse hot, but it's got a little kick. Happy birthday. Sixty-five, huh?"

"Yes. I am on officially on Medicare, and entitled to every senior citizen discount the state offers. Did you make cornbread?" he asked glancing at the counter.

"It's in the warmer, and I made a cake from scratch."

A few minutes later everyone sat in the breakfast nook to eat.

"How's the chili?" Emmy asked.

Father James took another bite and said, "Just enough kick to make it interesting. I hope it's not too spicy for you, Kenny."

"I added crackers to cool it down."

"Can I have another piece of cornbread, please?" Kevin asked.

222

Emmy handed him the platter. "I didn't know you liked it."

"This is a lot better than the box mix you usually make. You're a pretty good cook when you make stuff yourself."

"I learned from Mama Bertucci," Emmy said taking another slice of the moist cornbread.

"Are you keeping busy, Uncle James?" Heather asked. "Mom said you should retire now that you're sixty-five. Are you going to?"

He shook his head and replied, "I can't. There's still a severe shortage of priests. In fact, I might be transferred to another parish."

Emmy looked at him and asked, "Not a different diocese though. You don't want to move back to Kansas, do you?"

He shook his head. "My parents have made it clear I need to stay here with this part of my family. If they need extra care, they will move to SoHam."

"We could help with expenses if needed," Emmy said.

Father James laughed. "You've met them. Do you really think they would accept charity?"

Kenny smiled. "They are the most determined and independent people I've ever met."

"And very proud of the fact," Father James said.

"When will you be allowed to retire?" Emmy asked.

"I know three priests over seventy-five who still work on a limited basis. As long as my health holds out, I will continue to serve."

"You should have been a Nazarene. Our pastors are allowed to retire."

"I want to thank everyone for making time to be here," Tyler said. "I promise not to take more than an hour if I can help it, since this is my final board meeting with you. We should go through the reports and then get to the main item on the agenda."

Fifteen minutes later the reports were accepted.

"Okay, now in case you were not aware I will explain what happens when a senior pastor resigns."

"Isn't this in the manual?" Ramon Warlito asked.

223

"Yes, and in most cases the pastor is the only staff member, but here that is not the case. Obviously. The entire staff is required to resign, but the board can choose to rehire them. Either in total or individually. I should tell you up front Pastor Dickinson has accepted a call to be the senior pastor in Carmi, Indiana.

"He did tell us several weeks ago," Roger Goldman said. "It should be a good move for him. His family lives nearby and his parents are advanced in age."

"Also, Pastor Milhuff submitted his resignation and asked not to be considered for rehiring. He cited his health as the main reason. He and Ruth are moving to Florida as soon as they sell their home."

"We should thank him for the outstanding job he's done with the seniors these last few years," Dolores Hoffman said.

"I have a question," LaShae Mabry said holding up a hand.

"Yes, LaShae, what is your question?" Tyler asked.

"Should we pay Pastor Dickinson and Pastor Milhuff a bonus since they're leaving?"

Roger Goldman answered, "As a general rule, we have not done that in the past. Staff ministers are hired by the senior pastor and not the board."

"Doesn't the board set their salaries?" Robby Collins asked.

"We approve the salaries, but we don't actually hire them."

After a short discussion the board passed a motion to give the two men a bonus of two weeks salary.

"Okay, now you have the opportunity to rehire the other staff members. Please keep in mind when a new senior pastor is hired, they will have the option of retaining the staff or bringing in his, or her, own," Tyler said then chuckled.

"We do need people in place to continue working," Genna Ademilola said. "We could probably get by without replacing Pastor Wade and Pastor Harold for the time being. Especially since we have not resumed Sunday School."

"I agree," Lenore Toth said. "We really need to restart soon."

"We are working on a plan to reopen and still follow the state's policies," Terry Marjai said.

224

Again, after a short discussion, a motion was passed to rehire the current staff members at their current salary.

"Okay, that's all I have. Does anyone have anything else? If you need to discuss business without me present, I can step out."

No one could think of new business to discuss.

"In that case, I will entertain a motion to adjourn."

"How did it go?" Liz asked when Tyler returned home.

"Short and sweet. The board rehired everyone except Wade and Harold. I don't think they will hire a childrens minister until the new pastor arrives unless they resume Sunday School soon."

"That makes sense. The seniors take care of each other. Pastor Milhuff has been at a loss since the shutdown. He hasn't been able to visit people like before."

"I'm pretty sure he was planning to retire at the end of this year anyway. They've been trying to sell their house since June."

"Are you going to miss this church board?"

Tyler chuckled and said, "In a board of this size, I feel there will always be someone who disagrees for the sake of playing devil's advocate. Other than one or two members, this board has always found a way to reach a consensus on important matters. "

Liz grinned and said, "I bet I know who. At least Mrs. Thompkins isn't on the board. She would make your meetings miserable."

"The nominating committee is smart enough to know who shouldn't be on the board."

"Has Wyatt given you an answer yet?"

"No, but I think he's leaning toward staying here. Maybe."

Chapter Thirty-Two

"How is she doing?" Liz asked.

Darian Michaelis smiled at his young wife and newborn daughter then answered, "They are both doing great."

"It didn't take very long this time," Liz said.

"Dany woke me up at three this morning and she was born at five thirty."

"You are so fortunate she didn't have another long labor. Have you decided on a name yet? When I talked to her yesterday, she said you weren't sure but had narrowed the choice to three."

Darian scratched his forehead and brushed his hair to the side. "Three or four. Everyone has a different name they love."

"The decision is yours, and you don't have to decide immediately," Liz said then laughed. "You can call her Baby Girl Michaelis for a week or two."

"Yeah, that's not going to fly. Our mothers will insist we choose a name before Dany comes home."

"Em, I have good news," Kristen said over the phone.

"Did you and Wyatt decide if you're staying or moving to Michigan?" Emmy asked as she pulled more wrapping paper from the closet in the library. "You better not be leaving."

"Wyatt called Tyler an hour ago. We are not moving to Michigan."

"Good. He will remain on the staff at our church."

Kristen laughed and replied, "The church board had to rehire him. They could have let everyone resign."

"No way. There has to be someone running the church, and he's the logical choice. It could be months before we find a new senior pastor."

"It is possible the new pastor will bring his own staff, and we will end up moving anyway."

"That's a possibility, but you can't leave me," Emmy said. "I think it's time to toss the wrapping paper with fire trucks."

"It's nice to be wanted, but I don't think you have the final say, Em."

"Yes, I do! I'm stubborn, remember?"

"That you are, but you have to be open to the possibility Wyatt may not be hired by the new pastor."

"The board should make it a requirement of the new pastor."

Kristen laughed and said, "They should do whatever you say, right?"

Emmy giggled. "Sounds like a good plan to me. You can't move to Michigan. I don't know anyone there."

"You know Tyler and Liz."

"Besides them, I meant."

"We don't have to worry about it yet. We are staying here... for now," Kristen teased.

Ten minutes later Kristen heard the doorbell.

"I'll get it, Mom," Zach said. He opened the door and Emmy rushed past him.

"Who is it, Zach?" Kristen asked.

"It's me! Where are you?" Emmy asked.

"In the family room. What are you doing here? I told you we aren't moving."

Emmy rushed into the room. "You teased me. I thought I better tell you in person you have to stay."

"You are such a goof, Emmy."

"I know."

They both heard the baby crying.

"She must be hungry again. Would you like to feed her?" Kristen asked.

"Yes, please. You can fix her bottle, and I'll run upstairs and get her."

Emmy dashed upstairs and got to the nursery before Grace.

"Hi, Aunt Emmy. Did you stop by to feed Kayla?" Grace asked with a grin.

"I heard her crying from my house, and I sprinted over here as fast as I could." She picked Kayla up and the baby stopped crying.

"She likes you, Aunt Emmy. She fusses if I hold her."

227

"Let me hold my little sweetheart," Emmy whispered. "I bet your tummy needs some milk." Emmy looked at Grace and said, "Your mother breastfed you and Zach, and I nursed all my kids. It's a shame Kayla has to take formula."

"It's nice in a way. Zach and I get to feed her, too."

Emmy carried Kayla out of the nursery and down the stairs.

"Here's her bottle," Kristen said with a sad expression.

Emmy saw the look. "Hey! It's not your fault your... you know what I mean."

"I miss it in a way, but in other ways I don't."

Emmy sat in Kristen's chair to feed Kayla.

"Kayla, as soon as you learn to talk you need to tell your mommy she can't move to Michigan, or anywhere else for that matter."

Kristen shook her head and sat on the couch.

"He's here!" Larry Kimmerle told Tyler on the phone the next morning.

"That's great," Tyler said.

"Oh, I thought I called Liz's phone," Larry said.

"You did, but she was... occupied,, so I answered it. I saw it was you and guessed why you were calling. Hang on a second." He put a hand over the phone and hollered, "Liz! It's Larry. You should talk to him. I'm supposed to meet Wyatt to discuss some church business."

Liz raced into the kitchen and took the phone from Tyler. "I'll talk to you when you return."

He grinned and headed out.

"Did Allie have a rough delivery?" Liz asked. "Give me all the details."

"Where do I start?" Larry told her everything.

"Lawrence Dustin Kimmerle the fifth. Not many families keep up with a tradition like that," Liz said. "We will have to run down to Tennessee to see you guys in January. We're taking the whole month to get settled in Alexandria Rapids." She paused then added, "I wonder if the locals shorten it to something the way people here call the city SoHam?"

"It is a mouthful," Larry said.

"If not I will start a new tradition. Alexandria Rapids is too long."

"We will be here if you want to visit. How's Dany doing? Did they come up with a name yet?"

"Not that I've heard. She is getting bombarded with suggestions from everywhere. One of the cousins suggested Cleopatra Beyonce. Dany said no. Go figure."

"At least we didn't have to come up with a name," Larry said. "I better go. I have to make a dozen calls. Allie told me announcing it on Facebook was too impersonal. Our families would never forgive us."

"Tell Allie we will see her soon, and I will text her when Dany decides on a name."

"Merry Christmas, Mom," Dany Michaelis said. "Did Santa Claus stop by the house?"

"Have you chosen a name for my new grandbaby?" she asked. "Oh, Merry Christmas to you, too."

"Yes, but I can't tell you yet."

"And why not?" Mrs. Kimmerle asked with obvious surprise. "I am your mother. You should tell me first. Please tell me you haven't chosen something too unusual."

"We are not naming her Cleopatra," Dany said with a giggle. "Darian and I want to tell everyone at the same time. He's setting up a Zoom meeting. As soon as everyone is connected, we will reveal her name."

"You are being too secretive and overly dramatic, young lady. But I will wait like all your other distant relatives."

"Mom!" Dany said slowly. "Don't be that way. This is most likely my last child, and I want to be dramatic."

"I thought you wanted six babies."

"That's Lizzie. I couldn't handle that many. Tell Daddy to check his email for the Zoom info."

"I will. Please don't make us wait much longer."

"Oh, Mom," Dany said rolling her eyes.

Thirty minutes later everyone was in the room. The virtual room.

"Dany, how much longer are you going to make us wait?" Mom Kimmerle asked.

"Be patient, Karen," Dusty Kimmerle said. "It must be important, or else she would not make us wait so long."

Dany looked at Darian and shook her head. "Daddy, you are as bad as Mom." She looked at the laptop and noticed a new face had joined the meeting. "Hi, Emmy. How are you?"

"I'm fine. I hope you will forgive me for crashing the name reveal, but Liz said I should join in."

"It's absolutely all right," Dany said. She looked at Darian and asked," Are we ready?"

"Tell us before the hospital sends you home," Liz shouted.

"Okay. Her name is... Darian, hold up the card, please."

He grinned and held up a poster-size white card with the name above a photo of the baby.

"What?"

"I can't read it."

"What language is that?"

"Are you kidding?

Darian looked at the card and said, "Ooops! It's upside down." He turned it over and now everyone could read the name.

Addy Joy Michaelis.

Emmy bawled. Liz clapped her hands together as she lost control of her emotions. Dany beamed through eyes with ribbons of tears flowing down her face.

"It's a very special name for my precious baby," Dany said.

Chapter Thirty-Three

"Do you think Tyler will get emotional during his sermon?" Emmy asked on the way to church.

"I don't know. He's usually pretty good at keeping his composure. I'd say it's even money."

"I think he's going to lose it big-time," Kevin hollered from the back of the van. "I made a bet with Ben. I'm going to win his collection of football cards."

"Who cares about football cards?" Heather said disdainfully.

"Guys do," Kevin answered.

"We know Mom will be crying," Isabella said. "That's as predictable as the sun rising in the East."

"As guaranteed as taxes," Kevin said.

"A much of a sure thing as politicians wasting taxpayer money," Kenny added.

Emmy folder her arms over her chest. "I am not going to cry during the service. I am going to remain in total control of my emotions," she said then wiped away a tear.

"I'm going to be president someday," Kevin said.

Heather grinned and said, "I'm going to be the Queen of England."

"What about you, Isa?" Kenny asked.

"I think Mommy will be strong enough not to cry."

"Sucker," Kevin said.

"I didn't time it, but was that a shorter sermon than normal?" Kevin asked Ben after the service.

Ben shrugged as they walked out of the sanctuary and said, "Maybe he was hungry."

"Let's see how much food there is," Kevin said. "Come on, Taylor. Let's check out the gym."

The boys dodged the crowd and raced into the gym where tables were set up.

"Wow! They really spread everything out," Kevin said as he slid to a stop.

Genna Ademilola waved a finger at the boys. "You have to wait. Pastor Tyler and his family get to eat first."

"We know. We want to check things out, Miss Genna," Kevin said. "We know enough to wait."

"You are very smart young men. Would you take those bags of trash to the dumpster for me?" she asked.

"We're smart enough to know you tricked us, but we will do it anyway," Ben said handing a bag to his brother.

Kevin gave another one to Taylor and took the heavier bag himself.

Bruce Sutherland turned on a wireless mic and handed it to Genna Ademilola. Dan Belanger adjusted the volume.

"Is it on?" she asked.

Bruce nodded and said, "Please hold it closer to your mouth and keep your mask on." He grinned and whispered, "Nice mask, by the way, I've never seen one with red hearts on it."

She laughed and answered, "My daughter made it for me. Should I go ahead and talk?"

"Please do," he replied.

"May I have your attention please. I need to give you some instructions." She looked at Bruce and asked, "Can they hear me?"

"Only if you use the mic."

"Okay, I will try again. Because of the rules concerning COVID-19, we might need to eat in shifts today," Genna announced.

Some groans were heard from the teens.

"It will help if you wait until someone can escort your family to a table. We will try to fill all the tables, and then dismiss each one separately to go through the line and take your food. This isn't like our old potlucks. All the food has been catered and there will be a server behind each item," Genna said. "Oh," she said waving both hands excitedly. "Please wear your mask as you go through the line. Parents, please fill plates for your young ones who don't have masks."

"Tell them about the plastic silverware," Janelle Cornejo whispered.

"Yes, there are plastic knives, fork and spoons wrapped in cellophane at each setting. We have tried to eliminate people touching the utensils." Genna looked at her staff of volunteers and said, "Since Pastor Tyler is our special guest, I will pray and then we will begin seating everyone." She closed her eyes and began, "Precious Lord Jesus, our Savior and King..."

"I guess we have to sit with our families, Ben," Kevin said. "I'll talk to you later. Maybe we can sneak upstairs and play air hockey or something."

"Kevin Michael," Emmy said gripping his shoulder. "You are not sneaking anywhere. This is Tyler and Liz's last Sunday. The board will present them with a gift or maybe several. You need to stay with us."

"Okay, but can I go to Ben's house later?"

"You can ask Aunt Sloane. They might have plans."

Eventually, the tables were filled and the first shift was allowed to go to the single serving line to get their food.

"It's different today," Emmy said to Kenny. "Normally there would be serving tables in each corner, and there would be four lines."

"We have to adapt because of the virus," he answered. "Andy swore it would all go away after the election and President Rhodes was reelected."

Emmy grinned and said, "I guess he doesn't know everything."

"Don't let him hear you say that," Kenny said with a grin.

A few minutes later LaShae Mabry stopped at the Colwell table and said, "You may get in line now. Please wear your best Sunday-go-to-meeting mask."

"I wore my scariest one," Kevin said. "Is it working?"

"What is it supposed to be?" she asked staring at his homemade mask.

"It's an old man with missing and rotten teeth. Can't you tell?"

"I see it now," she said with a laugh.

Quick work by the hospitality and maintenance teams in setting up more tables in the smaller gym allowed everyone to be seated without too much of a wait.

Later, Roger Goldman used the wireless mic and announced, "Now that everyone has been through the line at least once, the board would like to take this time to thank Tyler and Liz for their service to our church first as interns, then as staff members and for the last nine, no make that ten years as our senior pastor." He gestured to Tyler and Liz. "Would you please stand by me. I think someone is going to present you with a gift." He looked at Carol Wisnewski.

She rose and pointed at Ryan Deighton. "You need to help me."

Ryan joined Carol next to Tyler and Liz. He took the microphone from Mr. Goldman, looked at Tyler and Liz, smiled and said, "I've been told it's a tradition to present the leaving pastor a new vehicle, but since you already own a 2018 Sienna we decided to go a different route. Could someone put the slide of the vehicle..."

The tech guys put the picture on the screens on each wall of the multipurpose gym.

"Are they really giving him a junk car?" Kevin asked. "It looks like it's been in a demolition derby."

"I think they're teasing him."

"Okay, so that's not really your gift," Ryan said. "The teens bribed me into doing it, so you can blame them. To get back to reality, Liz told us how much you owe on the minivan, so we decided to pay it off."

Carol handed him an envelope.

"There's supposed to be a check in here to pay for the van. You can verify the amount later if needed."

"Thank you, Ryan. We appreciate it," Tyler said and started back to his seat.

"Whoa! Whoa! Whoa!" Ryan said grabbing Tyler's arm. "There's more. Don't leave yet."

"Don't leave at all," someone shouted.

Tyler chuckled, looked at Liz and whispered, "That sounded like Andy Walker."

"I didn't know he was back from South Carolina," Liz said.

"Who is going to present the real gift?" Ryan asked Carol.

She took the mic, pointed and said, "Emmy, the board voted to have you present this gift. It was your suggestion, so you may have the honors."

"But I didn't know you were going to make me do it," Emmy said. "I don't know what to say."

"Emmy! Get up here," Carol ordered with a laugh. "You always rely on God for the right words for your books. You can rely on Him for the right words now."

"Do I have to," Emmy said.

Carol nodded. "Now would be a good time."

"Kenny, you do it."

He shook his head. "You need to do it, Em."

She bit her lip and made her way to the front.

"Here you go," Carol handed her the mic and an envelope.

"Lord, please give me wisdom and the right words so I don't mess this up."

Most of the crowd laughed because Emmy was just being herself.

She looked up at Tyler and began, "Okay, Tony was talking about what the church should give you and Liz as a going away gift. You already have a kinda new van, so that wasn't an option. Tony suggested several things which I thought were rather lame." She put a hand to her mouth and said, "Sorry, Tony."

"It's okay, brat," he said though only loud enough for the people close to his table to hear.

"So, I prayed about it and in the middle of the night, I woke up and sat up in bed. I scared Kenny because I hit him in the side to wake him up. He can sleep through a tornado, so it's not easy to wake him up." She paused because people were laughing and looking at him. "He asked if someone was breaking into the house. I told him I didn't think so, and said, 'I have an idea of what to give Tyler and Liz' and then said... I don't remember my exact words because I was kinda sleepy."

235

"You don't need to remember your exact words," Liz said.

"Okay. It was something like 'the kids need to go to college someday and it will cost a fortune.' He mumbled something and went back to sleep. I texted Tony... I guess I should have waited for morning because he texted back asking if everyone was okay. He thought it was an emergency." She looked at Carol and said, "I knew I would mess it up."

Carol laughed and said, "You are doing fine. Finish your story, and I want to read it in one of your books."

"Anyway, my idea was to set up scholarships for the kids to use for college, or whatever higher education exists when the time comes. Liz always said she wanted six kids, so I don't know what we will do if you have two more." She held up the envelope, looked at Carol and asked, "Is there a check in here or what?"

She shook her head. "It's a letter with all the information."

"Oh, I get it." She bit her lip then continued. "I think the board voted to set up the scholarships for each kid. Is that right?" she asked Mr. Goldman, who chaired the finance team.

He nodded.

"I was afraid it wouldn't be enough to get them through college, and I happened to mention it to Mr. Robertson..." She paused and turned away. When she faced everyone again, tears were cascading down her face. Liz hugged her and handed her some tissues. She wiped her eyes and said, "Sorry, but I get emotional occasionally. One of the last things he did before he passed away was to add what he called *capital* to the scholarship fund." She looked at Carol for guidance and asked, "Am I supposed to let Tyler open this so they can see how much Mr. Robertson added?"

"Yes, please, but you don't need to tell everyone else."

She handed the envelope to Tyler. "I know what he added, but I won't say anything unless you want me to. Should I wait for you to open it?"

Tyler rendered the decision mute by opening the envelope, pulling out the piece of paper, reading the information and putting a hand to his eyes. He handed it to Liz. She read it quickly and gasped, "Oh my."

236

Emmy smiled as she was crying and said, "Mr. Robertson contributed a substantial amount to the fund. That will help get the kids through college."

She reached out to hug Liz, and Tyler took the microphone from Emmy before she dropped it.

"I don't know what to say." He looked at the far wall, gathered his thoughts and said, "This has always been a giving church. Whenever there was a need, you supplied whatever was necessary to fill the need. Most of the time it was money, but there were other times when you provided labor to repair Russ Otto's porch that was damaged by high winds." He looked around, spotted another person who received aid. "You helped Arlene Connors when she needed to quit her job to take care of her ailing mother. You do so much for so many." He paused again and cleared his throat. "Leaving here would be impossible without God leading me to a new beginning. One of the last times I saw Mr. Robertson... it might have been the last time... I asked him for advice about the decision I had to make. He offered these simple words. 'You must be faithful to the call.' They might sound childish, obvious or even puerile, but they were the truth. I kept thinking of those words as I held his memorial service." He looked at the paper again. "We will not be selfish with this money. If another child needs it more than ours, we will share. Thank you, church, for everything you have done for us." He handed the mic to Emmy, took Liz's hand and walked back to his seat.

"Am I supposed to say anything else?" Emmy asked as she held the mic at her side.

"Nope, you did a great job, Emmy," Carol said. "I was afraid you were going to reveal the amount."

"I almost did, but then I thought Mr. Robertson wouldn't want everyone to know. That was his way."

"He was very generous," Carol said.

For the next hour people said goodbye to Tyler, Liz and the children.

"Mom, are we going to wait until everyone is gone to say goodbye?" Kevin asked.

"We don't have to," she replied. "Are we ready to go, Kenny?"

"I'm ready if you are."

"Let's say goodbye now, Mom," Isabella said. "There's no one in line."

Emmy led the way and hugged Liz. Kenny shook hands with Tyler. Heather and Isabella said goodbye to Natalie. Kevin talked to Grayson and David about the new fort he was building in the woods.

Emmy released Liz and picked up Phoebe. "I know you are too big to hold, but I wanted to see if I could still do it."

"I didn't let anyone else pick me up, but it's okay for you to do it, Aunt Emmy," Phoebe grinned and whispered, "I don't usually call you that, but all the Bristol Ridge kids do."

"I don't mind at all, Phoebe Grace."

The families talked until another group of people walked up to say goodbye.

"We should go, Em," Kenny whispered.

"Okay." Emmy hugged Liz and Natalie again.

Kevin nodded to the boys.

Kenny shook Tyler's hand again.

Emmy looked at Phoebe, clenched her jaw and said, "We will see you later, Phoebe."

She turned and walked away before Phoebe could see the tears.

Kenny put an arm around Emmy and whispered, "Why did you say that? It might be months or longer before we see them again."

"I know." Emmy wiped her face with his handkerchief. "But Phoebe doesn't like to say goodbye."

Check out these other titles by the author. Visit the website:
kennethleemcgee.com

The Emmy's Story Series

1. We Were 'posed to Get Married
2. One Of The Guys
3. A New Friend
4. Did You Like the Ravioli Tonight?
5. Completely and Forever: A Wedding
6. It's Time To Go!
7. How Difficult Can It Be?
8. Forever... Isabella... Forever
9. The Forgettable Year
10. Turning Thirty
11. Hello, I'm James
12. Remember The Struggle
13. But God! I Write Songs
14. A Lifelong Dream
15. Gideon's Tree
16. New Priorities
17. Christmas Surprise
18. God Is In Control

The Annie Mercer O'Dell Series

1. Roosevelt High
2. North Park College
3. Smoky Mountain Summer

The Rex Ford & Clay Horn Books

1. The Amazing Adventures Of Rex Ford & Clay Horn

The Stockton Woods Series

1. Sounds Like a Mournful Train Today
2. Sounds Like a Happy Train Today

Stand Alone Books

1. Growing Up In Kinmundy Junction
2. Grandpa, Lions and Kitty Cats: A Collection Of Short Stories For Children Of All Ages
3. The True Stories Of Ol' Melvin, Obadiah, Perkins MacGhee and other Characters

Crest Ridge United Nazarene 2020 Worship Team

Adult Group

Rebecca Deighton – piano & keyboards & vocals
Ryan Deighton – vocals & drums
Regina Collins – vocals
Liz Hammond – vocals
Julia Weishar - vocals
Heather Colwell – vocals
Isabella Colwell – vocals
Isaac Ladlow – keyboards & acoustic guitar
Adam Vicini – keyboards & vocals
Jared Brodie - keyboards
Nathan Kellett - guitar
Bryce Croft – guitar
Tyler Hammond – acoustic guitar
Mason Williams – bass guitar
Josh Belanger - bass guitar
Robinson Collins – drums
Bobby O'Connor – drums

Teen Group

Heather Colwell – vocals
Isabella Colwell – vocals
Marcus Dwyer – vocals
Sean Warlito - vocals
Tamia Sims – keyboards
Katie Farrell - keyboards
Nathan Kellett – guitar
Will Stockman – guitar
Josh Belanger – bass guitar
Austin Fields – drums
McKenzie Mahaffey - drums

www.ingramcontent.com/pod-product-compliance
Lightning Source LLC
Chambersburg PA
CBHW050733180626
46814CB00002B/733